JA [illegible] TON

BLUE SWORDS

BROKEN OATH

BOOK TWO OF THE CRIMES & CRESTS SAGA

Michael Terence
Publishing

First published in paperback by
Michael Terence Publishing in 2021
www.mtp.agency

ISBN 9781800942011

Dedicated to the Stroke Association
for all they do to support stroke victims and their families.

My profits from the sale of this book will be donated to the Stroke Association, UK.

CONTENTS

I

THE HUNT

Observing the tavern door, a local boy pointed discreetly to indicate that the weathered, rotten inn entertained members of the degenerate outlaws, the Shadow Crooks. The sound of men's laughter and merriment caused me to roll my eyes.

Throwing a coin down to the informative peasant child, I turned to Chenchi. "Let us get this over and done with, I grow tired of the chase. The child has described the turd to a tee, he is in there, I smell his lingering scent."

Nodding his head, Chenchi strutted out onto the main path of the village. Removing his sword from its scabbard, he cracked his neck. Locals began to run from our path as they looked between our tunics and our drawn swords. One child had been unable to scarper, freezing still at the sight of my companion, Chenchi. His muscular frame and enormous height was made even more frightening by his thick beard and bald head. Chenchi grunted at the gawking child, however I gave him a wink, keen to assure him that we were the good ones.

Our boots crunched through the fallen snow, until Chenchi faced the entrance of Crows Edge village tavern. The door buckled easily at the impact of his gigantic foot, causing the startled occupants to jump up from their tables. Scanning the room, I saw at least four obvious Shadow Crooks. Their weathered animal furs and muddied war paint complemented their attitude as they refused in an instant to surrender. The small handful of locals inside the inn gasped and sprinted behind the serving table.

The first Crook charged forward towards us, so consumed by mead he forgot to remove the small axe lodged within his belt. Seeing that the man was unarmed, Chenchi stepped forward and caught the miscreant Crook, gripping his hand around his throat. Raising him one handed from the ground with his sheer strength and might, he slammed him down on to a table, causing the wood to splinter and leaving the man clutching at his back in agony.

I stepped to the side and met two further Crooks, both of whom were armed with short swords and ready for combat. Composed, I swiftly sliced my blade down across the front torso of the one stood on the right-hand side, splitting him open from his chest down to his stomach. The one on my left-hand side did not fall so easily. Undeterred by my fatal blow to his associate, he stepped back preparing himself for a fight. His stance indicated he had some skill, perhaps self-taught or an ex regal guard gone rogue.

I could hear Chenchi grunting behind me, which assured me that the fourth Crook was being taken care of. My combatant remained poised, awaiting my first assault. Sweeping my blade towards him, I was keen to make light work of his defeat, however his deflection of my attack forced me to react with a swift second blow downwards towards his head. A medley of strikes soon forced the man to struggle to defend himself against my powerful, relentless blows. Eventually he stumbled back, leaving me no choice but to end our brief encounter. Seeing him open, I lunged forward, thrusting the tip of my blade into his throat and pushing the steel forward with force. As the blood trickled from his neck, his eyes widened with fear. I neatly withdrew my sword and my assailant slumped to the ground on his knees. The blood leaked through his fingertips as he gripped hold of the open wound in his neck. Seeing the life drain from his face, I felt nothing, neither sorrow nor pity for his death. I was just doing my duty.

Turning around, Chenchi plunged his sword downwards into his fallen opponent, twisting the steel to ensure he was dead. The blood splashed up, hitting his face as he stared over to me with wide eyes, displaying a sinister grin on his face.

Shouting at the cowering locals behind the serving table, I demanded to know if any other Shadow Crooks were present. A woman crept out from behind the table and stood shivering at the sight of us. Her red hair and tight, tattered purple dress reminded me of Jen, the tavern girl I had lusted over back in Stanford and whose murder was caused by the man I hunted.

She spoke with a stutter, "No sir, there are no others."

Chenchi pointed his finger "If you are lying you will be taken in for impediment, girl."

"I swear, sirs, there was only four here."

I intervened, "We believe you. The blood spilt here today was necessary, these beasts would have raped and murdered you as soon as they were done being served ale."

Groaning came from the floored man who Chenchi had put through the table. I stepped closer towards him, my boots crunching down on the toppled beakers. Gripping his furs, I yanked him to his feet, causing him to moan in further discomfort, "Where is that filth, Hota?"

Smirking, he looked at me, amused by my disgruntlement and undeterred by his defeat. "You are the one he seeks; you are going to need more men." said the Crook.

Chenchi had already grown impatient and marched forward, pulling the man from my grasp. Closing his hand around the man's throat, he slammed the loyal Shadow Crook against the tavern wall.

As Chenchi placed his blood-stained skin against the man's face, the Crook looked back at him and this time only horror filled his face.

"My friend asked you a question."

Gasping, the man stretched his neck, attempting to gain a breath of air. "He has gone back south," he managed to blurt out.

Chenchi turned to face me, unamused. "Two winters we have chased this bastard around the north and he hides in the south, right under our noses."

Stepping closer, I looked at the Shadow Crook. "You lie," I snarled.

He grunted from Chenchi's firm hold, "I do not, his following grows in the south, and when the time comes, he will crush the Crown and what is left of you Blue Swords. You, Jep, will be his final victory!"

The fact the Crook used my name sent shivers through my body, knowing it had been bandied amongst them.

Chenchi noticed my distanced thoughts and insisted on taking the man out to the wilderness to prise out more information.

"No, it sounds like it is us who are being hunted." I said.

"At least let me snap the filth's neck."

Contemplating my next words, decided on my actions. I leaned in closer towards the nervous Crook. "You give your master a message from me. Until I draw my last breath, I will seek him out and bring him to justice for his treachery and wickedness. Any man who dares rise against the Swords will be executed without trial."

Chenchi released his grip, sighing and shaking his head. The Shadow Crook rubbed his hands across his throat, pleased by his release. Ordered to leave, the man attempted to offer his gratitude for our mercy. However, Chenchi lunged forward, striking his forehead into the Crook's nose. The crunch caused the Crook to yelp and grab his bloodied face. I repeated my order for him to leave and he scarpered out of the tavern, as fast as he could.

"He deserved that at the very least," said Chenchi.

***

Leaving the village on horseback, Chenchi snorted as we rode onto the snow-covered path.

"Say it Chenchi, your grumbling is rather irritating. What is bothering you?" I asked.

Frowning, he glanced back at me and rested his hand across his thigh. "Two winters we have searched the north for that rat, all on pitiful intelligence of his whereabouts. These farmers are as treacherous as Hota."

"These farmers want rid of the Crooks as much as you and I; it is the Crooks that plague their lands, robbing them of their livelihoods."

Bringing his horse to a halt, Chenchi turned and pointed his arm back towards the village. "Jep, take a look at where we are: Crows Edge. This is as north as Thear will allow us to go. I can see the damned Wither Islands across the water. The turd most likely shelters there, licking his wounds."

"You heard the Crook," I said.

Shaking his head, he replied, "The Crook's tongue was littered with lies. The regal guards or our fellow Swords in Alma would have sniffed out any Shadow Crooks by now."

We rode on in silence as I was unwilling to continue our argument.

***

Two more days passed before we reached the familiar town of Whiten. Our stubbornness to break the awkward silence between us was expelled by our arrival at the town where my late tutor and I had visited whilst investigating Isaak's disappearance.

Chenchi rolled his eyes at the sight of the dilapidated village. To me it was just another underprivileged northern village, like my birth home Somerby. However, my companion had grown tired of the poverty that plagued the northern lands. Reliant on beverages to lift his mood, Chenchi insisted on attending the local tavern for ale. The weathered log hut was a rather dismal affair and resembled more of a peasant's home than an inn.

Chenchi sighed on entering the dingy tavern; the melancholy atmosphere matched its darkness. Three older looking locals sat around a table in silence, giving us a brief glance before sipping from their beakers. Chenchi called over to the scrawny looking man who stood behind the serving table and asked for ale.

Hearing the man's confirmation that the tavern was well stocked, Chenchi smiled back at me, "Well at least there is ale and no Shadow Crooks!"

Once seated, Chenchi wore his usual natural frown as he peered over towards the silent table of drinkers. "A funny lot, these northern folk. Not very welcoming to people."

"The winters are harsh up here, they're most likely jealous of your oversized gut," I replied, smiling at my enormous companion.

Chenchi peered down at his stomach, scrunching his face. "You think I am fat?"

"You may have just let yourself go a little since our confirmation, but then who am I to judge?"

By his sixth beaker of ale, Chenchi's mood had eased, his hand gripped my shoulder from across the table and his drooping smile had become somewhat infectious. I never did quite understand how a man of his magnitude struggled to handle his drink, and it was not long before his words turned more serious and sincere.

"He would have been proud of you; you know that don't you?" slurred Chenchi.

Knowing that he referred to my mentor Fulten, who had lost his life at the hands of Hota. I looked at him, while nodding sombrely in agreement.

Squeezing my shoulder, Chenchi attempted to compliment me further. "To think you were nothing but a stuttering farm boy who struggled to wipe his own arse, and now look at you, even I wouldn't want to draw my sword against you. Although when we return to Stanford, you must remove that patchy hair from your face. You look as if you have struggled to mature."

I was amused by his drunken humour.

A minute amount of coin handed over to the innkeeper had secured us a night on the tavern floor, however the cracks in the wood encouraged external elements to join us in the room.

Waking the following morning, I had decided that there was somewhere I wanted to visit before returning to Stanford, but I understood that my decision was likely to be controversial.

Saddling our horses, I looked over to a rather bleary-eyed Chenchi. "I am going to ride across land and return home."

Tutting, he was clearly unamused, Chenchi stared across at me. "Jep, the coldness from the north grows wearying, besides, the Governor will not be best pleased with our detour."

"I understand, but we have been gone a whole winter and a few more days will make little difference. I must look in on my mother and sister, they will be in need of silver. You can head back, I will face the consequence of the Governor on my return."

Chenchi sighed and refused to reply. As I mounted my horse Spike, Chenchi watched me.

"Tell me, do all these northern women look the same?" he asked.

"Yes, but they are much more spirited than the girls you have become familiar with in the south."

Chenchi grunted, then said, "I will come, but we stay for one night, that is all. Besides, alone you will only lose your head."

Gladded by Chenchi's decision to accompany me, I smiled down at him before we began our journey across the north. I was pleased at the thought of returning home. I had failed to look in on my family for two years now and it was time to see them again.

Chenchi's scrunched and dismissive expression said it all as he peered over the endless fields that lined our path, but as I breathed in the cold crisp air my lungs felt cleansed. The horses' hooves crunched on the snow-covered ground, making the ride feel rather therapeutic for me.

Chenchi had always hated needless talk, so I figured he must have been bored when he began to insist on making conversation, but his words were quick to gather my attention. "Is this the same path on which you began to seduce the Baroness?"

Turning to him, I frowned. "What nonsense you speak."

"Well, rumour suggests she is in need of another adventure," chuckled Chenchi.

Shaking my head and pretending that I was paying little attention, I replied as if I had little care of the Baroness' needs. "I am sure Lady Ivy is quite satisfied with Baron Asher."

Chenchi laughed. "The pig spends most his time indulging in wine and wetting the bed. He hides from his duty, the coward should step down."

Chenchi was right; I had become privy to the rumours that Baron Asher had never recovered from the night he abused Lady Ivy in the square and learnt of Gil's plot to overthrow his reign. Gil was his head guard and his power. Losing such a feared asset within his household had left the baron weakened. His reckless actions, humiliating the town's beloved Baroness, had had a detrimental impact on his people's confidence in him. Their witnessing of his thuggish head guard falling at the hands of a senior Blue Sword had left Asher feeling sullen and vulnerable. Lady Ivy had been reunited with her father but still refused to break her own loyalties, remaining committed to her cruel husband. This was something I had trouble understanding.

As the night crept upon us, the sight of the burning torches lighting up the entrance of Somerby was very welcome. In the centre of the dilapidated huts, I stopped and dismounted. Chenchi raised his eyebrows. "Why do we stop?"

Nodding towards the nearest tatty hut, I said, "This is my home."

Chenchi shook his head, "This makes perfect sense. Forgive me Jep, I have no interest in any emotional family reunions. Can you hear drums and the cackles of women? That must be the tavern. That is where you will find me, I am in much need of ale and love."

"I will join you shortly."

Tethering Spike to the post outside my home made me think of Lady Ivy and the last time I had attended the village. It was here that she had met me outside after our rather eventful evening in the local tavern. I began to reminisce about the kiss that we had shared and the flutters that had taken over my body that night.

Entering my family home, I called out to announce my arrival. A thud came from the rear chambers, situated on the other side of the fire pit. Emil appeared, her brown hair messily resting upon her shoulders. Red faced, she looked back at me with her mouth open.

Noticing the bed sheet that she had swiftly used to cover her body, I mirrored her bashful expression.

"You're back, we hadn't received news of your intended return," said Emil.

"Where is Mother?"

"She will be back shortly, she left to collect handouts from the market."

Footsteps came from my sister's quarters, followed by a male voice, "What is the hold up my love?"

The short and bearded man stared at me in horror, before attempting to neaten his untidy ginger hair. "Jep! We were not expecting your arrival," stuttered Abbot.

Looking between my sister and my childhood friend, I felt uncomfortable by the circumstances which I had just disturbed.

Abbot was unable to meet my eyes, prompting me to speak abruptly, "You bed my sister, at least have the decency to look at me."

"It is not like that, Jep," called Emil.

"Well come Abbot, do tell. What is it?" I asked.

Abbot stared down at the ground and began faltering his words. I over spoke his mumbling, "Do you treat my sister as you would a common whore?"

Emil interjected, "How dare you Jep, you have been gone for years and yet you feel you have the right to strut in here all high and mighty."

The door behind me opened. Mother entered, and instantly tears began to form in her eyes as she dropped the basket in her hand and reached out to embrace me. Pulling away, Mother glanced over to my sister. "Emil, your brother is present, you should dress yourself at once."

"You knew about this Mother? Why do you allow them to mate like dogs in our home?" I asked.

Reaching up to me, my mother clipped her palm around the back of my ear, "You will mind your manners in this house young man, besides who am I to stand in the way of love?"

Uneasily I turned back to Abbot, "Is it love you offer my sister?"

Abbot gazed across to Emil, "With all my heart."

"I need ale." I responded.

Mother began giggling at my sour expression, "You should show your gratitude to Abbot, it is he who has supressed others from taking a shine to your sister."

Abbot stood with his chest raised and looked back at me, smiling proudly at the compliments made by my mother.

Stepping closer to me, Mother rested her hand on my cheek. "You have the hot headedness of your father. It delights me to see you son, God continues to answer my prayers."

2

LOYALTY

Sitting on the bench across the table from me, my mother, Emil, and Abbot listened intently to the turbulent stories I told of my experiences in Stanford. Mother became teary-eyed on learning of Fulten's death. Emil froze with her fingertips pressing against her mouth, whilst Abbot shook his head in dismay.

"He was a good man, that Fulten. You know he invited Gibbon and I to try out for the Swords," Abbot relayed.

"He was the most honourable man to walk this land and I will seek justice for his murder."

My mother squinted at me, with a look of worry and doubt on her face. She had raised me and was aware of my stubborn mindset, a trait handed down to me from my father.

"Are you sure it is justice you seek, or is it revenge?" muttered my mother.

Standing from the table, I shook my head sadly. "Mother, I don't know."

Mother also stood up from the opposite side of the table. "You must allow God to hear your woes, my love."

Looking back at her, I took in her words and dropped my head sombrely. "I have, Mother, I have."

Abbot suggested we attend the Bull Horn tavern to celebrate my return home and to lighten the mood. I was keen to check in on Chenchi, so I agreed to his proposal. Emil leapt up, clearly excited by the thought of an evening's merriment. Mother declined the invitation, indicating she wanted to prepare our home for my companion's arrival.

Looking over to her, I said, "Tomorrow morning Mother, I will need to speak with you alone. There is something of great importance I wish to discuss."

My mother smiled at me. "Good night Jep, for now be with your friends and rest your mind."

The boisterous chants coming from the Bull Horn tavern indicated we were in for an eventful night. On entering, I saw that the local people's attention had been drawn to a table placed in the centre of the room. Beakers were being hit against benches and both men and women yelled in exhilaration.

Chenchi was seated bare-chested at the table causing the commotion. Some of the village girls admired his colossal muscles and defined physique. With his elbow firmly planted on the wooden table, his veins straining through the skin of his balding head and arms locked with another equally sized local, Chenchi's flushed face proved he was struggling to defeat his opponent in this recreational show of strength.

Seeing the moon-shaped head of Chenchi's challenger and the stool legs bulging underneath his large build, I realised that it was in fact Chenchi who was the challenger. Gibbon, my old childhood friend and the village's arm-wrestling champion was hustling my companion.

I purposely stood within Gibbon's sight, and he dropped his smug smirk at his upper hand over Chenchi when the shock of seeing me before him made him lose his concentration. Chenchi must have felt the easing of resistance and took his chance, slamming Gibbon's knuckles onto the table. Screams and jeers came from the spectators, who had clearly lost coin at Gibbon's accidental defeat.

Chenchi raised both his arms, yelling boastfully about his victory. Gibbon leapt up from the table, red faced and irritated. "You waste of a man, two years I have been waiting and you show your scrawny arse now."

Smiling, I pointed down to Abbot. "You allow this dwarf to court my sister? We are even."

Chenchi looked confused, bewildered by our greetings. "I was warned of this inbreeding in the north."

As always, Gibbon raced forward, lifting me from the ground and cracking my bones with his squeeze. Seeing him had raised my spirits and reassured me that our diversion was worth the potential reprimanding I was going to receive from the Governor.

Leaving Chenchi to mingle and flirt with the local women, I sat with Gibbon and brought him up to speed with current events.

Shaking his head, he stared back at me, sympathetically. "Fulten seemed a righteous man. I always knew that Baroness was going to cause you a mischief, you are lucky to be alive."

I began downing the remaining dregs of ale in my beaker.

"So, this Hota. Do you hunt him, or does he hunt you?"

"In truth, I do not know. Up until now I have been able to track his movements, but I have learned of rumours that he has ventured south. Until this is proven my family are not safe here, he will use them to avenge his father."

Sitting back in his chair, Gibbon raised his eyebrows, appreciating my concern. "You do know your mother will never leave; she is committed to the village."

"You should come," I said.

Frowning, Gibbon replied, "What, to Stanford?" Laughing, he then paused on seeing my serious expression. "You're bloody serious! I can't stand southerners; they are weak and needy."

I leaned forward, "You could become a Sword, the trials are to be held in Spring."

"Me, a Blue Sword? You mock me Jep," Gibbon replied.

"I was confirmed and you have as much ability as me. Come to Stanford, try out for the Swords," I asked.

"What about him?" Gibbon said, whilst nodding his head towards Abbot. "You know he loves your sister."

I looked back to see Abbot and my sister sat together giggling. Seeing her face shining like stars brightening the night sky from his delicate charm gave me comfort.

Looking back at Gibbon, I laughed, "He will make a fine stable boy."

Gibbon stood from the table and drank down the ale from his beaker, before slamming it down onto the table. Raising the empty cup, he shouted, "It is decided, we will teach those Southerners the ways of the North. To Stanford!" His energetic speech went unnoticed by the rather lively villagers.

The following morning, I woke with a rather drowsy head, and glanced over to see Chenchi unconscious on his back, snorting like a hog. Standing up, I peeked through the arch to see Abbot snuggled into my sister, resting on a bed. Rolling my eyes, I grunted.

Mother was already awake, heating milk on the fire pit. Stirring the pot, she smiled on seeing me approach. It was refreshing to see her preparing our morning beverage, it made me feel nostalgic. Remembering the conversation I needed to have with my mother, my mood dampened. Sensing my discomfort, she placed her hand on my arm and eased my torment, before insisting on waking my sister to continue with the morning chores and enabling us to speak.

Mother wrapped her body in a sheep's wool shawl, before we headed outside and began to stroll towards the market square. My mother smiled proudly, enjoying the attention she received of being in the company of a Blue Sword. Linking her arm into my own, she rested her head against my shoulder. I decided to remain silent, allowing my mother to enjoy the moment together.

Unfortunately, this was short lived by an unwanted interruption.

"Ah, the mighty Sword returns to attend his flock," said a voice in a pompous tone, prompting laughter from a second man.

The familiar voice caused an instant sneer to appear on my face as I set eyes upon my previous foe. The guard stood, poised as he brushed his fingertips across his moustache. Flicking back his wavy hair, he gave me a cunning grin. Steffen had been the cause of Lady Ivy's humiliation in the square, the night Gil fell at the hand of Sword Fawkes' blade. Steffen had arrived in Stanford on the invitation of Baron Asher, and it was whilst on their hunt that he had relayed lies of Lady Ivy's overindulgences whilst visiting my home village. Worst of all he had decided to pass on the information of Lady Ivy's willingness to spend the night with me in the slums.

Mother gripped my arm tightly, and feeling my tension she whispered for me to remain calm. "He has kept his word not to come within an inch of your sister."

Feeling my stomach tighten at his display of confidence in front of his armed companion, I was surprised to see Steffen's face suddenly drop at what had caught his attention behind me.

Turning, I spotted Chenchi stumbling towards us and rubbing his hand over his head, clearly suffering from the aftereffects of the previous evening's merriments.

"Where are you going?" I asked.

Buttoning up his tunic, he yawned. "I left my sword at the tavern in the hands of some farm girl."

Staring between the guards and I, Chenchi clearly sensed the stand-off as he glared over towards the men. "What is this?"

"This is the guard that informed the Baron of my so-called irresponsible behaviour towards the good Lady Ivy."

Steffen gulped as if he was frightened by the sight of the man mountain. Chenchi chuckled and approached the men, firmly clasping his hand down onto Steffen's shoulder, causing him to shudder uncomfortably. "I owe you a drink. It is because of your loose tongue, Gil lost his head," Chenchi said, as he wandered up the path, still laughing aloud.

Steffen's sheepish look reminded me what little sport he really was, and any further confrontation was a waste of effort. Giving him no further attention, my mother and I continued towards the square.

The morning traders bellowed out their offerings, keen to promote sales. Local children had their gawping mouths closed by their parents as they set eyes on the thick steel that ran down my thigh.

"What is it that unsettles you, Jep?" Mother asked.

Looking around, keen to keep the conversation private, I told her the thoughts that were tormenting my mind.

Staring over at the church, Mother paused with a dismayed expression on her face.

"You wish for me to leave, don't you?" she asked.

"I cannot protect you here, Hota will stop at nothing to seek vengeance. Until now I have been able to track him and keep him moving, yet it seems he has vanished."

"Can you not see we are already protected? Nobleman Skinner has guards to keep these Crooks at bay," Mother replied.

"Hota could slaughter these men even blinded."

"I will not leave nor run away and that will be the last word said on the matter. You have my permission to ask your sister, but I will not be driven out of my home by your feuds."

Ending the conversation, Mother began to walk away, clearly saddened. I ran to join her, knowing too well there was no way I could change her mind. Comforting her, I wrapped my arm around her back, offering no further debate on the matter. Once back at our hut, we found that Chenchi had arrived, pleased to have located his sword.

Noticing his clammy, reddened skin, I said, "It must be unnerving to misplace your sword."

He muttered back so he was not heard. "No, she would only return my sword if I offered her mine. Let us say the ale has now well and truly left my pores."

The unrest at leaving my mother and Emil unprotected continued to taunt my thoughts. I wandered out to meet with Gibbon who was outside his hut, excitedly mending the splintered wood on his door, "Just let me seal this, then I will be ready to head south."

I sighed "Gibbon, I must ask a favour of you."

Rolling his eyes, he looked at me with annoyance on his face. "I am not joining you, am I?"

I shook my head showing my intentions. "I need you to stay here and watch over my mother, Emil and Abbot. Mother refuses to leave and with Hota at large, I need someone that I can trust to ensure their safety."

Refusing to speak, he firmly slammed the wood back into place before huffing, "You are my oldest friend and have asked little of me in our time together. I will stay; besides, it will be nice to ram this Hota's head up his arse should he arrive." Turning to face me, he pointed. "But do not expect me to sleep at your home, I cannot listen to Abbot whispering sweet words in your sister's ear, night after night."

Wishing Gibbon farewell, I began to walk up the track towards the square. He called out to me, demanding that I was to be swift in locating Hota. Smiling back at him, I assured him that I would have Hota arrested by spring, so he would be free to attend the Blue Sword trials.

Relieved to see Steffen was not the one guarding the Grand Hall, I requested an audience with Nobleman Skinner. Whilst the guard went in to announce my arrival, I could not help but notice the melting snow dripping from the stone roof of the nobleman's home. The cracked stone walls reminded me of how deprived and vulnerable the village really was.

Nobleman Skinner greeted me at the door, appearing enthused by my arrival. Inviting me inside, he led me down the cold, damp corridor towards the dining hall. The modest fire in the corner of the room struggled to heat up the chilly hall. The past two years had not been kind to the peaceful nobleman, who now appeared frailer than ever. He limped towards his chair, catching his breath as he slumped his body down.

Peering over to the two boyish looking guards tasked with shielding the village, I felt even more uneasy.

Noticing my observation, Skinner coughed. "Do not let their youthfulness overshadow their abilities. I recall you sitting here before me, immature and enthusiastic. Now you stand before me a man, a man with saddened eyes yet filled with vengeful intent."

"I come in need of your aid; I am sure you are familiar with the events that unfolded in Stanford," I said.

Skinner rubbed his hands onto the arms of his chair. "I have heard whispers of rumours, none of which are favourable to you. I did however hear that a plot of treachery was exposed and that you have gained another enemy."

"I need to be assured that if that enemy attends this village, my family will be protected."

Skinner tightly gripped the arms of the chair, struggling as he lifted his body to its feet. Looking over to the young guards he flickered his fingers, dismissing them from his hall.

Pouring wine into a goblet, he offered the drink to me. I politely declined his offer.

"Do not allow this delicate appearance to fool you, Jep. Rest assured my mind is sharper than the blade you carry. I am aware of Steffen's wicked tongue, but the man has doubled my infantry in the past two winters. If any of these Crooks intend to cause harm to any of my people, they will be faced with my wrath. We Northern men and women are made from robust blood. If it is a fight they want, it is a fight they will get. I do however expect something in return for the protection of your family."

Peering over to the nobleman, I listened intently as he awkwardly stared back at me. Sighing, he spoke. "You are not to return to this village again, the arrival of Blue Swords undermines my presence and that of my men."

"This is my home, you cannot deny me my family."

"I can and I will Sword Jep, you forget who masks your past. Not all can hide from their previous misdemeanours."

"I don't understand."

"Guardsman Steffen has brought to my attention unexecuted warrants that read your name. Childhood has a habit of shadowing one's future."

"So you are blackmailing me?"

"No I am making a proposal. You desist from returning to Somerby and your superiors become none the wiser of your past."

Mulling over his request, I knew I was cornered and had to consider it.

Standing to my feet, the legs of my chair ground across the stone floor. I gave the nobleman a sour look, before stepping away from the table.

"You know I am a man of my word; I will keep your mother and sister safe, and guards will be posted to patrol the slums. It is with regret that my offer comes at a great price," said Skinner.

"If I learn of any harmful intent or ridicule of my family, I shall return and be assured, with regret I will remove your head."

Nobleman Skinner nodded his head, making very little of my threat, clearly putting it down to my annoyance at his terms.

As I left the Grand Hall, not only was I saddened by the nobleman's conditions, but I was also slightly bewildered by his reasons behind them. I decided that the agreement I had shared with Skinner would remain between us and as sad as I was to be leaving my home for the last time, I felt relief in knowing that between the village guards and my oldest, most trusted friends, my family would remain safe.

My final plea to my mother to join me on my journey back to Stanford fell on deaf ears. My offer of purchasing a horse from Skinner had excited my sister who was now left disappointed by our mother's decision to stay in Somerby. Chenchi had already saddled his horse and was keen to set off back down to the south.

I looked back at Mother with sadness displayed on my face. Silently, I felt the tears welling in my eyes. Mother stepped forward wiping away a tear that had loosened and ran down my cheek.

"You silly boy, come now, you are a Blue Sword, don't let that oaf see you cry." said mother.

"I will send you coin," I said, whilst clearing my throat.

"Do not whittle about that, we have what we need. All I ask of you is not to leave it two winters before you return."

Pulling her into my chest, I held her tightly, just like I did as a child after a disturbing night terror. I leaned around facing Abbot and my sister, letting out a sigh.

Pointing at my friend and my sister's new lover, I called to Abbot, "You guard them with your life."

Pulling my sword from its scabbard, I was uncaring of the consequences of returning to Stanford unarmed. "Do not use this to boast, it is to remain here, and I suggest you learn how to use it."

Abbot's face glowed as he held my sword out in front of himself, gripping its hilt. Even though the blade matched his height, his strength was enough to hold the sword upright.

Stepping outside on to the snow-covered ground, I noticed Gibbon staring at me from his hut. We met each other's gaze and nodded, before Chenchi began quizzing me on the location of my sword.

"Why would I need a sword, when I have the largest warrior in Thear for a companion?" I answered, dismissing his questioning.

Mounting my trusted horse Spike, I peered back at my mother and Emil, keen to leave and avoid any further emotional goodbyes in Chenchi's presence. Digging the heels of my boots into Spike's sides, we began to ride away.

Taking a final view of my home village, I took in a deep breath and inhaled the clear, crisp air. I was a man of honour now, and I had given Skinner my word that I would not return. However, in my heart I knew that once I had brought Hota to justice, not even my word would keep me from home.

3

BLOOD AT THE ALTAR

Chenchi smiled across at me as the hooves of our horses took their first steps onto the stone bridge. The regal guards greeted us respectfully upon our arrival onto the bridge. Chenchi looked up at the sky, relieved by the crossing into the south of Thear.

Sniffing, he took in a deep breath. "Smell that Jep, civilisation awaits."

I continued ahead, rather tired of his belly aching about the north.

Shouting, he called out to me, "Your sulk is undignified."

The snow had already begun to melt on the southern path, and I could not deny it was a relief to see patches of hardened soil. My worries about leaving my family had started to ease and my concern was now directed at facing the Governor on our return. I knew very well that he would be displeased with the time we had spent away from Stanford, especially as we had little to show from our travels, just a small trail of Shadow Crook blood.

Keen to avoid any unwanted attention, we decided to stay clear of the main path and Chenchi and I settled for the night in a nearby meadow, close to the notorious village of Hooks Cross. I had no desire for further conflict so thought it wise to spend the last evening of our journey somewhere secluded, giving me time to gather my thoughts before the final day's ride to Stanford.

Chenchi was quick to fall asleep, leaving me to endure his unbearable snoring. We had overindulged on our last bota bag of wine and the alcohol had set my mind racing. I started to think of a person that often entered my thoughts when I was alone. Laying on the hard ground, I peered up at the night sky and pictured Lady Ivy's face reflecting down at me through the stars. Ever since our intimate encounter at the lock up, after learning the fate of her father and her humiliation in the market square at the hands of her jealous husband, Baron Asher, the Baroness had kept her distance from me.

The rumours of the Baron's downfall were true. Since losing his wicked head guard, and discovering Gil's plans to betray his own ruler, Asher was winded and now carried the reputation of a spineless coward, spending his nights in torment. His appearances before the townsfolk had been sparse, and the Governor had made it no secret that he was relieved to have seen the end of the troublesome Baron Hill Festival. Asher's weakness and lack of leadership had not gone unnoticed within the town; locals often amused each other with puppet shows, mocking his rule. Daily petitions had been delivered to the lock up, demanding his abdication of the title of Baron. Luckily for Asher, he continued to have the support of the Crown, who often reinforced his troops of guardsman, halting any idea of a revolt.

It was Lady Ivy's loyalty to her husband that aided the peace, pacifying the people's hatred. She was the true ruler of Stanford, the people's ruler. Her undignified belittling, observed by the locals on that summer night two years ago, had only made the Baroness more favoured in the town. The thought of her soft angelic features, her long brown flowing hair, and mesmerising green eyes made my stomach flutter. I wanted to see her, to be close to her once again.

The clear blue sky and bright sun sparkled on the remainder of the snow that littered the fields. The path however remained clear and its ground hard from the frost. Seeing the giant stone walls that surrounded the rich and lavish town of Stanford reminded me of its true grandeur. Chenchi stared at the thick, wooden gate, his smirk an indication of his relief to be home. On our approach, Chenchi yelled to the gatekeeper demanding entry. The gate was swiftly opened by a youthful looking guard and another new member of the Baron's henchmen.

I pitied the boy, even though he was only a couple of years younger than myself. Seeing his fresh, claret tunic with the Baron's markings embroidered across its material made me curious to think that one day this immature guard could grow to become an enemy. Chenchi refused to acknowledge the boy, passing him arrogantly with his hand resting upon his thigh. On seeing the lad's cautious eyes raise up from the ground, I greeted him with courtesy. His shyness and youthful features reminded me of myself when I had first wandered into the town and encountered Hota, a man who was once a friend. I still found it difficult to comprehend his betrayal and dishonesty. Hota had treated me like a brother and if truth be told, it was his reassurance and encouragement that had strengthened my determination to become confirmed as a Blue Sword. As much as I loathed him, I missed the bond I thought we once had.

Halting outside the church, the exquisitely crafted stone tower impressed me each time I had the privilege of gazing upon its fine structure. Looking down the hill, black smoke filtered into the air from the Finch and Burn oak estates. The lively movement and noise of the crowd down in the market square could be heard from the top of the hill as they haggled for bargains from the traders. Lifting my head, I sighed, capturing the sight of the Grand Hall situated at the back of the town. Just seeing Lady Ivy's home made my stomach flutter once again. Its dense iron gates could be seen from where I was positioned. Forgetting the tyrant that resided there with the Baroness, I remained thoughtful of Lady Ivy, and hoped that the past few seasons had been generous to her.

The inquisitive and curious stare generated from the locals was something I had learnt to dismiss. Their submissive expressions were somewhat expected after the night they saw the Blue Swords' show of strength and witnessed our most capable swordsman end head guard Gil's wicked and vile reputation. The townsfolks' ongoing anguish had been fuelled by a well-loved local man's death, who was murdered in cold blood by the Baron's henchman. Pip, a respected trader, whose kind and considerate reputation had made him favoured amongst the people.

What was unknown to the citizens, including my fellow Swords, was that Pip was a Cavalier of Stanford, part of a secret society whose members were made up of a variety of influential people. It was the Cavaliers that had put their trust in me and led me to Isaak, Lady Ivy's missing father.

It was that same night Hota and his father had struck down my mentor, Fulten. I had now learnt the identity of four of the Cavaliers, who resided in Stanford, one being the late Pip, another being the town's priest, Father Arrend together with Lady Ivy's father, Isaak, and finally the West farm owner, Carre. Carre lived on the farm with his delightful wife and two young sons. It was Carre's family that had showed me such kindness on my arrival at Stanford.

Approaching the lock up, its weathered and damaged stone walls reminded me that I was that much nearer to confronting my Governor with a rather disappointing debrief. Chenchi looked back grinning, undeterred by the impending meeting with our superior Sword. The Governor was a formidable man; however, his temper was short and fiery.

Leading Spike into the rear courtyard, I looked across the long, unkempt grass which separated our quarters from the building. Enthused by its modest wooden walls and patchy straw roof, it was pleasing to know that tonight we would be slightly sheltered from the outside elements.

Sword Lev leaned against his horse, brushing down its rump. Lev's thick animal furs drowned his slight shoulders. Flicking back his blonde wavy hair, he squinted as we approached, giving us a timely stare. Smirking, he eyed me up and down, conjuring up a witty and humorous remark.

"Judging by the fluff on your face, my guess is that they have finally dropped. About time your body matured," chuckled Lev.

Chenchi quickly made an attempt to encourage Lev further, keen to divert the sarcastic Sword's attention away from himself. However, no one was safe from Lev's ridiculing.

"And look at you, Chenchi, you have frost bite on your head. Surely if you ask Jep nicely, he will oblige and donate some of his own newly developed hair. You boys have been gone a while; we were beginning to think you had grown over-fond of one another and deserted our ranks."

Pulling back on the reins of my horse, I led Spike into his stable, and then began quizzing Lev on current affairs within the town. He replied with his usual careless and flippant responses. "The people remain weary; Baron Asher now speaks to nature and the Governor remains as adorable as an infant pup. Little has changed and little will ever change within these over-privileged walls."

Crossing the courtyard, I heard wood clattering and high-pitched grunts coming from the far side of the gravel. Blair, the brash servant girl, danced around Fawkes, defending his combination of attacks and confidently lunging back towards him, returning precise and accurate strikes. A rare smile developed from the senior Sword's chiselled jaw, clearly proud of the girl's efforts. Fawkes caught our stares with his hardened eyes, and concluded their training, before brushing out the splinters of wood from his dark cropped hair.

Blair had changed; she had grown lean, losing her infant fat. Standing taller, with her golden hair tied up neatly in a bun, she looked like a true warrior. No longer did she wear her oversized and torn rags, now she wore a crisp white blouse, neatly tucked into her tight fitted leather trousers. Upon seeing me she smiled and dropped her wooden sword before sprinting towards me.

"What took you so long? Have you brought us his head?" She asked.

Fawkes called out to Blair, "You haven't finished, girl. Do you wish to become a Sword or not? There will be plenty of time for gossip."

Reprimanded, Blair cheekily grinned at me before racing back towards Fawkes. Giving us a nod, Fawkes discreetly acknowledged our return. Fawkes had saved my life on more than one occasion and had proven the rumours of his abilities and fearsome reputation to be true.

As we entered the parade room, Sergeant Hock was seated, sucking on the ligaments of a chicken thigh. Turning to face us, he gave us a half-hearted smile; our arrival had made no impact on his cantankerous manner. Leaning back into his chair, he extended his short legs, resting them on top of an unoccupied stool. Glaring at us with his beady eyes, he appeared smug.

"It's like seeing lambs awaiting slaughter. I imagine I will hear the Governor's anger from the dungeon, when he gets a hold of you two."

Isa appeared with a clay jug, pleased by our return. She began pouring wine into the Sergeant's goblet. The servant's entrance prompted Sergeant Hock to remove his feet from the stool and sit up straight. As irritable as our peer was, he was still chivalrous and was known for his respectful manner towards all women.

"Your daughter grows well, Isa," I said.

"She grows idle." She replied.

"Blair wants to better herself; she is determined to become a Sword."

"And who will have to dry her eyes when her body is the cause of rejection? Her mother, that is who."

"Nonsense," Called Hock. "I would much rather be faced with death with the girl by my side than these two fools. Now boys, be on your way, the Governor awaits you."

Wandering through the combat chambers, Chenchi insisted on me taking the lead up the stairs. The dingy corridor was still home to cobwebs and dampened scrolls, scribed from cold cases back when Detectors were housed in Stanford. Seeing the scrolls reminded me of my departed tutor's previous student, Detector Flint, a rather stylish and confident Blue Sword who now carried out his duties in the great city of Alma. It was Flint who had aided my rather fortunate victory over Hota's father, Ricard. I had declined his offer of mentorship in the city, keen to stay and learn my craft before taking the next steps to becoming a Detector. It was a decision at times I had regretted, however my focus remained on bringing my mentor's killer to justice.

Approaching the Governor's door, I looked back to Chenchi and took a deep breath. Chenchi sneered, clearly undeterred by our looming encounter. Raising my fist to the wooden door, the deep, rugged voice of our superior ordered us to enter his chambers.

He sat behind his table with his elbows wedged on to the wood, emphasising his muscular shoulders. The snarl on his face highlighted his menacing, squinting eyes.

"Don't sit down," he grunted.

I stood tall, unable to make eye contact with our fearsome leader, however Chenchi deliberately leaned against the wall, prompting the Governor to bite. "Are you wounded?" he called.

"No, just tired," answered Chenchi.

Speaking firmly, the Governor looked down at his table before raising his eyes and staring at my companion. "My wall needs no aid, so unless you wish for me to nail you to its stone, you will stand tall, man."

Chenchi did as asked and stepped forward, aware that the Governor was in no mood for his arrogance. Now stood, the Governor turned his back to us and peered out of his window, "I gave you a month, yet you were absent a winter. I can only assume you have brought our adversary to justice?"

"He had the upper hand, our sources failed us, and it seems they were loyal to the Shadow Crooks. We did, however, interrogate one of his men, who gave us word that Hota is here in the south," I replied.

Slowly clapping his hands together, the Governor turned to us, his cynical smirk transforming quickly into a grimace. "You captured one of his ill-bred followers and now have word that Hota, the leader of the Shadow Crooks, is this side of the river. Well, you men must be honoured," he replied, sarcastically, before raising his voice. "I lose one of the most prestigious men to ever wear our crest and I am left with you two. You are nothing more than a pair of uniform hooks."

"Sir, if you would just let us investigate this lead, we should need no longer than a week," I pleaded.

Stepping closer towards me, the governor leaned his face closer to mine. "It wasn't that long ago, pup, that you believed the man you stand with was the snake slithering within these walls." Moving away, he approached the table. "You will both remain here and get back to your town duties. I will send a seasoned Sword to follow up on this lead. Dismissed!"

"But Sir."

"Dismissed!"

Walking down the stairs, I felt agitated by his decision to remove me from the hunt. "He grows softer," Chenchi chuckled.

I felt agitated by his careless attitude. "Does it not bother you that Hota gains the upper hand with each day that goes by?"

"You heard the man; he is sending seasoned Swords to locate the turd. Fawkes will execute Hota by spring."

Chenchi was right. With Fawkes tracking Hota his days would surely be numbered, but I wanted to be the one that brought him to justice.

***

The blood trickled from her throat as she leapt up from the bed, watching me with sunken eyes. Her hair was drenched, sticking to her forehead as she whispered. "I bleed for you, Jep." The door was flung open behind me and the wind howled through the gap. The wooden floor shuddered and in rolled a decapitated head, the blood around its laceration dry and dark. Gil's widened eyes stared at me whilst Jen's cackles echoed throughout the room.

Waking, I sat upright, disoriented, and struggling to catch my breath. The nightmare had left me with my bed sheets drenched in sweat. I could not remove Jen's face from my mind as the room began to spin. Remembering the time I had found her murdered in the Viking Invader tavern made my stomach gripe. I needed to be sick, but my legs refused to allow me to stand. Dropping on the floor from my bed, I crawled on my hands and knees, bare chested, towards my chamber's door.

Drawing in deep breaths, I attempted to hold in the sickness, before vomiting in my mouth by the door. Outside I rolled on to the grass and emptied my stomach. Gasping for air, I was suffocating. I tried stretching my neck to open my throat, whilst the tears streamed down both cheeks as I imagined dying there on the ground, half naked. In a state of panic I inhaled, but no air entered my lungs.

I felt a hand touch down on my clammy back, and an unusual voice gently called for me to settle. "Breathe into it, boy, breathe into it."

His gentleness began to sooth me, allowing me to catch mouthfuls of air. "That's it, slowly inhale the clear air."

My stomach emptied on the grass for a second time, however this time it was a relief. The sheer fright had left my body and I was able to breathe steadily.

Turning my head around, I glanced at the man who had come to my aid. I felt shocked and horrified to see who stood over me. It was Sergeant Hock who had soothed my panic. Breathing heavily, I paused, unsure of what to say.

He patted my back, sighing and began to smile compassionately. "It happens to the best of us, eyes are not made to endure the sights we are exposed to. I suggest bringing out animal furs and embracing the winter air for a while."

Watching him walk away I could not reply, not even to express my gratitude. His unexpected act of kindness left me flabbergasted and took my thoughts away from the venom attacking my mind.

The following morning, I observed Chenchi as he prepared his tunic for morning briefing. His lack of reaction indicated he was oblivious to my restless night. As I entered the parade room, I saw that Fawkes and Lev were already seated, awaiting the arrival of Sergeant Hock. Lev chuckled on seeing Chenchi and I enter the room before leaning back in his chair. "It must have been pleasing to embrace one another in a warm bed."

Chenchi grinned, casually wandering towards Lev, allowing his smile to quickly transform into a chilling scowl. "What if we did embrace one another, maybe I like it or maybe I prefer scrawny blonde men who talk too much."

Lev's mouth dropped open as Chenchi's witty reply sparked uncommon laughter from Sword Fawkes. The parade room door opened behind me and Sergeant Hock entered, sour faced and unamused.

"Right, listen up, orders for today are as follows: Jep, you will take the day patrol and handover to Chenchi at dusk. It is about time you wanderers pulled your weight around here. Lev, anything to report from last night?" asked Hock.

"No Sergeant, only some of the local girls proved a little eager to toy with my baton."

After Hock dismissed us from the parade room, I took a second look over at him, attempting to gauge his thoughts on my previous night's predicament. He did not return the attention I expected to receive, instead he stomped out of the room, clearly with no desire to speak further.

Mounted upon Spike, I rode through Burn Oak Estate, no longer feeling phased by the attention gathered at the sight of my uniform. It had been a while since I patrolled the town, and in the meantime both my confidence and reputation had magnified. It had taken months to dampen the rumours of my love affair with Lady Ivy, and the people had stopped whispering about the night I fell to Baron Asher's head guard, Gil.

Entering the square, I peered over at the gathering of locals surrounding the trading stalls that neatly lined the cobbled ground. The smell of spices and garlic lingered in the air; however, someone was missing. Pip, the old man who served hot pork slabs and always offered me generosity. His act of heroism had cost him his life.

Pip had begun to expose Gil's intentions and treachery towards his ruler, Baron Asher. His association with the Cavaliers of Stanford had made him rather knowledgeable about the town's affairs. I had been sworn to secrecy by Father Arrend. The secret society of Cavaliers was to remain unknown for the good of the people. I had kept my promise and had refused to disclose the identity of any of its members, aware that both the Baroness's father, Isaak and my old friend Carre, were both members of the secret society.

Guiding Spike from the market square, we continued along the cobbles and entered Main Street. People stepped aside, making way for me and my stallion as I casually drifted down the path. With my hand resting on my thigh, I felt confident and bold, however this emotion soon left me as I looked across at the Viking Invader tavern and began mulling over last night's thoughts of Jen. Staring down the narrow walkway that ran alongside the tavern, my thoughts changed to my first night in Stanford. I remembered the evening when I caught Linc interfering with a local woman. My meddling gained me a beating that night, but it was Sword Fawkes who arrived and came to my aid for the first time.

A sweet high-pitched voice called my name, distracting me from my reflective state. It was welcoming to see her comforting face. Dam, Carre's wife, began walking towards me, followed by Rye, her farm hand. Her plaited hair and freckled skin matched her delightfulness, and her presence had a way of lifting the irritation from any mood. Rye was like me, a peasant boy who had been taken in by farmer Carre and provided for in return for his labour at Western Farm.

"Oh dear young man, you are in much need of some tender care," called Dam.

Leaping down from Spike, I embraced her and greeted Rye with a handshake. "I have missed you and Carre, is the grouch well?"

"He is, it would please him to see you."

"I have been absent this winter, my duties led me out of town."

"Searching for that coward, Hota?" called Rye.

Dam slapped his chest, reprimanding his quick tongue. "You mind your manners boy." Turning to me she continued, "Do not mind him, ever since you joined the Blue Swords he has been prepping for the next trials. I worry his eagerness to carry a sword has deflected him from his own chores. As you can imagine Carre isn't impressed at the thought of losing his best hand to the Swords."

I assured Rye that he would make a fine Blue Sword, before accepting Dam's offer to supper soon. Wishing them well, I continued with my patrols.

As my watch came towards the end, the night sky had already begun creeping over the uneventful day. Before returning to the lock up, I decided to head up the hill towards the church. It had been too long since I had offered my conscience to God and I was keen to clear my guilt in the hope it would prevent another restless night. Hazy light glistened through the stained glass windows in the walls of the church. Dismounting from Spike, I looked for the narrow path through the graveyard, which was just visible from the faint light of distant torches. Cold air howled from underneath the thick wooden doors, before I pushed them open. Scanning across the pews, the dim light was enough to allow me to confirm that the church hall was unoccupied. The altar was not visible, so picking up a candle I was able to illuminate my steps down the aisle.

Bitter coldness swept through the feet of the benches catching my ankles and riding up my trouser legs. The chilliness was worsened by the whistling wind passing through the church. I called for Father Arrend, only to receive silence. Squinting, I looked over to the archway on my left, expecting to see the priest appear.

Startled by the feeling of skin brushing my hair, I gripped the hilt of my sword and pointed the flame towards the unexpected intrusion. Its light exposed horror as the chilliness became even more bitter. Father Arrend was present, his eyes staring into nothingness, his torso stretched from his neck as the rope cut into his throat, leaving his body hanging from the beams that lined the church roof. Barefooted, he hung lifeless, dressed only in his night robe.

The blood had drained from his face and his legs felt cold and stiff to the touch. With his death in no doubt, I bowed my head before him and began to offer my prayers. The town had lost yet another honest and noble man.

4

THE BARONESS

Ending my brief prayer in front of the holy man, I stood and became emotionless towards the hanging corpse, allowing instinct to take over. Hastily walking to the church door, I looked across the misty graveyard and noticed a shadow reflecting from the street flames onto the church wall. Calling out to the stranger, I heard the gate squeak and felt relief that they had not ignored my request.

A nervy high-pitched voice responded from the path. "Can I be of help?"

Recognising the boyish person, I was relieved to see that he was an official. His oversized, claret tunic indicated he was one of Asher's guards.

"Is all well, sir?" he stuttered.

The young guard was clearly anxious about my summons and I now recalled where I had seen him before. He was the gatekeeper, the guard whom Chenchi had so arrogantly dismissed.

"You must attend the lock up at once, call for more Swords to attend here immediately."

"But sir, I am to relieve at the gate."

"I care little for your gate, you will go at once."

"I can help, I am armed."

"A man hangs inside these walls, the only need I have of a sword is to cut him down. Now go and hurry."

The youthful guard looked at me wide-eyed, and paused in panic.

After I had repeated my command for a third time, he turned and clumsily stumbled before sprinting out of the churchyard.

Returning inside the church, I wandered around the edge of the hall lighting all the candles. I kept taking a fleeting look at the dead priest and before long found myself beginning to stare at his hanging body. My mind had become accustomed to processing brutal deaths, but this was different. It felt as if his wide, dead eyes followed my steps. I tried to imagine possible events before his death; the father stepping up on to the now toppled stool which lay beneath his feet, and looping the rope around the rafters, preparing his own demise. The shivers that ran down my spine felt unnatural. I was confused. We lived in a time that every move we made led us closer to death, yet our beloved father had made the decision to secure his own destiny and cut his life short.

I began examining the ground below Father Arrend. Studying the stool before slowly looking back up at his body, I shook my head and began speaking to him. "You fool, your act of desperation baffles me."

Scanning the altar, nothing appeared untoward nor out of place, and all the ceremonial instruments remained intact.

Moments later the church doors crashed open and Fawkes, along with Chenchi, marched down the aisle towards me.

"When did you discover him?" asked Fawkes.

"Moments before the guard called on you."

Frantically looking around, Fawkes quizzed me further. "Any signs of a disturbance? A struggle?"

"No, all seems in order," I said. "What are you suggesting?"

"I am suggesting nothing, it's called investigating. Has he left any parchment? Any indication of his reasons?"

Fawkes had a way of making me feel nervous and inadequate. Clearing my throat and carefully considering my next words, "I am yet to examine his chambers."

Chenchi looked over to Father Arrend and tittered. "Kind of hypocritical don't you think? A man who preaches of relishing life, then takes his own."

Chenchi's answer came from a gruffly toned voice at the front doors of the church. "Even a holy man can know sorrow, it will do you well to embrace compassion, Chenchi."

The Governor strode towards us between the benches, frowning as he eyed a shamefaced Chenchi. Paying little attention to my presence, he insisted on receiving his update from Fawkes. Satisfied with what he had initially heard, he approached the priest and went on to make the sign of the cross over his forehead and chest.

"Jep, cut him down," The Governor ordered.

I nervously glanced at Chenchi who raised his eyebrows. "I will take the legs, Jep."

Righting the toppled stool, I stepped up level with Father Arrend's body. Gawping across at his neck I noticed patches of purple bruising, discolouring the skin. Leaning up, I began to tug at his robe, to examine him further.

Chenchi was breathing heavily and began to gag whilst holding up the priest's legs. "Stop undressing him Jep and get on with it, his bowels are weaker than your sword arm."

The damaged texture to his skin ran along his collarbone and down to his shoulders with red scratches covering the lighter bruising.

I called to the Governor and Fawkes, "Sir, the skin around his collar is spoilt."

Fawkes looked over at me, irritably. "The impact of his fall has stretched the ligaments; it will cause pigmentation. Hurry along, Jep. Give the father the dignity he deserves."

As I sliced my blade through the rope, Chenchi stumbled, accidently allowing Father Arrend's body to slump onto the ground.

Sergeant Hock entered the church hall and witnessed Chenchi's mishap. "Damn you man, have you no respect?"

I lowered my head, offering Chenchi no reassurance. Hock stomped closer, nudging Chenchi aside and lowering himself, knelt beside the late Father. Straightening the priest's legs, Hock then brushed his fingertips over his eyelids, closing them and removing Arrend's chilling lifeless stare. The Sergeant's sadness reminded me of the time I knelt over my tutor's dying body. Fulten had fallen close to the spot where Father Arrend now lay.

I was not aware of the closeness our sergeant had had with the priest and felt upset at witnessing Hock's grief. However, I could not help but take another look at the markings on the Father's neck.

Riding back to the lock up alongside Chenchi, I was keen to express my thoughts surrounding the priest's injuries. Chenchi was quick to dismiss my concerns with mockery, "You should speak with the Governor, but please let me be there to witness his reaction."

"Are we not investigators? Should we not consider all possibilities?" I questioned.

Sighing, Chenchi gave me a sour look. "Jep, no one can fault your spirit, but there was a time when you considered me a traitorous killer. Sit back and follow the guidance of our superiors."

"So, you think I am a fool?"

Chenchi brought his horse to a sudden halt, showing his willingness to engage with me further. "You have potential, but you are reckless and allow your judgement to be directed by emotions. All I am saying is give yourself time to learn, respect the rank structure. A reputation is built on tolerance."

Moving our horses on, I began to ponder on Chenchi's advice, finally concluding that he was right. My silent reflection was interrupted by Chenchi's observations. "Although did you notice how the Sergeant reacted? I was unaware of his fondness for the priest."

"Hock has faith, and seeing Father Arrend in such a way, I feel his faith has been tested," I concluded.

***

Purposely drinking several beverages, I was keen to do all I could to ensure I had a restful night. The mood in the parade room had remained rather sombre as we raised a beaker of ale for the departed Father. Even Lev refrained from attempting to lighten the tone, as he understood his humorous approach to these tragic circumstances would have been tasteless and not well received by the Sergeant.

The following morning, the winter sun pierced through the cracks of my chambers. Chenchi was absent as he remained committed on his night patrols. I made my way over to the parade room, and Sergeant Hock was already there awaiting my arrival.

"You need to get straight out, there has been an attack on one of Asher's guards," he ordered.

"An attack? By a local?"

"No, worse, it was at the gate. Outsiders must have been disgruntled at being refused entry so attacked the guard. Head to the Grand Hall, take over from Chenchi and gather an understanding of this assault at once."

"Sergeant, with all due respect, I fear my presence will not be welcomed at the Baron's residence."

"I have a dead priest and a guard who has been savagely attacked; I care little for your quarrels with Asher. You will go without further debate."

Arriving at the gates of the Grand Hall, I was met by one of Asher's guards. Clearly unaware of my history with the Baron he politely welcomed me before escorting me across the gravelled courtyard.

"Your man is with Markus. They are in the guards' quarters; his disfigurement is awful," said my escort.

"Yes, Chenchi is not easy on the eye."

The guard frowned at me, displeased with my distasteful humour. "Not your companion's, the boy's."

The guards' quarters were located to the side of the Grand Hall, the wattle and daub outbuilding stretched the distance of the Baron's home itself. The structure was well kept, the walls effectively constructed with woven lattice, finished with a neatly laid straw roof. Entering the compound, sturdy wooden bed frames lined the walls leading to an archway at the end of the room.

The guard stopped and pointed to the archway. "The boy has been placed in the armoury; his whining was disturbing the men."

As I walked between the beds, I saw that at least eight guards were present, and my intrusion had garnered their attention. Some offered me brazen stares, recognising me from the night in the square where I once challenged their late leader, Gil. One guard stood from his bed as I passed, his heavy build, along with a deep scar running from the front of his hair line, making him even more intimidating. Spitting close to my feet, he was keen to make me aware of his thoughts at having me present in his chambers. Choosing to ignore the insult I walked by, following the groans that came from the armoury.

Chenchi met me at the door and began muttering in my ear. His words were missed as I observed the youthful guard who was being treated by the town surgeon. It was the boy I had sent to fetch assistance on my discovery of Father Arrend's death. He grunted, whilst biting down on a peg as the doctor attempted to realign his splintered face with thread. The blood had dried on his sheets and now stained the floor. Chenchi nudged my shoulder to regain my attention and ordered me outside.

We made our way outside, hearing the yelps from the guard echoing through the chambers. Walking back through the Baron's men, the reception had changed as they nodded and acknowledged Chenchi, who himself had once served amongst them.

"They feel me responsible for Gil's death," I whispered to Chenchi.

"It is not Gil's death that displeases them."

"Ricard? He was planning to betray them."

"Ricard was like a father to most of these men, and you plunged a blade into his back. Do not expect to receive hospitality here," said Chenchi.

Outside, Chenchi began to relay the circumstances of the guard's attack. Hearing that the man, not much younger than myself, had received an axe in his face as a consequence of his bravery through refusing entry to some savages, left me feeling uneasy.

"I haven't been able to get much from the boy, just that they were outsiders," said Chenchi.

"Shadow Crooks? Do you think Hota may be close?" I responded.

"Your theory is not all that far-fetched. But we cannot assume anything until the boy has been properly questioned."

I looked at him with broad eyes. "Father Arrend's death has to be part of Hota's reprisal. He was the one that aided Isaak, leading to Ricard's death."

Chenchi frowned. "Here you go again, coming up with your notions and without evidence. The boy was attacked outside the walls and also after the priest was discovered. You must calm yourself; I will brief the Governor. When the boy is able, you will need to interrogate him."

Chenchi left the Baron's grounds, leaving me standing outside the guards' chambers. My mind began to race with dread at the thought that Hota could have potentially returned to Stanford and was waiting for the right time to fulfil his father's ambitions. Sighing, I heard the crunching of gravel as light footsteps approached me. As I turned my heart faltered, seeing her pure skin and long brunette hair flowing down her back. Her tightly fitted green satin dress complimented her hourglass figure. Witnessing that angelic smile, framed by dimples, made my stomach knot with nerves.

Lady Ivy smiled, making me assume she was pleased by my presence. I felt my cheeks redden and my thoughts became stagnant. I found myself lightly tapping the handle of my wooden peace baton. Lady Ivy giggled at my fidgeting.

"Do you plan to draw your baton on me, Jep?"

Clearing my throat, my voice stuttered as I struggled to know where to place my hands. "The winter has been kind to you, my lady,"

Lady Ivy pointed to the stubble on my face, commenting on the change in my appearance. She told me that I looked rugged and found my new unkempt form endearing.

Her flattery caused my words to jam in my throat, as I was left speechless by her appearance. Luckily, the Baroness's charisma had a way with awkwardness, and she swiftly led the conversation.

"The attack on the gatekeeper is alarming. Poor Markus, he is an enthusiastic young guard. Are you here to question him?"

"Yes, my lady. It is imperative we learn the identity of his attackers."

"I have listened to the poor man's cries throughout the night and then I wake to learn that our dear Father Arrend has departed us, such tragedy."

Lowering my head, I contemplated telling her my suspicion that Hota could be responsible for the guard's assault but considering I had not seen Lady Ivy for nearly a year, I wanted to keep the conversation clear and pleasing.

"Is your father well, my lady?"

Lady Ivy smiled. "He thrives, he has taken charge of the grounds here. It felt fitting, considering his experience in farming. I assume your mother and sister remain prosperous?"

Laughing, I shook my head. "My sister chooses to lay with Abbot now."

The Baroness chuckled, biting her bottom lip. "Now that is not a relationship I anticipated. But good for her, Emil deserves happiness."

The much softer mood and flowing conversation was short lived. Baron Asher appeared through the door of the Grand Hall. He stood glaring over at me and his wife, before staring up at the clear, blue sky and inhaling. Seeing his beady eyes and black beard, along with his rounded gut hanging over his belt, brought back my feelings of hatred towards the man.

Walking down the steps towards the courtyard, he turned his head, inspecting Lady Ivy and I as we stood together. "Now isn't this a delightful sight, two devotees reunited and rekindling their love."

Lady Ivy tutted, before turning to face him. "What displeased you, my lord? Sword Jep is here to interrogate the guard."

"Ha, the boy needs to learn to fight if he wishes to remain a representative of mine. As for the Sword you entertain, he is not welcome on my grounds."

Lady Ivy gritted her teeth. "Sword Jep is here to investigate and investigate he shall. If you didn't rely so much on your winery, you would have better control of your town and less need for your reliance upon the Blue Swords."

My stomach clenched at Lady Ivy's defiance. Anticipating confrontation, I foolishly gripped the hilt of my sword.

Asher stepped closer to his wife, placing his face close to her own. "You will do well to mind your tongue woman; I have no need for a Baroness these days, nor her snivelling father."

Lady Ivy met his hostility and appeared undaunted by his threat. "Will you parade and degrade me before the townsfolk again or just lightly chastise me?" she asked sarcastically.

Asher growled, clenching his fist that was resting by his side.

Looking around the Baroness, he glanced down at my hand that was still gripping my sword's hilt, before sniggering, "You are welcome to the worn whore; you can hump her in the stables."

He leered back at his wife. "You are familiar with being ravaged outside, are you not?"

Lady Ivy remained firm and stood her ground but refused to embark on any further unpleasantries.

As the Baron turned to walk away, the confrontation de-escalated, as did my nerves. I looked at Lady Ivy offering my sympathy.

"We have grown tired of one another, but that is not your concern. He is still my husband."

A hostile voice called from inside the guards' chambers, unaware of the Baroness's presence. "Markus is able to talk now, just do not attempt to slay him whilst he is wounded, I know you have form for stabbing men in the back."

The muscular and scarred guard appeared, and his jaw dropped open horrified that his antagonistic words had been overheard by Lady Ivy. "My lady, I wasn't aware of your arrival."

The Baroness scowled as she approached the guard. "This man saved the life of my father; you will do well to remember that and treat him in the manner in which he deserves."

Lowering his eyes to the ground, he replied, "Yes, my lady, I offer the Sword my apologies."

Lady Ivy turned to me grinning, pleased with the now obedient guard's reprimanding. "Do not leave it so long," she whispered.

As she walked away and made her way up the circular stairs to the Grand Hall, my gaze remained fixed on her.

Coughing, the stocky guard called to me, putting an end to my view of the Baroness. "When you have finished, Markus has settled."

The untidy stitching running between the wounded guard's eyes was a consequence of his haunting disfigurement. The surgeon finished wiping away the blood that leaked from the wound. Leaning around to face me, the surgeon queried the necessity of my questioning Markus at that moment. I replied that time was of the essence and I needed to speak to him without delay.

Unsatisfied with my response, the aged doctor gruffly answered, "Do not think that I will repair any tear to the stitching." Glancing down at Markus, he insisted that the guard gently moved his head to answer my questions. "If you talk, they will rip."

Leaving us alone, I leaned down next to Markus. "He is right, do not speak, give only a small nod if you agree. Did your attackers enter the town?"

The guard gulped before shaking his head, leaving me to sigh in relief. "Are you aware of Shadow Crooks?"

Swallowing again, he nodded his head slowly, prompting my next question. "Was it Shadow Crooks that attacked you?"

Lifting his shoulders, he shook his head, agonised by the movement. Ignoring the guard's pain, I eagerly pressed him, keen to be convinced that it was not Hota's men that assaulted him. I raised my voice, abruptly describing the common appearance of a Shadow Crook.

Unable to reply due to excruciating discomfort caused by his wound, Markus appeared to be made uncomfortable by my demeanour.

"Don't you Swords have any compassion? The boy has been maimed, and you determinedly interrogate him. Have you no shame?" said the muscular guard, appearing from his chambers. "If it was Crooks that assaulted the boy, he would be dead, and they would be running wild around our town."

The hostile guard was right. Knowing Hota's venomous thoughts of the Baron, if he was responsible for the attack, Markus would not have been spared. Considering the state in which the guard lay, I had no choice but to delay my questioning.

Leaving the grounds of the Grand Hall, I peered up at the window positioned above the wooden doors of the hall. Lady Ivy stood there, gazing back at me, her figure shining in the rays of the winter sun. The feelings I had learnt to numb had now returned, and I remembered why I had fallen for the Baroness.

5

THE BRAWL

Returning from the Grand Hall, Sergeant Hock was far from impressed with my debrief and the lack of response to unanswered questions left him even more ill-tempered than usual. Since his brief acts of empathy on finding me unwell outside my chambers the previous night, Hock's tone had completely changed and not only had I been given the day's duties, I had now to assist Lev and Chenchi with their night patrol.

"I want presence in the town. The people must know that we shall not tolerate strays or acts of violence. What of the scene?"

"The scene?" I asked.

"Where the guard was struck down. Have you examined it for clothing, blood, weapons? Anything that could give away the identity of his attackers? I do question your confirmation at times. I suggest you get a beverage, then make your way to the gate and examine it properly."

Hovering over the rotten fruit left on the parade room table, I picked up a sodden, miscoloured apple. Biting into its soggy texture, I heaved at its sour taste. Grunting came from the adjacent room, so I wandered through to find Blair striking one of the haystacks with a wooden training sword.

The speed in which she sliced her weapon through the air would catch any able warrior off guard. Her delicate footwork was the result of being educated by Fawkes. He treated the girl as if she were his own daughter, and his love for Blair's mother, Isa, was no longer regarded as clandestine amongst the Swords.

"You are fast; I would not want to be on the receiving side of your blade," I commented.

Turning to me, Blair smiled before wiping the sweat from her reddened face. "Well stay on my good side then. Mother grumbles that I spend too much time practising and not enough time completing my chores."

"You should listen to her. Mothers always know what is best for their children."

Blair scowled at me, before turning back around and continuing to strike the hay. Her mood had changed, and it was reflected in her careless and angered attacks.

"Did I upset you, girl?"

Blair stopped and lowered her training weapon, and after catching her breath she spoke bitterly. "A girl I may be, yet I am a girl that is as able as any man and any Blue Sword. I will not allow myself to live my life a servant."

I shook my head, "Why the self-pity? Do you think that being a Blue Sword is not to serve? We serve them, the people. We tolerate them and their idle whines. You are a child and no matter what you think, your mother will only want you to achieve greatness. Now stop whimpering and strike the damned haystack."

Blair fed off my words and again began attacking the target. As I turned to walk away, she yelled out to me. "Oi Jep, when did you finally grow a pair?"

Laughing, I was pleased to hear that cheeky humour she so often applied to conversations.

As I arrived at the entrance of the town, the guard that now patrolled granted without question my request to open the gate. Frost covered the hard ground, making the leaked blood from Markus's wound easy to locate. The spotted trail led outside the main gate and became heavier within a few steps from the town's wall. Resting upon the hardened grass was a thin silver-chained necklace, attached to a chipped coin. It was not something I had seen worn by a Crook, since at first glance its value appeared to be beyond their means. But then their reputation as thieves could have easily seen it in the possession of one of the bandits.

My gut feeling was still telling me that the guard's attack and Father

Arrend's unexpected death had all the hallmarks of Hota. I stared across the grass away from the town, aware that the forest on the horizon led to the main road. Squinting my eyes, I snarled at the thought that I was being watched, the small chance that Hota looked on from the tree line. I wanted him to know that I was not afraid, and I was ready to meet him again.

The light began to fade as I stepped back through the gate into the town. One of the Baron's servants had already begun lighting the torches and the slender, elderly man reminded me of Pip as he stretched up to open the metal bracket of the torch. Catching my eye, he gave me an unpleasant look and grunted, "You might want to get to Main Street, they are brawling like wild dogs."

Placing the necklace into my leather purse, I sprinted towards the square. The sound of jeers and chanting could be heard as I ran across the market square onto Main Street. Outside the Viking Invader stood at least twenty men exchanging punches and carelessly attacking one another. A few locals had congregated to ogle at the fighting. Pushing my way through the gathered onlookers, I discovered Sword Chenchi and Sword Lev standing in front of them, laughing and pointing as they made light of the brawling men.

Lev stood casually with his arms folded, muttering up at Chenchi who winced and screwed his face up at the men's assaults on one another.

Seeing me, Lev grinned. "Jep, come see this pathetic attempt at manhood. These travellers fight worse than you."

"Why do we not intervene?"

"It is merely a handful of peasants beating their chests at some randy, wandering merchants." Turning to face the gathering of locals, Lev yelled so all could hear. "Do our fine people not deserve some entertainment on this cold winter's evening?" The crowd responded, cheering, clearly amused by the disturbance.

Looking over at the commotion, I noticed a peasant man cowered on the ground covering his head with his arms whilst two strangers stood over him, repeatedly raining punches down upon his body. The band of travellers were easy to identify, their clothing slightly more glamorous than the torn and muddied rags worn by the local peasants. Their well-repaired tunics and clogs indicated they had access to silver.

The peasants' intoxication gave the travellers the upper hand and it wasn't long before the fight had become one sided. Watching the cowering man on the ground, I saw he now groaned and had begun begging for mercy from his adversaries.

Growing anxious, I peered back at the boisterous and excitable spectators. I observed Chenchi, who appeared equally thrilled by the scuffle.

I asked whether we should intervene.

"Jep, what will we achieve? They will only turn on us. Let them fight, the mess can be cleared swiftly."

Appeasing my peers I continued to hold back the crowd, keeping a close eye on the floored peasant. Violent clashes continued between the rest of the men, with each man refusing to back down and accept defeat. It was apparent that our presence had gone unnoticed.

Suddenly I heard a firm voice call from the crowd. Catching my attention, I turned to see Sergeant Hock scowling at us and at the belligerent group of scrappers.

Shouting, he called out to Lev, Chenchi and I. "You stand here and allow this viciousness on our streets, and you dare to call yourself Swords? Raise your batons and move forward at once, that's an order!"

On his command, I charged straight towards the two travellers beating the local man. Both men took a step back on seeing my intention to intervene, however their demeanour did not give me the impression they were ready to end the fight. One ran his hands either side of his head to remove the hair from his eyes. Both standing tall, they stepped closer, keen to engage me.

Lunging at them, I crouched, lowering my stance so my head was in line with their waists. Swiping my baton into the legs of the first man, I heard the cracking of bone as my weapon struck his shins and forced him off his feet. I stood upright and swiftly spun my body around, striking my baton across the shoulders of the second traveller. The strike caused him to tumble over on to the ground, leaving him and his companion wincing on the cobbles.

Their victim was bruised, nothing more, and scarpered at the first chance he could get. Observing the remaining brawlers, the circumstances were much the same. Most of the peasants had fled, leaving around ten brave travellers up for a fight and now turning their attentions on us, the authorities. One landed a punch to Chenchi's face, and it was amusing to see the traveller's enraged expression change to horror at the little impact his assault had made on the brute. Chenchi's eyes opened widely, displaying nothing more than annoyance at his assailant's attack before gripping hold of both the man's arms. He squeezed the man's body tightly and the traveller squirmed, before feeling the impact of a head butt from Chenchi's abundant forehead.

Lev danced around three of the defiant merchants, gliding between them effortlessly as he promptly delivered baton strikes back and forth. His rapidity and precision left his adversaries with little time to react as Lev targeted their torsos with bold blows, leaving them crippled on the ground. Lev peered arrogantly down at them, clearly satisfied by his own performance.

Hock had placed one of the travellers chest down on the ground and was in the process of locking the iron hinges around his wrists, securing him in black coated shackles. Unbeknown to the Sergeant, an unoccupied brawler crept up behind our kneeling superior, and was moments away from delivering a cowardly attack. Lev yelled to Hock, warning him of the oncoming assault.

Before we could intervene, Hock promptly spun around, his eye line now level with the assailant's waist. Reaching up, he cupped the traveller's crotch, brutally gripping hold of the bulge in his trousers, and with clenched teeth he continued to yank and twist his hand, leaving the merchant yelping in agony.

After an uncomfortable yet satisfying pause, Hock released his hold on the traveller, causing him to slump onto the ground, weeping as he held onto his crotch.

Still kneeling, Hock spat across at the incapacitated man. "Spineless bastard." Rising to his feet, he scanned his eyes over the other fallen brawlers. "Jep, search them for weapons. Chenchi, back to the lock up, I want all of them shackled. Lev, if any of them even utter a murmur, stick them."

The crowd began to disperse on the orders of an irate Hock, and I began patting down the reprobates. Starting my search of one of the merchants, I could not help but notice his eyes staring back at me. Whilst shaking his head, he attempted to remove his long, black hair from his eyes. I sensed he was eager to talk, and he watched me behind his weathered skin. "We offer no more hostility; it was merely a bit of entertainment for a group of tired and travelled weary men."

"I am not sure my sergeant agrees," I replied.

Brushing my hand up his sides, I removed a brown satchel from his shoulder. The cracked leather was thick and its contents heavy. Pulling it open, I exhaled on seeing what was inside.

"We trade jewellery, the finest in Thear," confirmed the merchant. "I would be glad to bargain some for our pardons."

Pulling loose one of the tangled necklaces, I examined it more closely. Its silver chains were neatly linked, bearing a coin with a carved image of a rounded shield, divided by a sword and a stag's head. The rim contained lettering, with which I was unfamiliar. Pulling out the necklace found at the scene of the guard's attack, I confirmed its description was identical, however the one I had in my purse was much more misshapen and chipped.

The long-haired trader, noticing me comparing the coins commented, "I see you are already in possession of one of our niche ornaments."

I took a long and silent look at the merchant, and he appeared uncomfortable by my stare. "I suggest you remain quiet; these items are now evidence."

"Evidence?" he replied, frowning. "I will have you know these items were all obtained by honest means."

Searching the remaining men, only a couple of clubs and more jewellery were found. Having been escorted back to the lock up after being met by some hostile locals wanting the blood of the travellers, each man was placed into the dungeon and caged. Sergeant Hock took great pleasure in parading up and down in the front of the cells, advising them on his lack of tolerance for such ill-mannered behaviour. Most of the detainees had only just attained adulthood and trembled at Hock's reprimands. However, the long haired one with whom I had spoken seemed rather comfortable, resting his forearms on the iron bars of the door, refusing to take his eyes off me. I started to feel slightly apprehensive of his unknown thoughts.

Once in the parade room, Lev was keen to re-enact his gallant display over the prisoners. Blair sat listening intently, entranced by the account which Lev so boastfully relayed. Fawkes smirked, encouraging Lev's dramatic story telling.

"Straight for the balls I tell you, the Sergeant has no compassion," chuckled Lev.

Hock entered the parade room, bringing Lev's description of the sergeant's actions to a sharp end. Breaking off a hunk from a loaf of stale bread, he began chewing on the crust, uninterested in making conversation with the rest of us.

Following him outside into the courtyard, he turned impatiently at my interruption as I pulled out the necklace I had located at the scene of Markus's assault from my pocket. He looked at me, frowning.

Holding up the chain, I said, "Sergeant, this is what I found on the bloodied ground, where the guard was set upon."

"And what of it?" he questioned.

"It matches the jewellery traded by the merchants we house in our dungeon."

Grabbing the necklace from my grip, Hock turned it back and forth, squinting as he examined its appearance.

He took a deep breath. "There we have it, the boys' attackers. Not bad Jep, not bad at all."

He wandered off across the gravelled yard with the necklace dangling from his fingertips. I called out to him, keen to learn of the travellers' planned fate.

"An unlawful assault on a Baron's guard is an assault on the Crown itself. I would imagine that knowing Asher's current predicament, he will insist they are hanged in the square to satisfy the people. They will not receive an honourable death."

Dissatisfied, I asked, "Should we not at least interrogate the guard further?"

Hock chortled. "We may make a Blue Sword out of you yet. At first light return to the barracks and speak to Markus again. If there is no other conclusion, these degenerates will be handed over to Baron Asher."

6

TRUDA

Smoke drifted from the homes on the estates, making the air heavy and potent. Blood from last night's brawl stained the cobbles outside the Viking Invader tavern and locals stood idly by, chatting about the affair, as if it was theatre.

Ice reflected off the iron gates securing the Grand Hall. The guard on the other side eyeballed me on my approach. His face was scarred, war torn, making his heavy build even more intimidating. The guardsman casually began unlocking the gate, refusing to make conversation; his hostile manner was somewhat similar to the previous day. With a grunt, he raised his finger, pointing towards the barracks.

Walking past him, I paused, wanting to reinforce the circumstances of my past actions and speak of the reasons surrounding his irritation towards me. "Your duty would have required you to put an end to Ricard's treasonous plot. If anything, I saved you from having to finish him."

The fierce guard strutted towards me and spoke, his voice gruff and dominating. "At least he would have seen my blade coming. There is little honour in thrusting steel into a man's back."

He turned back around and began locking the gate, indicating his unwillingness to entertain me any further. Entering the barracks, the beds were all abandoned except one. Sitting upright on it was the young guard who had been savagely attacked two nights previously. He looked over at me, taking a second glance at the crest on my tunic. Swelling had formed around his face, surrounding the wound, leaving him disfigured. The stitching had held the severed flesh in place, however the colouring of the skin indicated it was infected.

Markus squirmed as he attempted to sit upright further, leaning his back against the cold wall.

"Can I get you anything?" I asked.

"No Sir, it looks worse than it is."

"Are you able to talk?"

"I can, slowly. My tongue works fine, it's my mouth that's the problem, please excuse my impediment."

Pulling a stool from the armoury, I sat beside the young guard's bed with my hands cupped over my thighs. I looked down at his linens. They were damp from the sweat that seeped from his pores caused by his fever, a further indication that the wound was infected.

"We have apprehended a band of men that could have been involved in your assault, it is vital that you give me the accurate appearance of your attackers," I insisted.

Groaning, Markus began to fidget before looking at me with concern. Pressing him to break his silence, I relayed the importance of the interrogation.

"They were traders," he stuttered, "All seemed rather shrewd in what they wore. They insisted on entering the town to sell trinkets and charms. When I told them they would have to wait for first light to enter, they became agitated and forceful." Gulping, the boy continued. "I fled, they caught up with me and then one drove an axe into my face. That is all I remember."

Sighing, I glanced up at the roof of the barracks, allowing myself time to briefly process his account. "Why not run back into the town?"

Markus's eyes flickered, and he began twitching his legs. The guard seemed anxious about my challenge to his attempt at escaping. "They had blocked the entrance, I had met them outside, how was I to know of their malice?"

I placed my hand on his forearm and called for him to settle, his over-exertion from his reply had caused him to over-use his mouth and blood had begun leaking from the sewing over his lips.

"That is all, rest easy. These beasts will be brought to justice."

Stepping out from the barracks, I heard the sound of water trickling against the wall of the Grand Hall. Looking across, I saw Baron Asher stood unsteadily on his feet with one hand spread out against the stone, aiding his stance.

Relieving himself, he looked around and caught my eyes. Curling his upper lip, he called over to me. "You had your fill of the boy? I expect to have those merchants delivered to me by dusk."

Turning, I intentionally dismissed his condescending demands. Hearing him step closer through the long grass, his heavy panting indicated he had become infuriated by my arrogance towards him.

He leant his face closely towards mine, I could feel the warmth in his breath and smell the stench of stale wine. "You forget your place Sword; you forget who I am."

I snarled, eyeing him up and down, before focusing my sight on his stained beard. "You are nothing more than a drunken fool, lost and ungracious."

"You illegitimate in-bred peasant, how dare you address me in such a tone?"

I moved away, ignoring his petty insults, leaving him disgruntled at my snubbing of his title. The gate was being opened, allowing entry to two guests, both on horseback. Glancing to the female rider, she noticed me looking over to her, prompting her to return a cunning smile. Her skin was as white as snow, and her blue eyes were piercing over her high cheekbones. The hooded, silken black robe she wore lined her slim figure perfectly.

Bringing her horse to halt beside me she pulled back her hood, revealing her enchanting beauty, complemented by her long, shining black hair. Stepping down from her horse, she smirked at me, scanning me up and down with her sky-blue eyes. Her arrival had calmed Asher and he refrained from any further slurs.

"This town does offer the most intriguing of men," she said in a delicate yet teasing tone.

Unable to deny her beauty and seductiveness, I coyly offered her good day, before continuing to walk towards the gate.

Calling out to me, she spoke flirtatiously. "I do hope we meet again, Sword. Let us hope that our paths are destined to intertwine."

Leaving the Grand Hall, it took me a while to become undistracted by the mysterious stranger's charm and I began pondering on her purpose for visiting Asher's household. Thinking back to Markus, I knew that I would have to relay my findings to Hock, in turn determining the fate of our captives. However, something did not feel right. Markus's hesitation had not sat right with the conclusion I was faced with.

***

The dungeon was astonishingly quiet considering it housed a band of highly-strung travellers. Sergeant Hock was absent from his table situated in the centre of the vault. Tapping came from one of the cage doors and I turned to see the mature, long-haired merchant who appeared to have assumed authority over his fellow tradesman.

"Did you speak with the guard?" he asked.

Nodding my head sombrely, he reacted to my sullen expression by dropping his head and sighing.

"So, it is to be our deaths that will restore order, and I am sure will provide some well needed amusement for your townsfolk."

Overhearing their master's comments, pleas came rushing in from the other merchants, all keen to offer their innocence in Markus's attack. The commotion escalated, with sobs and jeers directed at me from the other side of the iron bars.

I shouted for silence; however, my command fell on deaf ears, the elder tradesman watched between me and his distraught companions.

"Enough!" he yelled. His authoritative tone had the desired effect. "Sword, I am your man, I struck the boy with the axe."

Moving closer to his door, I gripped hold of the bars. "Why are you doing this?"

Glaring back at me, the aged merchant looked around at his associates, and whispered an apology, before leaning back and spitting in my face. "Let me out of here and I will show you how I did it, you whore's son."

I looked at the other travellers to see their confused reaction at their superior's unprecedented conduct and confession.

"You will hang, they will not offer you a noble death," I said, unconvinced of his confession.

The entrance gate to the dungeon suddenly came crashing open. Lev, Hock and the Governor stormed into the chambers. Sergeant Hock looked at me, noticing me wiping the spit dripping from under my eye. Removing his peace baton, he slammed it against the bars of the cage door, demanding order and threatening to break bones.

"This man has confessed. He claims to be the suspect who assaulted the guard," I relayed.

"Well then he will be the last to hang," said Hock.

"Release the others," demanded the Governor.

"But Baron Asher will want any accomplices too," replied Hock, dumbfounded.

"I care little for what he wants, we have a confession. Let them go."

Looking over to the merchant, he continued to watch me, and then lowered his head, discreetly.

"As for the rest of you, your presence in this town is no longer welcome. Lev, escort them to the gate, any resistance, cut them down," ordered the Governor.

I followed the Governor from the dungeon, and he halted in the courtyard and turned to me. "Jep, I sense you are about to offer me a dilemma."

"Governor, that man did not attack the guard, he is a trader, not a thug."

"Once again you attempt to undermine the truth. I often wonder if you learnt anything from Fulten."

Pausing I stood, silenced by his reaction. Taking in a deep breath, the Governor stared at me with his piercing, sharp eyes. "Father Arrend, the attack on the boy, do you think of me as ignorant to the situation? I assure you I am aware that history tends to repeat itself. My first observation was that the church was not ransacked of all its plunder, a clear bluff by whoever murdered Arrend. The merchant's confession is merely an act of principle, a true leader will always take the responsibility."

"So, you will free him?" I asked.

He looked around, before replying. "No, he will hang so the others may go free, and we will display our own bluff for the whole town to witness. Time will be our ally, young Sword. Patience is something you need to learn."

As the Governor marched across the courtyard, I stared at him in awe. His understanding and experience had floored me and at the same time made me rethink my ignorance towards his authority. Chenchi was right, I was far too pre-emptive; it was time I learned to trust in the knowledge offered by my senior Swords.

***

Both Chenchi and I had been summoned to the dungeon. Sergeant Hock awaited us, alongside the prisoner shackled in iron chains. Chenchi gladly yanked the chain, pulling the merchant towards him. Leading the aged, long-haired tradesman to the stables, I demanded we walk with the captive.

"Let's drag the turd," growled Chenchi.

"There is no need, we shall take him on foot," I insisted.

Grunting in dismay, Chenchi did however respect my request. Our presence in the town with the tradesman did not go unnoticed by the local peasants. Recognizing the brawler, children began calling out to their parents as we walked past, and a gathering of eager onlookers began to build. I looked back at our detainee, noticing him struggling to maintain the pace at which my companion led him. The iron of the cuffs had begun digging into his skin, causing red sores to appear on his wrists.

The handful of spectators walked alongside us, lining the edge of the path. A few of the men began to spit on the ground at the sight of the merchant, shortly followed by jeers and chanting. Facing the more boisterous of the bystanders, I scowled, giving them an angry stare, forgetting their unfamiliarity with the truth. However, I was struggling to accept that I was sending an innocent man into the hands of our merciless Baron.

Chenchi demanded entry into the Grand Hall and once inside the compound it was not long before Asher's henchmen began to arrive, keen to see the attacker. The burly, heavy guard strutted across the gravel to meet our prisoner. Scrunching his mouth, the brute peered down at the merchant, glaring at him with chilling eyes. The elderly man glanced back at me, looking for reassurance which caused me to look down to the ground, shame faced since I could offer no such thing.

Leaning back, the muscular guard swiped his arm, hitting our captive with the back of his fist to his cheek. Falling to the ground, the prisoner struggled back to his knees, before spitting blood from his mouth. Chenchi stood beside the grounded man, smiling back at his equally sized and previous associate.

"Easy Seiloff, there will be nothing left to hang," said Chenchi.

Embracing each other, grasping arms, Seiloff looked behind Chenchi and begun eying me. "I enjoy seeing you, old friend, however the company you keep is unfortunate."

"Jep is a good man. Do not be fooled by the sparse hair that grows on his chin."

Seiloff chortled, before moving his uncomfortable expression away from me. Reaching down, he took a firm grip of the merchant's long hair before dragging him away from the courtyard. Chenchi began walking back towards the gate. Calling over to him, I insisted on seeing Markus, keen to check on his recovery. Chenchi grumbled, ordering that I was to make my visit brief.

Inside the barracks, Markus was still laid on the bed, resting from his injuries. I nudged his shoulder, and he opened his eyes, startled by my intrusion. Getting straight to the point, I told him that his alleged attacker was now housed in the guard's dungeon. Unable to make eye contact with me he groaned in pain, once again disturbing the stitching that ran down the centre of his face.

"Long black hair, old and haggard, is that really the man that struck you?" I asked.

"Yes, that sounds similar."

"You will identify him," I said.

"Enough, you will torment my guard no more," called a gravelly voice from the entrance of the barracks. Seiloff stood, watching me with malice before nodding for me to leave. Giving Markus a final unsatisfactory look, I approached the gigantic guard.

"You lead these men?" I asked.

"I do."

I became distracted by the sword that had been fixed above the doorframe, losing my train of thought. At first sight the weapon appeared nothing more than ornamental, until I squinted, examining its fine craftmanship more closely. Its thick, steel blade had been forged precisely, each edge containing three curved patterns, which matched the design of its bronze hilt.

Seiloff took a glimpse at what was hindering my reply. "You recognise the sword?" he asked, smugly. Snorting, I refrained from answering, knowing full well I had crossed steel with it in the past. "You say treacherous, we say inspirational, Ricard was a man of honour," muttered Seiloff.

Now meeting his eyes, I raised my upper lip. "I took his life; I have no qualms about taking the life of another spineless guard."

For a few moments neither one of us withdrew our sight from the other, however uncomfortable the standoff. Leaving the quarters, I could not help but feel relieved. Seiloff was a mountain of a man, and the encounter had left me feeling uneasy.

Chenchi awaited me on the far side of the compound, keen to get away from the Grand Hall. As I made my way to join him I heard the sound of heavy breathing, with the occasional murmur coming from the rear of the guard's barracks. As always, my over-inquisitiveness got the better of me and I quietly crept around the wall, keeping close to the stone, keen to discover what was causing the sound. I was not naïve; I knew full well what action was responsible for the over energetic panting.

Amongst the long grass that curled against the rear of the guard's chambers, the Baron stood with the ties of his linen trousers wrapped just below his knees. Witnessing his bare white, pimpled buttocks was a somewhat difficult sight, as he thrust his hips, vigorously, into the rear of a slender, black haired woman. He ogled down at the girl, red faced and clammy, his eyes bright as he rubbed his chubby hand down her back, forcefully.

The picture was nauseating; yet knowing the girl he humped was not Lady Ivy pleased me. Unresponsive to Asher's efforts, the black-haired woman flung back her head at the pulling of her hair. Seeing me observing the uncomfortable intimacy, she raised one side of her mouth, grinning, staring back at me with her high cheek bones and mesmerizing blue eyes.

Startled, I turned around, swiftly walking away from the barracks. Chenchi noticed me approaching, sheepishly fast paced.

"Let me guess, you been caught conversing with the Baroness?"

"It is not I that is being over familiar. Asher, he mounts a woman over behind the garrison."

"He is a Baron, what do you expect? He mates with all the servant girls," said Chenchi, brushing off my claims.

"This was no servant, I met her yesterday. She seemed of importance and rode in company with protection. Something about her, I cannot describe, her silk black hair, blue eyes as clear as a summer sky, she is somewhat enthralling."

"You speak of Truda," replied Chenchi.

"I know not her name."

"She has been sent by the Crown, from Alma. It appears our Grace wishes for Asher to be reinvented, learn some new manners. Some say she is an adviser, someone to realign our Baron's power. I am yet to see her, but I hear she is easy on the eye, seductive. Her guardian goes by the name Eruk, and rumour speculates the man was a Blue Sword once, fearless and gallant."

"Why turn his back on his pledge?" I asked.

"Not all wish to be a slave to the Swords Jep, besides most would pay nicely for the protection of a retired Sword."

7

APPEASEMENT

The night was being unkind, my mind felt repetitive as I visualised the aged merchant's gaze. His innocence was clear and yet his valour could not be criticised. Sick of the silence and restless moments in my bed, I put on my uniform and headed for the stables. Spike was eager to stretch his legs, stamping his hoof onto the gravel as he awaited me, impatiently. Keen to avoid Fawkes on his night patrol and face an inquisition of my intentions, I rode Spike across the boggy mud tracks, behind the Finch estate. Following the river that ran through the south of the town, the journey time to the Grand Hall was doubled, however it allowed me to pass through unnoticed.

The ride over to the Grand Hall was peaceful and it gave me a chance to breathe in the clear air from the night sky, whilst observing the tranquil flowing of the water. The guard on the gate was rather concerned by my late intrusion, however seeing my uniform he granted me access to the dungeon, after I led him to believe that I was there to put further charges to the captured tradesman. I followed the guard through the grounds, his burning torch lighting our path around the outside wall of the building's main structure.

Tethering Spike, I insisted that I needed no further escort. Hitting my fist against the iron doors of the Baron's dungeon, I demanded entry. An elderly man limped towards the iron doors, squinting as he attempted to clap eyes on me. The flames from his torch were distorting my vision, causing me to raise my hand to my eyes.

"What is it? Why at this hour must you attend?" the elderly man asked.

"I have reason to believe your prisoner is responsible for more crimes against the town, now open the door, old man."

Watching him turn the key, I felt relief as the hunchbacked jailer opened the rigid door. Seeing my crest, he refrained from his initial abruptness and invited me inside. Rats scurried across the straw covered floor at our steps, and the stench of dampness from the moist walls was unbearable.

Surprised by the lack of guards present, I was keen to confirm who was in attendance. "They leave you alone with these men?"

He looked at me with his boil covered face and crinkled skin, "With this man, you mean? He poses little threat, the guards have beaten him that hard, he will be lucky to make his own death."

"I must speak with him, alone."

"If I leave this place unattended, it will be I that is strung up tomorrow," the old man argued.

I moved closer to the jailer. "Look at the tunic I wear, be assured I was the one who dragged him here, besides, do you truly believe that I am in the habit of freeing criminals?"

"I suppose not, but make it quick, I must relieve myself anyhow."

Waiting for the old man to hobble from the dungeon, I listened to hear the gate lock before stepping closer to the occupied cell. Heavy breathing came from inside the cage, and the merchant was cowering in the far corner, looking back at me, beaten and downtrodden. His groan caused him discomfort and he began coughing, violently.

"Can you walk?" I asked.

Struggling, the merchant got to his feet and limped closer to the cage bars. He held his forearm tightly into his stomach, moaning with each step he took.

His once elegant tunic was now stained in blood, leaking from the wounds that had been inflicted on his bruised and battered face. Barely able to lift the lids of his eyes due to his swollen skin, he murmured quietly, questioning my reasons for attending.

"I don't suppose you have come offering me a pardon?" he smiled, uncomfortably.

I glanced down at the floor. "I am afraid not." Looking back at him, I asked, "Why do this? Why not plead your innocence and demand a trial?"

The merchant gripped hold of a bar with his able hand. "I have lived well and experienced adventure. I have met kings, queens, fools and whores. I now grow tired, tired of the scroungers, sick of the infestation that breeds throughout this once beautiful land. I knew the risks coming here to trade, we all did. Your town and its Baron have quite the reputation for being corrupt and unjust."

"You didn't harm the boy, if you were to demand trial, it would give me time to learn the truth," I stated, concerned by the miscarriage of justice about to be enacted.

"And deny the people their amusement? The Baron needs this, it is a way of offering pleasure and satisfaction to the townsfolk, along with a warning of regimentation. If I had not offered a confession, all my companions would be facing the noose. Your enthusiasm to learn the identity of the guard's attacker is pleasing, but we both know this cannot be achieved by noon tomorrow."

"So that is why you confessed? Out of heroism?"

"I have never been an honest man, so why change now?" he laughed, before coughing painfully.

The main door to the dungeon slammed shut. Several footsteps approached from the walkway.

A deep voice called from the shadowy doorway of the chambers. "You shouldn't be here Sword."

Staring back at me was Seiloff, the guard with the scarred face. Straightening his back the crown of his head just slightly missed the stone archway above him. "What do you want with the prisoner?"

A gentle, calming voice called from behind him. "And what business is that of yours, Seiloff?"

Red-faced and embarrassed, the gigantic guard turned around, lowering his head, he made way for his challenger.

Appearing from out from the passage, Lady Ivy entered the dungeon. Her eyes sparkled as she glimpsed over to me, giving me a discreet grin.

"My lady, he converses with the captive," complained Seiloff, this time lowering his tone.

"He is a Blue Sword and will converse with whomever he wishes. Your ongoing animosity towards our allies can only allow me to assume you are jealous of his rank. Are you not satisfied with being a nobleman's guard?"

"I am, my lady," replied Seiloff, peering up at the ceiling whilst biting his tongue to prevent him saying anything more that might antagonise the Baroness'.

Leaning closer to the guard, Lady Ivy whispered. "Well show some dignity then, man."

Seiloff nodded shamefaced, accepting his reprimand.

"Leave us," ordered Baroness Ivy.

Seiloff gave me a sour look before acknowledging Lady Ivy's demands and departing from the dungeon.

"Now that is a leader," said the merchant through his cell bars.

Lady Ivy approached the cage, observing the prisoner. "I assume your wounds are a consequence of my guards?"

"I gave as good as I got, my lady."

"I cannot excuse the crime of which you have been convicted, but you are to meet your judgment tomorrow and I wish to offer you my blessings."

"Thank you, my lady. If you are the last sight I am to see, then I will die a happy man," he replied.

My chuckle caused Lady Ivy to give me a stern look as if she were dissatisfied with my encouragement of the tradesman's charm.

Offering my farewells to the weary merchant, he grinned, giving me some advice. "Do not over complicate your investigation. Just like life, you need to keep it simple and not allow yourself to overthink. You are a worthy man, Sword."

On the arrival of the hunchbacked jailer, I claimed it was time I should leave. Lady Ivy insisted on walking me to the gate. As I untethered my horse, the Baroness began gliding her hand down Spike's neck, smiling and relaying her fondness for him. Holding his reins, I pulled him along behind me, whilst strolling beside Lady Ivy.

The glistening stars lit up the courtyard of the Grand Hall. Baroness Ivy came to a standstill halfway between the front doors and the gate, keen to converse away from the ears of the guard patrolling the entrance.

"Does it not alarm you, the thought of your husband witnessing us in conversation at this hour?" I asked.

"No, I am assured that he grunts in his bed, his belly filled with wine and a stranger by his side," she replied.

"And this does not concern you?"

Giggling, Lady Ivy looked back at me. "No, I very much enjoy my rest away from his noisy gullet."

"You have changed, you are stronger. It pleases me to see you this way," I said.

Lady Ivy paused, gazing across at me, her eyes fixed on my own. The intensity reminded me of the night we kissed outside my family home in Somerby. I felt my heart begin to race and my stomach flutter.

Baroness Ivy glanced up at the starry sky, "We have all changed, Jep. When my father disappeared, I longed for his return, having taken our previous time together for granted. Your absence in my life recently has made me long for you more."

I took a deep breath on hearing the words that fell from her mouth, my heart felt as if it was lined with gold. I wanted to take her in my arms and kiss her, just like we had done before. However, even though we were out of earshot, I was well aware of the patrolling guard's presence.

Lady Ivy offered me goodnight and began to walk away, before unexpectedly turning back to me. "Jep, my heart has never left you and I have come to accept that it never will."

Watching her moving across the courtyard, I mirrored her observations of the night sky. It was yet another of those stolen moments that I had always sought after with Lady Ivy. I looked back at Spike, who stared at me through his black eyes. "If you could talk my friend, I suspect you would have a lot to say." Mounting his back, I rode out the gates of the Grand Hall and made my way back to the lock up.

***

That morning, the town felt chilly and my mood reflected the greyness above me. My encounter with Lady Ivy had been subjugated by the thought of having to witness an innocent man die, only to appease the animosity that bred throughout the town I served. Once again, the crest embroidered onto my tunic had no influence over the politics that continued to plague Stanford.

The market square had been cleared and the gibbet placed centrally for all to observe as if it was a rare, lavish ornament. Its structure was simple; two wooden planks had been crossed either side, harnessing a beam of solid oak. On a first sight, its initial appearance was rather simplistic, but catching sight of the two ropes that hung down tied into nooses made its presence much more daunting.

The townsfolk had arrived en masse, and the atmosphere remained animated. A handful of Asher's guards were already lining the gibbet, ushering away any excitable children who played, daring one another to climb the fixture. It was Fawkes who had been allocated the day's patrol along with me. I had attempted to discourage my companion from attending the execution, but his eagerness to deter any disorder took priority over my own longing to be as far as way as possible.

Bringing our horses to a standstill, Fawkes insisted on overlooking the square from the track.

Scanning his eyes over the boisterous crowd, Fawkes tutted. "Look at them, they're as pathetic as the man that hangs. Most of them starve, yet they arm themselves with fruit to inflict further indignity upon the soul to be punished."

Fawkes peered over to me, screwing up the corners of his mouth. "And yet nothing from you, Jep? I was waiting for you to voice your overactive imagination on these circumstances."

Thinking back to the advice given to me by the Governor, I was keen to conceal my own thoughts. "I care little for the punishment, I grew up in the north; hangings were common and most of the time unjust. One would hang for taking a piss," I replied, carelessly, attempting to appease him.

The gathering people began to separate at the entrance of Main Street, Seiloff led the group of riders as they cascaded onto the square.

Yelling down at the spectators, Seiloff demanded they make way for their ruler, Baron Asher. Central amongst the horses, Asher and Lady Ivy rode side by side, Baron Asher dressed in a ceremonial doublet and Lady Ivy in an elegant coral gown. The presence of the Baroness was Asher's protection from the jeers. Even though the locals had grown bolder in their opinions, Baroness Ivy remained in favour and her presence inspired the people, for they truly adored her.

Following behind, Asher's advisor and secret mistress Truda entered the square, her black satin dress matching her loosely flowing dark hair. She observed the people haughtily, raising her eyebrows and grinning over at her guardian. Eruk made little of the lively crowd, examining the marketplace, ensuring he was familiar with the settings as any experienced protector would. Giving little away, his expression remained dead pan, conduct that you would expect from a retired Blue Sword. At first sight, he did not appear noble nor elegant, he was a solidly built man, but short, and his hair thin and grey.

Fawkes commented on my gawping at the new arrivals. "Do not be fooled by his underwhelming form, Eruk has quite the reputation. He served with the Governor at Alma for several years and is one of the few men to ever retire from the Swords."

"He doesn't look like much," I said.

"And that, Jep, is why you will not see retirement."

Seiloff called for silence, his grave tone echoing throughout the square. Stillness from the bystanders was achieved. "Bring forward the prisoner," he bellowed.

The people turned to face the entrance of the square and on seeing the doomed captive, began to hurl profanities towards him. The merchant sat upright, unsaddled on a horse that was being directed by a guard pulling at its reins.

The aged merchant looked down at the hostile crowd, expressionless and taking in the heckles that were directed towards him. Rotten vegetables began splattering against his head, thrown by angered locals on seeing him emerge. The merchant offered them no reaction and remained calm and poised in his final moments. A child ran into the path of the oncoming horse and pulled back his arm, flinging a handful of browned cabbage up at the prisoner. The guard smirked up at the weary eyed traveller, showing him no compassion.

Lining up the captive directly below one of the dangling ropes, Seiloff called for a ladder. The townsfolk cheered as Seiloff climbed up bringing himself level with the merchant's head. Lowering the noose down towards the beaten man's crown, he pulled the rope firmly, untangling it from the merchant's long hair. Tightening the noose, Seiloff stared out at the crowd and raised both his arms, generating further excitement from the spectators. The Baron smiled, amused by the people's enthusiasm.

Guiding his horse forward, Baron Asher blocked the prisoner's stallion. Slowly he lifted his hand, indicating he expected silence. "Hear me! Gaze upon this criminal, whose act of terror will not go unpunished. I offer this death as reward for your loyalty and patience." The Baron then glanced over to Truda, who eyed him back, with a conceited expression displayed on her face. "Let this be a warning to any person who wishes to undermine our prosperous town. I will consider no final words."

Nodding his head, he indicated for the bard to begin striking his drum. The quick concussion of beats amplified the atmosphere, making the punishment more of a spectacle. The crowd whispered to each other in anticipation, whilst I caught the merchant offering me his final vision. It was haunting to meet his eyes, knowing his death was only moments away. He raised one side of his mouth, giving me a slight smile, before tilting his head down at the horse beneath him.

It was difficult to watch, knowing the man's innocence, but I knew it was necessary. As the bard firmly struck his final beat, Seiloff clapped his hand powerfully on the horse's rump, causing it to startle and jolt forward. The merchant's legs were flung into the air, but the impact of his body straightening was not enough to provide him with a quick death. Instinctively he began thrashing, his mind not allowing him to give in to his fate. I attempted to steer my horse around, keen to leave the square, only to be called back by Fawkes.

The merchant's momentary redness had now flushed away as his face became pale. His eyes were beginning to sink indicating his body had finally submitted and he was at his end. Seiloff prodded at the hanging corpse before nodding to the Baron, confirming death.

The crowd started to disperse, however some insisted on distastefully spitting at the merchant's hanging body. Truda and Eruk rode towards us, Truda's unique, beguiling features and Eruk's glorified reputation making me feel rather inferior as the duo approached.

Fawkes showed little appreciation towards Truda, his attention preoccupied by the veteran Blue Sword.

"A successful hanging, don't you think?" commented Truda, in an arrogant tone.

"They all hang the same," replied Fawkes.

Truda raised her chin, pompously. "Yes, quite. It pleases me to see the local Swords endorsing their Baron. And you," she said, giving me a cunning look, "I believe we have met before."

Bashfully, I looked over to Fawkes before clearing my throat, thinking of her physical encounter with Baron Asher which I had witnessed the previous day.

I began to stutter, thinking of the correct and cautious words to use, however Truda's response was calculated and perfectly timed. "Yes, at the Grand Hall. It was in the courtyard after your meeting with the wounded guard. I felt the animosity between you and our noble lord."

"Jep has somewhat of a history with Baron Asher," replied Fawkes, displaying his annoyance at her directness.

"That is why I am here, to advise the Baron on his current mishaps. I guarantee that the animosity between our ruler's house and your establishment will be a thing of the past."

Fawkes gave Truda little indulgence and quickly diverted his attention towards the retired Blue Sword. "It is an honour to meet you, Eruk. My Governor has often spoken tales of your valour."

"The old sparrow leads you still. It would please me to see him."

"Sparrow, Sir?" I interrupted.

Looking back at me with a frown he remarked, "You have no need to call me Sir, my title is no grander than your own. We called the cantankerous old bastard 'Sparrow', after his love of birds, a pastime I can only assume he has not shared amongst his men. Although behind that scorning face of his is a fierce warrior, the best I have had the privilege to serve alongside."

Truda grew tired of the reminiscing, expressing her discontent with an overly exaggerated yawn. "Oh! Do forgive me. I grow weary of stories of egotistical men. I do hope you will be attending the banquet at the Grand Hall."

"I feel you may be pressing this new-found alliance," said Fawkes.

"That may be so, but your Chief arrives in three days. I do not believe he would be impressed by your absence."

Eruk looked at Fawkes, rolling his eyes, before being belittled by Truda and ordered to retire to the Grand Hall.

Once they were out of earshot, I turned to Fawkes. "The Chief is due here? Did you know this?"

"No, and neither does the Governor. We had best return and bring him up to speed."

8

BLOOD IN THE NIGHT

It came as no surprise to learn that I had been allocated the night patrol for that evening. Both Chenchi and I were still being ostracized for our extended tour beyond the town. That and the fact we were still the greenest amongst our peers meant we were still liable to be allocated the worst of the watches.

Already familiar with the news Sergeant Hock was about to relay, I was keen to see the reaction of my companions as we sat listening to the morning briefing. "Chief Muir is set to arrive in Stanford within the next two to three days, and as we received no word directly from our establishment in Alma, I can only assume we will be in for an unannounced visit. So, now that we have the upper hand, I expect this place cleaned up, the armoury fully stocked and our charisma on full charm."

An interruption came from the combat room, behind where Hock was standing. "There is little need for that," said the Governor, appearing through the archway. "We provide our chief with no illusions or misconception of our struggles. We are two men down and feasting on handouts. Once he discovers the truth, maybe then he will aid us with more wealth. We will, however, all be attending the banquet provided by the Baron's household. There you will mask our unsettled past with Asher and for one night refrain from animosity towards them."

The Governor looked at me, making his point. In truth, the hatred I held for Asher had been surpassed after discovering his love affair with Truda. Besides, the thought of spending the evening catching a glimpse of Lady Ivy made the whole situation rather appealing.

The crescent moon illuminated the courtyard as I led Spike from the stables. Whispering into his ear, I had become accustomed to sharing my thoughts with the animal.

Casually I ventured up Main Street, relieved to see the paths free from drunks and mischief. However, like any peaceful setting within Stanford, it always had potential to be ruined by the inconsiderate behaviour emanating from the Viking Invader tavern. The dramatic slamming open of the doors, and the stumbling peasant woman who appeared, indicated not all was well.

On seeing me, she staggered closer, slurring and drooling as she spoke. "Kind sir, you best get in there, trouble is brewing."

"When is it not?" I said.

"It's those pesky merchants; a few of them sit in there parading their manhood. Carre, the farmer has challenged them; if he loses it, be assured all hell will break loose."

Tethering Spike outside the tavern, I heard the plump, hardened peasant woman call back to me. "If you would rather turn a blind eye, my lovely, a lady would be most grateful for a ride on that horse of yours."

Leaving the woman cackling in the street I pushed open the door to the tavern. It was the first time I had been inside since discovering Jen's body in her quarters. Taking a quick glance at the serving table where I remembered lapping up her playful behaviour, I felt my stomach gripe. My attention was quickly drawn away by the deep voice of a stocky man yelling at a table accommodating three seated merchants. It was, as expected, Carre.

The instant silence caused by my arrival attracted the attention of Carre, who leered back at me, behind his thick, ginger beard. His heavy frame towered over the table of merchants, who remained poised and undeterred by my presence.

"It is a stranger I see before me. Jep my boy, come embrace me!" bellowed Carre.

I couldn't help but feel thrilled to see the grouchy farmer, for it was Carre who had offered me compassion when I first arrived in Stanford. Meeting him with my arm held out, he gripped hold of me, adamant on giving me an overbearing hug. The stench of stale mead from his breath hit my face, and his unsteadiness on his feet forced me to hold up his weight.

Carre rested one arm around my shoulders as he turned back to the merchants. "See these bastards, Jep? They think they have the right to drink amongst us, even after the disregard they have shown our beloved town. I say lock them up," he wailed, prompting a cheer from the onlookers.

Placing my hand on Carre's chest, I gently and discreetly told him to leave. Carre scowled back at me, pushing my hand away. "You had spirit once boy, but you allowed those Swords to weaken your bones."

Moving closer to him, I whispered, "I swear to you, if they do not leave, I will hang them myself on this night."

Huffing, Carre waved his hand in my face, contemptuously, before stumbling out from the tavern. Approaching the table, the three merchants sat undeterred by my attempt at engagement. Sipping on their ale, they sat upright proudly.

"Why do you taunt these people? You were banished," I asked.

Their refusal to speak angered me further, making me repeat my question, this time more abruptly and therefore prompting a response.

"You allowed an innocent man to be executed, and we grow tired of your oppression," said the merchant seated opposite to where I stood.

Looking down at the table, I noticed a short wooden club, resting beside the man seated with his back to me.

My tolerance grew weary at their facetious tones, at which point I ordered the men to leave the tavern so that I could escort them to the gate. The merchant by my waist remained silent, whilst the one opposite began arguing against my demands. The third one, who was seated furthest away and continued to casually drink from his beaker, also refused to acknowledge my order.

Impatiently I leaned over the table to the third merchant, taking hold of his cup before yanking it from his hand, and spilling the contents over the table. The spillage caused the fluid to splash on the lap of the stout merchant seated by my waist. Seeing his bald head lean forward and his hand reach for the club on the table, I swiftly removed my peace baton, crashing it down onto the man's knuckles. He yelped, clinging on to his injured hand. The slender, vocal tradesman began lifting his body, attempting to get to his feet. As his head came upright, I took hold of his greasy hair tightly and forced his head back down, smashing his head on to the wooden table, and leaving him to slump onto the ground.

The third merchant leaned back into his chair, with his hands raised, peering up nervously at the end of my baton. I slowly stepped around the table, my boot crunching down on to the broken clay beaker as I stalked towards the vocal, belligerent merchant, who was now floored and submissively staring up at me nursing his bloodied nose.

I looked down at his pointed chin and sharp features. "I don't recall locking you up on the night of the brawl?"

He stuttered, "We were not present, we came for the execution, to pay our respects."

The spirited onlookers called for more punishment as they cheered on our confrontation.

"As you can see, your kind are no longer welcome in this town. You will now leave the tavern and head straight to the gate, never to return. Do I make myself clear?"

"Very well, we wish for no further conflict."

The three merchants walked dejectedly ahead of me as I rode behind on Spike. Making our way to the gate, two of the men remained silent, with one only making the occasional whimper at the pain caused by his injured hand. The more petulant man began wiping away the blood from his face with a rag.

He seemed keen to make conversation and express his point. "Does it not concern you that you have hanged an innocent man?"

Sighing, I stared down at him. "You told me you were not present at the guard's attack, so how could you possibly know if he was innocent?"

"Tomlin was a righteous merchant. He refused to trade in goods that were not of genuine worth, and he wasn't capable of violence."

Looking blankly at the slender, sharp-featured merchant I decided not to engage further in any form of debate, knowing as well as he did that Tomlin's death was nothing more than a spectacle, a way to appease the townsfolk and for the Governor to show a bluff to the true assailant.

Once at the gate, the Baron's guard on patrol began quizzing our arrival. "Sir, forgive my obstruction, but I am under strict orders that the gate is to remain locked until daybreak. It is the Baron's orders; he wants the town on lockdown. Rumour is there is a special guest making his way here from the city."

"These men are not welcome in this town and will only bring further disorder." I insisted.

The guard eyeballed the injured merchant's. "Leave these pathetic turds with me, any trouble and I will deliver you their balls."

Grunting, I glimpsed over at the three merchants, who all appeared relieved not to be heading out into the wilderness during darkness. They knew that bandits and outlaws prowled the woodlands, keen to pick off any carriers of riches travelling through.

"Then they remain here and are banished at first light, do you hear?" I said.

"I have seen infants with more fight in them. Do not worry Sword, I can handle three merchants."

"It has been a pleasure, Sword. I do hope that one day our paths may cross again," called the slender merchant in a rather haughty tone, whilst offering back my rag that he had used to clean his wounded nose.

***

Riding back towards the town, passing the edge of the Burn Oak slums, I noticed a figure take a quick glance at me, before picking up their pace. Squinting, I was able to get a brief glimpse of the girl's face, covered by the hood of her tatty robe.

"Stop right there, girl," I ordered.

The young girl slowly turned around, before pulling back her head cover and staring back at me, sheepishly.

"Blair, why do you roam at night? Your mother will not be happy with this discovery."

"Please Jep, I beg you do not speak of this to Mother, she will go wild."

"What are you up to?"

"Nothing, I can't sleep, that is all," she replied.

"Answer me, Blair, or you leave me little choice."

"For crying out loud, Jep, fine! But do you swear not to tell my mother?"

"No, I don't. Now answer the question, what are you up to?"

Blair tutted and rolled her eyes, before conjuring up another false answer in her head. Not fooled, I insisted on the truth.

"The boy, Markus," she whispered.

"The wounded guard?"

"He isn't a guard, he is a gatekeeper, and he is my friend. I have known him for years. The others, they belittle him and taunt him, treat him like a lame dog. I just took him a few leftovers from our feast, that is all."

"He is my age, what is he doing entertaining a child?"

"He is only a couple of years my elder, besides, it isn't like that, we are friends. Anyway, I hate boys, I would cut his hand off if he tried it."

"So, Markus really is just a boy. The guards, they will lock you up for poaching," I said.

Laughing, Blair answered. "The guards have no idea, I sneak in from the meadow and before that we used to meet outside of Asher's hall. Well, until he had his face opened up."

Thinking back to my own childhood and the acts that my friends Gibbon and Abbot and I used to get up to, I could only find her deceitfulness amusing.

Pressing for a response, Blair whined, "Come on Jep, don't let on, he's the only friend I have got outside the lock up."

"Very well, but I know nothing. If Fawkes finds out he will have mine and the boy's heads."

"Fawkes won't find out. Anyway, he likes to give off the impression that he is hardened. But you should hear the sweet nothings he whispers to Mother," chuckled Blair.

Smiling, I ordered her back to the lock up. I couldn't help but admire the girl's boldness and adore her witty charms. Blair was spirited and fearless, and under Fawkes's guidance she would make a formidable member of the Blue Swords.

The birds began to whistle from the trees, and seeing the sun rising on the horizon came as a welcoming sight. The cold frost was harsh, and I was pleased to be nearing the end of my tour. Spike had also begun to grow fatigued as he trotted sluggishly down Main Street. Planning to ensure the merchants had moved on from the town, I approached the market square.

A small group of local traders had gathered around something that had caught their eye. On seeing me arrive, one called out to me, "You there, please come."

Heading to the commotion, I jumped down from Spike, ordering them to make way so I could see what had garnered their attention so intently.

Looking down I saw a pool of blood, coagulating on the cobbled stones. The source of this harrowing sight lay still and lifeless on the cobbles. The ginger hair had reddened further from the blood and I was quick to recognise the victim. Carre lay face down on the cobbles. I leapt down, struggling to pull over his heavy body.

My heart plummeted on discovering the extent of his injuries.

"They got you, you should have gone home, man," I muttered, whilst examining his daunting injuries.

"How long have you been here? Why leave him face down?" I shouted.

The onlookers gasped at seeing the swelling and injuries to his face. Blood smeared over his skin, as his swollen, purple eyes made him barely identifiable.

I screamed his name, attempting to rouse him. One of the traders pointed out his chest was barely rising, from his shallow breaths. My mind became foggy, at the impact of seeing my friend in such a state. Slowing down my thoughts I was able to begin to think rationally and examine the blood on the ground next to where Carre lay. It still flowed from his wounds and was far from congealed, and considering the frost was near to freezing his blood, it meant the attack had happened recently.

Carre was known to voice his opinion vehemently, however his popularity made this violent assault even more implausible. It was doubtful it would have been a townsman. He had fought with the merchants in a drunken argument and that was enough to make them the prime suspects.

"Get him on my horse and take him to Western Farm. One of you head straight to the Grand Hall and demand the surgeon's attendance," I ordered.

"I don't think the Baron will care for the troubles of a drunken farmer," a voice responded.

"Baron Asher will care, for he owns the farm and without Carre, we all go hungry. Go now."

Getting to my feet, one of the morning traders asked me where I was going, appearing rather surprised by my eagerness to leave. I gave him a chilling look. "I am off to punish the men that did this."

Sprinting up the hill past the church, I could see the ravens lining the town's wall. Their excited calls made it apparent that food was in their sight. The guard that had been patrolling at the gate sat upright against the thick, wooden doorway, and just Like Carre, blood stained his clothing. His bloodied state and widened stare were a consequence of the laceration to his throat, as blood drained from his neck, leaving him ashen and disturbing to the eye.

Panting from exertion, my breath puffed from my mouth in a white cloud, made visible by the cold. The foot gate was unlocked, and I stepped outside, snarling as I looked over at the woods that lined the horizon opposite the town. The marks of several footprints disturbed the long grass leading away from the wall, where the merchants had made their escape. Finally, they had rid us of their presence, but not before leaving my friend battling for his life.

Racing back past the church, my heart pounded as the cold air sharply hit my lungs. My legs felt out of touch with my mind, as I felt a wave of terror rush through me. Stopping, I leaned against the fencing surrounding the church yard, with my hands cupping over my knees. I leaned over, feeling as if the ground was beginning to rise and capture my body, leaving me feeling paralysed and suddenly unable to move. Looking about, I desperately hoped that nobody was around to witness my moment of uncontrollable panic.

Eventually, I was able to steady my breathing and my mind began to re-engage with reality, allowing me to stand upright. Glancing up at the blue, wintery sky I gathered my composure and began to breathe more easily.

***

The door to Western Farm was ajar. Walking up the path, I could hear the commotion from inside as Dam yelled for water and cloth. Being a farmer's wife, Dam was used to the sight of gore. I was surprised by her lack of excitability and seeing her tending to her husband's wounds reminded me of the robust character she was. Directing her farm hand, Rye, with instructions on what she needed, she had the matter under control as much as circumstances would allow.

Noticing me at the door, she called out. "Jep hand me a knife, I need to cut off his clothes. His skin is like ice, I need to wrap him up in fresh rags." Placing my knife in Dam's hand, she told me to help move Carre, so she could remove his clothes.

Taking another look at the horrifying wounds that now disfigured my friend's features gave me further shudders. Staring across the table to Dam, I assured her that the town's surgeon was on his way.

"Tell me you caught up with the savages that did this, Jep?" asked Dam.

I was unable to make eye contact with her, "They have already fled the town."

Dam scowled back at me. "My husband lays here struggling for breath. Swear to me you will find them and kill them."

"You have my word, Dam. I will bring these men to justice and they will pay."

"I will help you. I will cut each one to the ground," said Rye.

"Rye, get the boiled water from the pot, place it outside, it will cool quicker," ordered Dam.

The surgeon arrived, and casually entering the farmhouse, he strutted towards us, unhurried and gracefully. Standing beside Carre he peered upon the injuries down the length of his nose, whilst undoing his long, tightly fitted doublet.

"All shall leave," he instructed, calmly.

Dam glanced over to me, taking direction from my nod.

Outside, Dam took a deep breath before her bottom lip began to quiver. Rye moved closer, embracing Dam, as she rested her head on his chest, offering her comfort as she sobbed, quietly. I stared over to Rye, who looked back at me with vengeful eyes.

Moments later, Dam manged to compose herself, and clearing her throat she pleaded with me to prioritise finding her husband's attackers. Hearing the sound of children's laughter coming from the field, I watched Carre's two sons playing and teasing one another.

With my eyes on the children, I made a promise to Dam, "With every breath I have, I will find them and slaughter each one."

9

THE CHIEF

Riding back, I kept my head lowered, signalling that I was in no mood to hear the whines of locals complaining about their affairs. Baron Asher's henchmen sat upright on their horses, positioned unmoving outside the front of the lock up. The guards whispered to each other on seeing me pass by. Two unfamiliar horses had been tethered inside the unoccupied stables. I wandered onto the courtyard, hearing raised voices coming from inside the parade room.

As I entered, my arrival prompted silence and I saw that Baron Asher was seated at our banquet table, picking at the remains of last night's meal. Witnessing me enter he grunted, unimpressed by my attendance. The Governor stood in the corner of the room, grimacing and clearly irritable. Truda stood next to the Baron and was the only person to greet me with warmth. She peered back at me through her clear blue eyes, before brushing back her long black hair, which flowed neatly over her shoulders and rested against her tightly fitted corset.

Asher turned his back to me and began chewing on a chicken thigh.

"Any word on the farmer?" asked the Governor.

"The surgeon is there. But judging by his condition, Carre will be lucky to make dusk," I said.

Baron Asher got to his feet and began casually picking the ligaments of chicken meat from his teeth. "We have a problem then, don't we Governor? My guard murdered, another viciously attacked and now potentially a dead farmer, who I will have you know is favoured very much amongst the locals," he said, whilst pointing the bone of the chicken impolitely at my senior.

"Your point?" asked the Governor.

"My point is that you have failed to maintain order. I will have no choice but to disclose this lack of control to the Chief on his arrival."

The Governor stepped forward, hitting his clenched fists on the table. "I care little for what you relay to the Chief."

"Very well. Come, Truda," ordered the Baron.

I moved clear of the door, keen to avoid any engagement with Asher. However, he saw his opportunity to tease.

He leaned his head towards me, making me feel repulsed by the stains of food on his beard. "It seems mischief has a habit of following you, boy."

Truda waited for the Baron to step out of the room into the courtyard. She offered the Governor good day, before whispering in my ear, "I am quite fond of mischief."

The Governor paced up and down the parade room floor, angered by the Baron's insolence. "Stout pig!" he growled, "I will assume that the merchants have fled, Jep?"

"Yes Sir, their tracks are clear, they headed into the woodland."

Rubbing the bridge of his nose with his fingertips, he looked back at me, pausing. "Do you still believe these merchants are responsible for the priest's death?" he asked, taking me by surprise that he would request my council.

"It is not that farfetched, Sir."

He sighed before responding, "Go to your quarters, get some rest. I will send the rest of the men out to get rid of any other outside traders before the Chief's arrival. Come nightfall, you will check on Carre, and inform me of his condition."

The Governor then marched out of the parade room.

Mirroring his sigh, I sat in the chair by the table and began pondering on the facts of Carre's assault and somehow attempting to establish in my mind why the merchants would be so keen to murder an innocent priest. I was in a quandary and my mind felt hazed as my stomach began to knot at the thought of who would be capable of causing such despair.

***

Knocking at Carre's door, I felt uneasy about learning his current condition. Even though I had unintentionally remained distant from the farmer after learning of his involvement in the Stanford Cavaliers, I admired the humble love he displayed for his family, and his generosity to me had never gone unforgotten.

Dam pulled back the door slowly, her eyes puffed and reddened. She looked at me, offering nothing but an empty stare and it was then my heart sank. Behind her stood the surgeon, by Carre's side, fastening up his doublet before brushing his hair back behind his ears. Carre lay still, his torso covered by a woollen blanket. Dam invited me in, and I slowly walked up to the table where I had previously left him. His eyes remained shut and the swelling around his sockets had increased, his nose remaining bent and out of shape.

"My things," called the surgeon.

Noticing Carre's stomach rise underneath the blanket gave me a brief moment of hope for the farmer's fate. I turned to face the surgeon. "What of his condition?" I asked.

"Take a look for yourself, his good luck and strength keeps him alive, for now. I expect if he awakens, he will be in a state of incapacity. I will return at the end of the winter, if he lasts that long," said the surgeon.

Sitting down with Dam and Rye, we all watched Carre and remained silent. Rye began clenching his lips and blurting out his plans to hunt down his master's attackers. I agreed with Dam that he was needed on the farm, now more than ever, yet his lust for vengeance was more than justified. The man idolised Carre and looked at him as a father figure. He was as broken hearted as the farmer's immediate family.

I walked closer to Dam, placing my hand gently on her shoulder. "If you need anything, whether it be supplies or labour, just ask. I will check in on you frequently."

Dam gazed up at me, whilst a tear ran down her cheek. "You find them, Jep! You find the men who did this to my husband. That will bring me peace."

***

As I entered the Governor's chambers, he eyeballed me from behind his table. My communicating Carre's condition to him had little impact on his display of emotion.

"What now?" I asked.

Glaring back up to me with his mouth set sternly, he replied, "What is it you propose to do?"

"Find them, sir. They will be on foot, no more than a day away."

"I will have word sent to the city to be aware of their arrival. I imagine they will return there at some point to gather more supplies," he responded, whilst continuing to read a parchment on his table.

"But Sir, I could cut them off en route!"

The Governor huffed and shook his head. "The Chief is to arrive within the next day, I have a town on the brink of a revolt and a lack of Swords to maintain order. You are staying right here and will continue with your duties. If, Jep, you were so keen to wander, maybe you should have taken the offer of a scholarship in the city."

Understanding his predicament and observing his deflation, I felt it wrong to press the matter further. Before leaving, I heard him take a breath and readied myself for further instruction.

"Your history with Asher's household must not become apparent at the banquet, you're a noble Sword, I expect you to act as one," demanded the Governor.

Nodding, I acknowledged his order.

The following morning, I was awoken by a loud thud on the door. Chenchi called out my name, insisting I get to the parade room pending the Chief's imminent arrival. Hurrying across to the parade room, I discovered it was filled with all my companions. Isa and Blair rushed to make the table presentable for our leader's pending arrival.

Lev was seated, smirking as he casually leaned back in his chair with his hands behind his head. "All this commotion and for what? Our great ruler prioritising the company of the Baron over his own men."

"I hear that he struggles to mount his horse, that he requires an aid, due to his stumpy legs," laughed Chenchi, garnering a chuckle from

Lev.

"The tree does have humour and here was me thinking you were slightly lame, Chenchi," said Lev.

"You will mind your tongues," ordered Sergeant Hock, as he passed through the parade room.

Lev smiled back at Chenchi, before muttering, "You know what these shorter folks are like, they feel the need to pat each other on the back."

Fawkes challenged Blair on her lack of effort in assisting her mother, leaving the irate girl to roll her eyes back at him. Sergeant Hock returned, relaying that the Chief was approaching and ordered us to line up in the courtyard.

"Right, this is it, best behaviour, that goes for you too, Lev," demanded Hock.

As we formed a neat line, Hock strutted up and down, focusing his attention mostly on me and Chenchi, straightening the single chains that hung from the breast of our tunics. The Governor led the Chief and his band of Swords as they entered the courtyard and dismounted from their horses.

"Lev," called the Governor, "see to the horses."

Lev wandered towards the group of fellow Swords, unhurried and undeterred by the company that met him. Sergeant Hock joined the line, demanding that the remaining three of us were to face forward and await our leader's greetings. Seeing Chief Muir approaching our line, I realised Lev was right in his description of our peer. He was unexpectedly short, but his demeanour and bluster made up for his surprising lack in height. He had a firm stare, one that looked through us. His hair was wavy and neatly groomed, matching his grey patchy beard which had been finely trimmed. He spoke with a hint of arrogance, but his tone was effective and dominant.

Standing in front of Chenchi, he eyed him up and down, impressed by the sturdy Blue Sword.

"Well bred, very good," he said to Chenchi, who responded quickly and respectfully.

Moving onto Fawkes, Chief Muir raised an eyebrow and gave him a partial grin. "Sword Fawkes," acknowledged the Chief.

"Sir, it is a pleasure to receive you in Stanford." said Fawkes.

"Your reputation has been voiced in the hall of my chambers, Sword Fawkes. Be assured the pleasure is all mine."

Next, the Chief stepped sideways along the line and stood facing me. I took a quick glance at the Governor who stood uneasily beside our ruler. Chief Muir stared at me closely, before casting his eyes up and down over my attire.

"You must be Sword Jep? For such an immature Sword, you have created quite a stir," he said.

"Stir, sir?" interrupted the Governor.

"Indeed. Exposing a plot of treason and also saving the father of your Baroness. Keep up the virtuous effort," smiled Chief Muir, before turning to enter the lock up.

Sergeant Hock sprinted forward to open the parade room door, leaving the Governor to walk beside the Chief. I glanced at Chenchi, exhaling and feeling relieved that the initial encounter with our leader was over.

Fawkes was the first to fall out of line and he made his way over to greet the band of Swords who had travelled with our Chief. Four men met us, all dressed in the same uniforms we wore. Two of the men, who were of similar age to me, were clearly young in service and thrilled with the opportunity to meet neighbouring Swords. Smiling, they greeted us with handshakes, all of us taking a discreet look at the number of chains displayed on one another's tunics.

Like myself, the third sword wore a single chain, however he was much older and battle-scarred. His weathered skin and greying hair expressed seniority and experience. The final uniformed man brandished two chains on his chest, signifying he was a Sergeant in rank. His haughtiness was apparent by his refusal to shake the hand of us fresher and greener Swords. The only one of our men to receive an acknowledgment from the Sergeant was Fawkes, a man well recognised amongst all the Blue Swords.

The Sergeant began brushing his fingertips through his moustache, frowning whilst he examined the rear of our lock up as he began paying particular attention to our rundown shacks that were scattered over the unkempt grass.

A familiar voice called from the stables, "Fear not, Sergeant Mosely, you will be resting in the comfort of the Grand Hall, along with the Chief."

Detector Flint appeared, offering me a smile. He was exactly how I remembered him, immaculate in his appearance, with his black, curly hair that co-ordinated with his tightly fitted black doublet. He spoke with confidence and poise.

Paying little attention to the others, he approached me first, keen to greet me. "It pleases me to see you, Jep. Yet I cannot help but wonder why you are yet to take me up on my offer of mentorship. I guess I will have to bide my time before I can get you to the city. Please, I wish for you to meet my companion, Amir."

Amir appeared from the stables, dressed in the same black doublet as Flint. He was very similar to Flint, smartly presented and self-assured. His complexion was olive and his hair covered by a rolled white cloth. Holding out his hand, he gripped my palm, tightly.

"Amir is one of Thear's most relentless Detectors. If he wants you, he will find you," said Flint.

"I can't imagine he is that hard to hide from with that white rag on his head," called Lev, contemptuously.

Amir grinned, not allowing Lev the satisfaction of a reaction. However, the same could not be said about Flint, who reacted sharply to his friend's ridiculing. "That rag is a mark of his God. It would do you well to leave the sanctuary of your stable on occasion, just so you may experience real life," he snapped.

"Don't mind him," I said to Amir. "It is only the horses that offer him love and comfort."

"Come, while the Chief is on his tour, we shall drink. We must become reacquainted," said Flint.

Our modest parade room became overcrowded with people, making it difficult to hear what Flint was saying. Standing, sipping ale with the Detectors, I began communicating my lack of success in locating our old comrade, Hota.

Detector Amir spoke softly but to the point. "You are well

informed; Hota remains concealed in the south. I fear his following grows, as does his lust for control."

Part of me felt relieved knowing that Hota was in the south and far away from my family home, but hearing Amir confirm that Hota was close by, I pondered over the recent misfortunes that tormented our town.

As I brought Flint up to date with Father Arrend's death, together with the young guard's assault, and the fact that Carre was currently fighting for his life, the Detectors looked over at one another tensely.

"This could quite easily be the work of the Shadow Crooks," advised Flint. "I will inform the Chief when the time is right. But for now, we celebrate."

10

THE BARON'S FEAST

Walking towards the Grand Hall, I felt a surge of apprehension at the thought of being in the company of Lady Ivy and Baron Asher. Chief Muir had already left to attend the evening celebrations, along with Flint and the rest of his guardians. Making our way down Main Street, Chenchi winked at the local women who showed him relentless amounts of attention as they admired the brute in his finery.

"What keeps you so silent? Aren't you excited by the thought of setting eyes upon the Baroness in a dainty, tight fitting corset?" he teased.

"I am more concerned with the reception Asher will give me."

Chenchi laughed, "Forget the turd, he will be filled with wine and wetting his pants by the time we arrive."

From across the river, smoke slowly rose into the air from the Baron's grounds. Torches illuminated the bridge that led over to the gates of the Grand Hall. The breeze drove the smell of garlic and spices, filtered by the scent of burning wood, caused by a roaring bonfire that brightened up the courtyard. The atmosphere was already spirited; sounds of drums being beaten could be heard, dramatized by the bards who vigorously played their lutes.

Two of Asher's henchmen stood guard by the opened gate, alongside a small handful of servant's keen to direct us to the festivities. The Baron's men demanded our swords, prompting Chenchi and I to give each other a rather curious look.

"By order of Baron Asher, no man shall carry arms at the banquet," insisted the patrolman.

Chenchi leered down at the man. "If you can take it, it's yours."

The second guard nervously intervened. "Sirs, we mean no offence, your leader has agreed to the Baron's terms."

Chenchi placed his face close to the guard. "The last time I left this behind, I had to hump the person who had it. Don't make me have to come back and hump you."

Leaving our sword belts behind, we made our way across the courtyard. The layered petals that had been scattered across the courtyard had now been ground into the gravel, causing the decorated ground to appear untidy. Seiloff was manning the front doors and initially grinned on seeing his old partner.

Chenchi excitably held his arms out to the side. "Seiloff, you pigs arse! Mark my words, if I do not get lucky this evening, I will be taking you to my chambers."

"The room is heaving with wenches, you will have the choice of many, old friend," replied Seiloff, before fixing his gaze on me. "Shame you had to bring the 'chancing slayer' along. I hope they removed your blade. Wouldn't want you stabbing any more men in the back."

"Easy boys," said Chenchi smiling. "This is a celebration after all."

Entering the hallway, I eyed Seiloff, who reflected my expression of hostility. "The 'chancing slayer', what kind of nickname is that?" I asked Chenchi.

"You should be pleased, it's better than what they used to name you, Jep."

Seeing Asher's animal hunting trophies decorating the walls reminded me of the first encounter I had ever had with the tyrant. Hota had kindly brought me to the Hall, in order to bid for my refuge. Asher and his late henchman, Gil, had mocked and belittled me in the presence of Lady Ivy, and it was from that day on I had begun to loathe both of them.

The music mellowed once we arrived closer to the Great Hall, lightened by the soothing sounds of harp strings being played. The Great Hall expanded as far as the eye could see. The ceiling was held up by thick stone pillars with finely carved lintels. Candles had been spread throughout, assisting the central lantern-surrounded fire, lighting up the room. Two lengthy stilted tables had been placed lengthways side by side, both covered in luxurious foods such as roasted quail, eggs, cheese and fresh, colourful fruits. Clay jugs of wine separated the cuisine along with flowered wreaths, making it all seem rather pretentious.

The top table was positioned horizontally, overseeing the entire room and occupied by our leader, Chief Muir, who sat in the middle next to Baron Asher and Lady Ivy. The Governor had also been seated at the top table, along with Sergeant Hock and Sergeant Mosely at the Chief's side, leaving Truda, who sat beside a rounded, well dressed older man at the Baron's end of the table. Only one seat was left empty, situated at the far end.

Seeing Hock whisper to the Governor, I knew they had already laid eyes on me, unnerved by my arrival. Unable to control my stare, I looked over and unintentionally fixed my sight on Lady Ivy. She smiled and chuckled, entertained in deep conversation with the Chief, who had clearly been won over by her gracious charms. She beamed, radiating beauty with her hair plaited, held by pale green petal combs that complemented her silky, green tinted gown.

Chenchi gave me a subtle nudge with his elbow, directing my awareness to a bitter looking Hock, who was nodding for us to be seated. Guests indulging on the luxuries that littered the tables had occupied most of the seating. Detector Flint was already engaging in conversation with other members of his band, leaving no spare places for me or Chenchi. Two spaces remained unoccupied on a bench at the far end of the hall and thankfully farthest away from the head table.

Taking our seats, the whole bench juddered at Chenchi's movement, startling the other invitees. Sat directly opposite I was relieved and thrilled to see a recognizable face grinning back at me. Isaak, Lady Ivy's father, appeared happy to see me seated close by. The man whom I recalled as being frail and weathered, raised his beaker towards me, now healthy and refreshed.

Standing to his feet, Isaak insisted on gaining the attention of the closest guests on our table. "This man before you is the reason I stand here, he allowed me breath and better still, he united me with my daughter. To Sword Jep," he cheered, whilst raising his mug.

"Hear, hear," called the people who listened intently, although you could see their confusion at what they were actually toasting.

Eruk, Truda's guardian, was seated next to Isaak, and he gave me an approving nod before sipping on his wine. The music created a quiet background of ambiance, allowing all to speak amongst each other unhindered. The gathering was civilised, most were still coherent and refrained from groping the servant girls who wandered back and forth, topping up the jugs of wine and revitalising the feast.

Chenchi sat upright with his back straight, scanning the room for potential intimate partners. Isaak was keen to make conversation and tactfully discuss the fate of his two Cavalier comrades, Father Arrend and Carre.

"There is no way Arrend took his own life. The man was holy, and very stubborn. I trust foul play has not been ruled out?" Isaak asked.

Looking around the table, I felt uneasy about discussing current investigations within the potential earshot of unfamiliar bystanders.

Sensing my discomfort, Eruk, a now retired Blue Sword, interrupted Isaak and came to my aid. "Enough, Isaak. The man is here for merriment, not to listen to the woes of us old timers. I will find it an insult if I see you without a drink in your hand."

Giving me an understanding nod, Eruk had managed to deflect the conversation and at the same time appease the Baroness's father, who immediately began engaging in a much lighter topic. The wine flowed and the discussions were pleasant with the retired Sword and Isaak. Chenchi began charming the table, and the more he indulged in ale the more he became over-familiar with some of the women who shared our dining arrangements.

The sounds of the gentle harp came to an end, and a young bard appeared. He stood before the room dressed in a doublet with oversized sleeves and a feathered hat, confident in his approach to obtain his audience's attention. The bard began singing softly, in tune with his lute, before sounding tales of a weary traveller, full of might and heroism.

He theatrically flicked his fingers over the strings of his instrument, adding dramatics to his tale, before introducing the legend of which he spoke. "Sirs and Ladies, I give to you, your champion, Bracken."

The wooden doors at the side of the hall were flung open and a brute of a man who made even Chenchi seem an average size entered with his hands held high. Bracken's muscular frame was flaunted by the flexing and stretching of his gigantic arms and shoulders. Chenchi frowned, put out by the titan who boasted and flaunted himself before us. The local women ogled back at Bracken in awe, seduced by his abnormally large physique and long shining hair.

The Chief clapped, impressed by the entertainment, leaving me to take a sneak glimpse over at Lady Ivy, who looked back at me discreetly, with a tiny smile on her face. The bard continued to boast about his associate, only to be disrupted by the Baron.

Asher stood to his feet, grabbing at the side of the table to aid his unsteadiness. There was a slur in his speech as he addressed his guests. "My hall is filled with Thear's most elite warriors. Who among you will dare challenge this giant? Thirty silver pieces to the man who stands before Bracken and can lay him down."

The room erupted with cheers and excitement, including from our own Chief, keen to see the potentially violent exchange. Feeling Chenchi edging forward, I grabbed his arm, advising him not to make a fool of himself. He looked back at me, grinning as he tried to step up, keen to answer the challenge of the wrestler. But before he was able to take the chance to walk out from the table, a voice called out, casually accepting the task.

"If all I must do is ground this oaf, my Lord, I will oblige in taking your silver," called the well-known self-assured voice.

As I turned to see who had answered the challenge, I noticed the Governor place one hand on his forehead, unimpressed by the man who had volunteered to fight Bracken.

Sword Lev strutted to the front of the hall, arrogantly grinning, whilst playing along with the excited audience and stopping before the unimpressed wrestler. The young bard chortled, eyeing up the disparity in mass between the contestant and his champion, as both Lev and Bracken stared back at one another.

Lev confronted the guests and pointed a single finger back at his colossal opponent. "A titan, a legend amongst men, you say? He braces like a lion, growls like a wolf, yet I bet he still shares quarters with his mother."

The spectators roared with laughter, encouraging Lev to further ridicule the gladiator. "Judging by the purity of this man's hair, I am certain he still drinks from his mother's breast and from looking at the closeness of his eyes, his sister's too."

Bracken scowled back at Lev, growling at his derisive statements. The Governor stood, ordering Lev to be seated. However, he was silenced by an enthused Chief Muir who confirmed he wished to see the fight.

Seiloff handed the Baron a leather purse, prompting him to slam it on the table. "You speak loosely, Sword. Now ground this man and take my hefty prize," shouted Asher.

Lev approached the head table, smirking at the Baron. "But, my Lord, I wish for much more than your coinage. For me to slay this beast, I will need to be assured that I am to receive a secure invitation to dance with a lady who sits at your table."

"Easy, Lev," called Sergeant Hock, reacting to the Baron's frown and a flabbergasted audience.

Turning back towards the head table, Lev continued. "Please, my dear Baron, I offer no insult, I would not dare request the hand of your sacred wife. Although I do know some that would," said Lev, whilst biting his lip and facing back to the guests.

Lady Ivy caught my eye, and her expression equalled my mortification at Lev's reckless tongue. Baron Asher screwed up his face, breathing heavily through his flared nostrils. However, Lev had played the crowd beautifully and they began to further encourage him, laughing at his disrespect and carelessness.

Prancing alongside the table Lev halted, standing directly opposite Truda. "My lady," he addressed her, "I will defeat this titan, but only if my incentive is to be offered your hand in a dance."

Truda rolled her eyes, unimpressed by Lev's forwardness. The Baron became even more enraged, spitting as he ordered for the duel to begin, prompting a cheer from his guests.

Without warning, the wound-up wrestler charged at Lev, giving him no time to react. Gripping the back of our companion's tunic, he lifted Sword Lev into the air effortlessly, tossing him towards one of the banquet tables. Lev crashed head-first on to the leftover food, knocking over drink beakers and spilling ale.

Fawkes was seated close to where Lev landed and never even flinched at seeing his fellow Sword in difficulty. Standing to his feet, Fawkes offered Lev no sympathy at the consequences caused by his own actions. Instead, he took hold of his disoriented associate and lifted Lev's body, pushing him back towards his brute of an opponent. The crowd continued to cheer and chant, excited by the exhibition, although I could not help but feel that Lev had caused trouble for himself by taunting the wrestler so severely.

Bracken once again gripped hold of Lev, this time scrunching the collar of his tunic. Lev observed the brute, wide eyed, as Bracken raised the Sword off his feet and threw him through the air for a second time. The people applauded as Lev was hurled onto the stone floor. Bracken roared, flexing his shoulders and clenching his raised fists.

Baron Asher stood clapping, admiring the shameful Sword's defeat at the hands of his entertainer. Everyone gasped at seeing Lev rise to his feet, and stumble back towards his almighty opponent.

"Stay down you fool!" yelled Eruk.

But Lev ignored his words of advice, and instead faced off again with Bracken and stood poised. The wrestler lunged forward, keen to grip hold of our Sword once again, however this time Lev moved swiftly, avoiding his adversary.

Clenching his fist, Lev slid to the side of Bracken and struck him on his jugular, leaving the wrestler gasping and stunned. Lev spun himself back around, now standing directly in front of the brute before thrusting the heel of his foot into Bracken's groin. The spectators responded with a jeer, before Lev landed a finishing blow to the incapacitated and hunched over combatant. Driving his knee into the face of the bent over wrestler, Bracken's head was flung back as blood sprayed from his nose, leaving him floored and defeated.

Many heckled but some applauded, the room erupting in noise, indicating the guests had been amused. Lev staggered across to the head table and presented himself to the Baron. Nodding, he removed the purse from the table and raised it in the air, prompting an even louder cheer from the room. Leering over to Truda, Lev gave her a superior look, before throwing the purse of silver on to the chest of the fallen behemoth.

"Showboating turd," groaned Chenchi.

I joined in the clapping, for Lev was a master of performance, and far too self-assured, but as always he had provided an amusing spectacle, and I couldn't help but slightly admire his ability to deliver such entertainment.

Asher had spared no expense, as the evening continued with troubadours telling stories of heroic knights and mythical creatures. Everywhere I looked people were enjoying the event, admiring juggling acts, musicians and hawk displays. The drink continued to flow, and behaviour declined. Locals began gambling on dice, creating disputes, and ale started to free the tongues of many, one of those being Isaak, whose voice began to stutter under the intoxication of wine.

Isaak was kind and had always offered nothing but delicacy, however the drink had ignited his blood and he began speaking with rage and intensity.

"I told her to flee with you, you know," he said, leaving me feeling stunned by his honesty. "Yet she remains loyal to that arse of a man."

Eruk, who was also weary eyed, rested his hand gently on Isaak's shoulder. "Easy, Isaak, not all ears are defective."

"I care little for what they hear. When I was forced to leave this town, do you know how many times Asher's men attended Edgar farm? They did not come, no one came but Crooks. That pig has plagued my child for too long, I will rejoice in his death and relieve myself on his stone."

Eruk snorted, "You will be required to wait in line, my friend."

The bard came to an abrupt stop and the room was silenced by a drunken Baron Asher, who struggled to lift himself out of his chair. "Hear me! Join me in wishing Chief Muir prosperity and good health." Raising his beaker, ale began spilling from its edge due to the Baron's unsteady hand. "Our history is spoiled, but not irreparable. That is if your Swords stop mounting my whore wife," roared Asher, glaring over at me with blood-shot eyes.

Lady Ivy peered down at the table, horrified by the content of the rambling fool's speech. Truda leapt from her seat and took hold of the Baron's arm, whispering in his ear. He frantically pulled away, ordering her to be seated, before scanning the room, unable to focus on anyone or anything. The Governor looked at me, before shaking his head and looking away. The Chief glowered up at the unsteady Baron, his eyes wide in disbelief.

Belching loudly, Asher continued. "This is my town, and I will be heard. My beloved wife would rather bed a peasant boy than lay with her own husband, and you sons and daughters of whores call *me* barbaric?"

Chief Muir jumped to his feet, taking hold of Asher's arm, angrily demanding he sit back down. In his drunken and uncoordinated state, Asher did not take kindly to being manhandled and pushed the Chief back, drawing a gasp from the onlooking guests. Fawkes raced towards the head table with a carving knife tightly clenched in his hand. He pointed its tip towards the Baron's throat. Shocked, the Baron fell drunkenly back in his chair.

Seiloff charged around the table to meet Fawkes at the front, with his blade half drawn from his scabbard as he weighed up Fawkes's intentions. All the Swords in the room, including myself and retired Sword Eruk, jumped from our seats.

Chief Muir yelled, demanding order, backed up by the Governor who commanded Fawkes to withdraw.

Chief Muir called calmly over the table to Seiloff. "Do not allow the ramblings of a bibulous fool to influence your next move. Secure your sword, Guard, and my man will yield. Then you shall assist your Lord to his chambers."

Seiloff did as asked, aiding Asher to his feet, who offered no resistance after witnessing the intense encounter. Lady Ivy retreated through the side door, unable to tolerate any more humiliation.

Truda took to the floor. "Do not be alarmed, truth must not be mistaken with ignorance. Now, let the festivities continue," she called.

Isaak got to his feet, keen to see to his distressed daughter, only to be held back by Eruk gently holding his arm. "Allow her to breathe, the Baroness is suffocated enough."

Exhaling, Isaak scowled over to Asher's empty chair. Gathering his composure, he leaned back into his seat and began swiftly tossing back his drink, before calling for more wine.

Eruk was a seasoned man, and in tune with the current atmosphere, he lightly redirected the conversation towards my own path, keen to hear how fate had led me to Stanford and the Blue Swords. He listened intently to my story, admiring my passion and drive.

"I never had the pleasure of meeting Sword Fulten, though his name is spoken of highly and his repute offers nothing but honour," responded Eruk.

Eruk continued with tales from his own time serving in the city. He reminisced proudly about the service he had provided for many years.

"Alma is grand and prosperous. Fitting for a young sword as yourself. Take my word, you would be met with many opportunities."

"Detector Flint has offered me a scholarship to train and become a Detector," I said.

"And you rejected this proposal?"

"No, not exactly," I answered, glancing awkwardly over to Chenchi, who laughed along with a group of equally vibrant locals, apparently unaware of my conversation with Eruk. "I just postponed it. I have much to learn here and people to whom I owe my life."

Eruk grinned, "When you do arrive at the city, be sure to present yourself to me. I will ensure all your needs are taken care of personally."

I nodded my thanks as Isaak changed the subject, his voice even more disjointed and saliva accumulating in the corners of his dry mouth. His daughter's mortification, along with his inebriated state, had left him in a rather sour mood.

"I should go up there and slice a knife across his gullet whilst he sleeps," Isaak slurred.

Eruk shook his head. "What you suggest is not only murder, but treason against the Crown. Now, you are drunk and seeking vengeance for the mistreatment of your daughter, so I will allow those words to be forgotten on the understanding that you retire for the evening."

Isaak began to sob. In his heart he wanted his precious Ivy released from the ongoing torment placed upon her by the Baron, but he knew she was trapped and powerless to leave the life in which he had helped to imprison her.

"Come my friend, let me see you to your quarters," said Eruk gently.

Keen to clap my eyes on Lady Ivy and not miss the chance of an encounter with the Baroness, I interrupted. "No, I insist, let me escort Isaak to his chambers."

"Do you think that is wise?" asked Eruk.

"Asher will be unconscious, and Isaak and I have history. I will take him."

"Very well." agreed Eruk.

Leaving the banquet, Seiloff gave me a suspicious look as I departed the hall with Isaak. Leading Isaak up the stairs, I was curious about what to expect as we delved deeper into the Baron's residence.

II

TEMPTATION

The concrete slabs had been laid precisely, merging into the walls and neatly raising the spiralling stairs. The stone walls had been cleared of any dust and were well preserved. Woven coverings lined the floors of the upper corridor adding further luxury to the interior. My eyes wandered, taken aback by the splendour of the settings in which I found myself. I curiously peeked in each room we passed, keen to get a glimpse of the Baroness.

Isaak came to a sudden standstill, wobbling as he struggled to gain his balance. He had recognised the entrance to his own chambers, however his intoxication forced him to squint at the door as he found it difficult to see straight.

Gawping back at me baffled, he started to mumble, "Leave with her, offer my daughter the life which she deserves. Grow old together, turn your back on this hideous place."

Isaak patted my cheek with the palm of his hand then sighed before staggering into his chambers. I scanned the corridor, considering whether to press further on with the hope of meeting Lady Ivy.

Without stopping to consider the consequences I stepped forward and continued down the hallway. Once at the end of the corridor, I was met by a much wider oak door that had been left partly open. Peering through the gap, I could see an open balcony on the far side of the chambers and voices could be heard laughing from outside. The bed was unoccupied and remained neatly made, prompting me to step foot into the room, without thought or care.

The grandeur of the chambers was like nothing I had ever seen before. The walls had been covered by carved wooden panels, to keep its stone structure hidden. The unlit fireplace was deeper than my own quarters at the lock up and it boasted the Baron's silver emblem, which had been hung above. I had become enthralled with the splendour, forgetting whose room I had intruded into, until a softly spoken voice startled me.

Baroness Ivy called my name, standing before me dressed in a white cotton gown. Her hair was now unplaited and flowed down the back of her night dress. She looked at me with her leaf green eyes and smiled.

"If they find you in here, I fear we will both lose our heads," she said.

"Where is he?" I asked.

"Who? My devoted husband? He sleeps in the Lord's chamber, the far side of the hall. Many full moons have passed since I accompanied him there. He appreciates variety, and it fits my desire to not entertain him further. Fortunately for us both, the guards do not patrol this side of the Grand Hall, so the question is Jep, have you come to seduce me?"

Gulping, I felt my heart begin to pound inside my chest. Lady Ivy was aware of my apprehension and helplessness to reply, and she began smiling at me, relishing my unease.

"I am sorry Jep, it is wrong of me to tease. Will you stand with me, by the balcony? The light is dim, you will not be seen."

Cupping my hands over the cold stone railing, I looked out over the courtyard, observing many of the guests walking away from the grounds. The bonfire had died down and only the embers remained, faintly illuminating the gardens. Lady Ivy wrapped a heavy robe around her shoulders and joined me on the balcony.

The sound of adolescent laughter caught my attention and I noticed Blair, cheekily ridiculing Markus, the wounded gatekeeper.

Baroness Ivy giggled on noticing my frown as I watched their inoffensive play outside the guards' barracks. "Does it upset you to see them together?"

"It does, I disapprove of his interest in the young girl."

"Markus is a mere boy. His responsibility has been forced upon him far too prematurely," Lady Ivy advised.

Seeing Blair's happiness did give me a sense of warmth. She looked like a child should, full of contentment.

"Does he heal well?" I asked.

"He does, the boy has youth on his side."

Changing the subject, I was keen to warn her of her father's deposition, and the advice he had offered me. Lady Ivy stared out across the grounds, before looking up at the night stars, thoughtfully.

"Is the idea so ludicrous, Jep?"

I gazed back at her, frowning, baffled by her remark. "Run away? You and I? It is all I have ever dreamed of since I met you."

Lady Ivy peeked down at my hand resting on the stone of the balcony, before placing her own palm on top, interlocking her fingers between my own. We gazed intently into each other's eyes, before I moved closer to the Baroness, as I placed my hand around the back of her head, gently stroking her hair. Leaning towards her I kissed her lips, tenderly. Lady Ivy returned the kiss, passionately touching my back, as the kiss became more and more intimate and intense. Our bodies clung tightly together, both feeling the excitement of yet another stolen moment together.

Pulling away, the Baroness rested her head on my thudding chest and let out a breath. "Stay with me?" she asked.

"I can't, I wouldn't risk putting you in danger." My heart screamed, wanting to continue this moment for ever, but the consequences of us being discovered together would be excruciating, and I was not willing to put the person I loved in jeopardy that way.

Kissing her forehead, I moved back, refusing to look away from her as we both mirrored one another's craving expressions.

"Leave with me Jep, let's disappear into the night, create our own destiny, together."

Chuckling, I took her comments as only idle words, until I realised that she had neglected to drop the serious look displayed on her face.

"I do not speak lightly or impulsively. Why stay here and live through the torment of never being happy together?"

Pausing, I was speechless. Unable to find any words to reply with. Baroness Ivy sensed my hesitation and pressed me for an answer. "Your father, Asher, your position, and that's not even considering the Swords. I would be a deserter. I fear wine influences your thoughts, my lady. Where would we even go?"

"I have much wealth, we would be together, allowed to make our own decisions, we could breathe free air. If I recall, you once made a similar suggestion."

"That was before Hota slaughtered my tutor. I have a duty to the Swords. I cannot just leave."

"And you stopped his father, Jep? I fear I will lose you to this unending conflict. The thought alone is unthinkable."

Gently holding her arms, I kissed her once again. Our intimacy now flowed naturally and felt less impulsive.

"You will never lose me. My heart will be with you for eternity, that is my oath to you," I said.

We both remained silent, just embracing the tender moment of holding one another close. The circumstances felt serene and imaginary. Baroness Ivy had offered me everything I had dreamed of, and I could not quite believe the magical circumstances in which I had found myself. Gently taking my leave, I quietly left her looking pensively into the distance.

***

On entering the banquet hall, I found Seiloff stood before me, regarding me with a bitter expression. Looking behind me at the door I had emerged from, he scoffed. "You were gone a while, I do hope you did not wander, seeking forbidden temptations?"

"I only proceeded to direct a drunken and saddened man to his bed."

"We shall see," said Seiloff smugly.

Leaving Seiloff sour faced, I returned to the table, keen to usher Chenchi away from the celebrations. He sat with a local woman on his lap, smooching and forgetful of his audience. Irritated by interruption, he argued, but finally agreed with my proposal to leave.

Looking across the table and nodding towards Eruk, Chenchi laughed. "Look at the state of him and to say he was one of the most adept Swords to have ever served."

I chuckled on observing Eruk seated, with his forehead resting on the table, his snores and grunts causing the beakers to rattle on the table beside him.

Outside, I turned around and peered up at the balcony to see Lady Ivy's silhouette standing hidden in the darkness. My mind raced with possibilities and decisions that would have to be made. Lady Ivy was someone who always outweighed any other of my priorities and that someone I would give everything up for. Choosing between her and the Blue Swords would be the hardest decision I would ever make.

***

Chenchi groaned, rubbing his thumbs into his eyes, grumbling at the ache that throbbed in his head. The morning mist had lifted, indicating we had overslept and prompting us to dress with haste. We walked towards the parade room, and I noticed the two novice Swords in Chief Muir's band standing sheepishly, refusing to make eye contact with us.

"Did I cause them an injustice last night?" mumbled Chenchi.

"Not that I recall, although I suspect there are many husbands seeking your blood this morning."

As we entered the overcrowded parade room, everyone went silent, including Lev, who echoed the expression of the novice Swords outside. The Chief gave me a hostile frown, as did Sergeant Mosely and his battle-scarred companion, Sword O'Hara. The Governor exhaled, and for the first time his fierce expression was muted with awkwardness.

"Anyone below the rank of Sergeant, out," ordered Chief Muir.

I turned to leave with the rest of my associates, only to be called back in by the Governor. "Not you, Jep, you will stay."

Confused, I watched as the room began to empty, before being ordered to take a seat. Sergeant Hock stood nervously behind the Chief and the Governor, unable to look up from the ground.

"Sir, may I ask the reason for this?"

Interrupting the Governor's uncommonly gentler tone, Chief Muir spoke firmly. "The Baroness's father is dead."

Gasping, I rubbed my hand across my forehead, immediately thinking of Lady Ivy's despair at the news. "How?" I asked.

"Well, I was hoping you could assist us with that question, since we are reliably informed by a guard that you were the last to see him," replied the Chief.

I stared up at the Chief, scowling. "You don't believe I am responsible for this tragedy? I helped the man to his chambers."

The room fell silent, answering my question. I felt my heart plunge into my stomach, as I began protesting my innocence. Sergeant Hock backed my pleas, reminding everyone that it was me who had saved Isaak's life previously.

"A great deal can change in time," responded Sergeant Mosely.

"I did not kill Isaak."

"You did escort him to his room, and then it seems there was a delay in your return. So do tell us, what took you so long to aid an old drunk to his bed?" asked Mosely.

My unwillingness to offer the truth, and risk my encounter with Baroness Ivy being discovered, gave them even more reason to suspect my involvement.

"Can I ask how he was killed?" I requested.

Chief Muir stepped closer, spreading his hands on the table in front of me, snarling as he spoke. "Suffocation, a flawless murder. So, answer the question, what took you so long to return?"

Dumbfounded, I was tongue tied and unable to react to their satisfaction.

Chief Muir nodded his head subtly at Sergeant Mosely, who stepped forward taking hold of my arm. I pulled back resisting, again pleading my innocence. Hock yelled, demanding if this was all necessary.

"Sergeant Mosely, you will take command in the dungeon. No Sword enters unless it's under my authorisation," demanded the Chief.

"I will not allow this," responded the Governor.

"Obstruct and you shall join him," barked the Chief. "Sergeant Mosely, shackle Sword Jep and relieve him of his weapons,"

As the Sergeant applied the shackles, I grunted on feeling the iron bite down onto my skin and grind against my wrist bone. Mosely pulled me up to my feet, his roughness indicating that he had already made up his mind on my involvement. I offered no further physical resistance, and allowed things to play out with little argument, though in truth I felt helpless and afraid.

As Mosely escorted me to the dungeon, Chenchi charged over on seeing me in shackles, shouting, "What is this outrage? Release him at once."

Mosely hesitated, observing my vast companion's objections and foul temper. He stared back at the Governor, seeking reassurance that he would control his man. The Governor huffed, and reluctantly demanded that Chenchi was to yield.

"What is the meaning of this? Answer me, damn you!" Chenchi yelled at the onlooking senior Swords.

Sergeant Hock snapped out of his bafflement, calling for order and insisting that everyone was to convene in the parade room.

As Mosely led me into the empty lock up, its damp stench got up his nose, causing him to spit. His encounter with Chenchi had rattled him and he took out his frustrations by being rather more vigorous, manhandling me into the dungeon. Frantically looking around, he grew irritated at not being able to find the keys to the cell doors. Nodding my head in the direction of the table, I indicated to him where they were kept, and he leant over and reached for the hanging set of keys, above the centre table.

Unlocking the iron barred door, he instructed me to turn and face the rear of the cage. Feeling the shackles release was a slight relief, however I felt dejected at being pushed forward into the cell.

Slamming shut the cell door, Mosely sneered at me through the bars. "I have never taken well to corrupt Swords. They bring shame upon the crest."

Astounded, I was unable to respond. The narrow light from outside diminished with the shutting of the external door and I was left in darkness. The muffled voices outside could be heard over the sounds the scurrying of the rats that housed themselves in the dungeon. My initial fright had now turned to frustration. I had been locked up for a death I had not caused, my treatment was unjust and the more I tormented my own mind with the facts, the more ill my thoughts grew towards the organisation I served.

12

STAINED HANDS

My eyes had slowly shut, and the adrenaline began wearing off. I was startled by the sound of a thunderous, bellowing voice outside. It was Chenchi, assuring me that he would seek justice. His words were followed by the sound of Sergeant Hock's reprimand, reminding him of the orders he had been given not to converse with me.

The outside door to the dungeon creaked open. The splits in the stone wall gave limited light, but enough to see Detector Amir appear from the passage. He handed me half a loaf of stale bread through the bars, and placed a beaker of water on the floor, within arm's reach.

He didn't speak at first, but just eyed me through the cage doors, weighing up my reaction to the quandary I was in.

"Detector Flint swears your innocence," he said eventually.

"What about you? What do you think?" I replied, whilst tearing off some bread from the loaf.

"I am yet to decide. This town you serve, Stanford, its corruption is renowned throughout Thear. Your encounter with Hota only reaffirms this town's ability to breed treachery. Yet I do trust in my partner's judgement, so for that reason, I greet you with an open mind, until I learn otherwise."

"It is the Chief I need to convince." I said.

"To the Chief you are just another member of his Swords, replaceable. He has come with one aim, to reunite the local Blue Swords and the Baron's house, a conflict you have severely added to, with your uncontrolled behaviour towards his wife."

"I unearthed a plot of treason; he would have been overturned if it wasn't for Fulten and I."

"Nevertheless, I fear that you may be nothing more than an offering."

Tossing the hardened end of the bread to the floor, I shook my head. "I get strung up for the murder of the Baroness's father, not only does it remove me from this web, but my name will forever remain tarnished in the eyes of Lady Ivy."

Amir turned up the palms of his hands and shrugged his shoulders, "And then peace is restored. Flint was right, you do have good understanding."

"So, I am to confess to a murder I did not commit and take this with the skin of my arse on display to spank?"

"Not at all. Luckily for you, one of the most tenacious Detectors in the land is your ally. Flint will solve this conundrum. In the meantime, you will need to remain strong, your test will start at noon." Amir looked through the bars at me one last time before leaving. My mind flooded with a surge of rage at the thought of being left to rot by the ones to whom I had offered my loyalty. I began thinking of Fulten, and of my sadness at not having him here to offer me his counsel.

***

The sun had risen, its rays splintering brightly through the cracked walls. I could hear footsteps coming from the courtyard and was intrigued as to who would be next to arrive at the dungeon. Hearing the key turn in the external gate I got to my feet and rested my hands on the cell door. Sergeant Mosely and his sideman, Sword O'Hara strutted towards me, heavy footed and with grave expressions on their faces. I knew instantly that my test was just about to begin.

O'Hara eyed me from the other side of the iron bars, his eyes squinting behind his ferocious visage. His skin was covered in deep scarring, making his lean build even more threatening. He ordered me to face the back of the cage, whilst he unlocked the cell door. Once satisfied I presented no threat, he entered and reapplied the shackles on my wrists.

Sergeant Mosely refused to make eye contact with me. Clearly, he had already come to the conclusion that I was guilty of killing Isaak. Tilting his head towards the centre pillar of the dungeon, O'Hara pulled on the bar of my shackles.

On each side of the squared, central column were chains, all attached to ringlets that had been bolted into the walls. O'Hara locked the chain onto the hinge of my shackles, securing me to the wall. I now stood fastened to the stone, defenceless at the hands of my interrogators.

"It is in your interest to speak the truth. Now tell me, why did you take the life of the Baroness's father?" asked Mosely.

"I aided a drunk and rambling man to his room, that is all," I said.

Sergeant Mosely looked at Sword O'Hara. He puffed out his breath, before nodding his head. O'Hara stood before me, glowering through his menacing and unblinking eyes. Pulling back his fist, he punched me in the stomach, causing me to fold over and splutter. His knuckles felt like hammers striking my body. He was well seasoned and knew how to administer punishment.

Mosely leant down, gripping hold of my hair and forcing me to look at him. His teeth were tightly clenched as he growled for my confession to causing Isaak's death. Still coughing, I remained silent, attempting to make sense of the situation I had found myself in.

"Well lad, it seems you have lost your tongue, let's see if my Sword can help you find it," said Mosely.

"Enough," called a voice from the entrance. Sergeant Hock stood, astonished by the treatment I was being made to endure.

"You shouldn't be here," insisted Mosely.

"The Chief has authorised that the prisoner be brought water," Hock replied.

Shaking his head, Mosely offered no further argument. Isa walked in, horrified at what she saw and began tipping water slowly from the jug into my mouth. She seemed saddened by the state in which she witnessed me. Clearing my throat, I asked on her daughter, Blair. Isa gave me a sympathetic smile, before answering that I was in Blair's thoughts.

"Right, be gone woman. This man has a confession to make,"

ordered Mosely.

"Not at your hands," blurted Hock. "The Chief has agreed that Jep will speak with the Detector before any further interrogation."

O'Hara stepped back, making a swift acknowledgement of the Chief's instructions. Sergeant Mosely leaned his head down closer towards me. "I will beat this out of you, boy."

Leaving me secured to the wall, I was left alone in the dungeon. The sun weakened as the day passed, leaving me sitting on the cold stone floor in darkness. Every footstep I heard on the gravel outside caused me to jolt upright, eager to see either Flint or Amir appear.

No one came. I was left chained to the wall like an animal awaiting slaughter. As night fell, so did my morale. Staring into blackness, my only company was a passing rat that scurried across my foot. My wrists ached from the shackles and all the time I could not help but wonder why I remained bound, rather than being returned to my cell. My faith in my companions was diminishing.

The following morning, I was awoken by the sound of the creaking dungeon door. Squinting from the light, I felt disorientated. I peered down at the passageway to see Flint walking towards me.

Crouching down to me, he grunted, angered by the condition in which I had been left. "I was told you had been returned to your cell. Bastards!" cursed Flint.

Removing the shackles, he assisted me to my feet. The chill had numbed my bones and I struggled to stand unaided. Flint gently lowered me onto a nearby stool, before picking up the jug of water, which had been purposely left out of my reach. Pressing it against my lips, the dryness in my throat caused me to choke as I attempted to drink the water.

Flint propped himself against the table next to where I was sat. Crossing his arms, he began to sigh, showing his turmoil and annoyance at the circumstances.

Clearing my throat, I spoke with a crackly voice, "You haven't asked me if I did it."

Flint gave me a half-hearted smile. "If I thought you were a guilty man, I would not have spent an entire day pleading with the Chief to be allowed to speak with you. What were you doing that night, Jep?"

I paused, looking up at him timidly.

"Isaak is dead? They are treating it as murder, but we all know the man has lived a long life compared to most. What took you so long to return to the banquet? Without answers, they have your balls under a guillotine."

Staring at the floor, I was still not willing to divulge my encounter with Lady Ivy, at the risk of her being shamed. Flint watched me, awaiting my response, but soon grew irritated by my lack of an explanation.

"Damn you Jep, the only thing they have is a guards account of the length of time it took you to return to the hall, you are being framed. If only you could account for this in some way, they would have no choice but to consider other suspects or possibilities."

"I got lost," I said.

Flint scoffed. "The only place you got lost was in the Baroness's chambers."

Looking up at him, I knew the truth was written all over my face and Detector Flint was no fool. His observations were flawless, just as one would expect from a hardened Detector.

"Jep, if you do not disclose the truth, you will hang."

"I will not give her up, Flint, I cannot."

"Then you will become the pawn that the Chief needs to heal this feud. Asher will rejoice at your death and the Chief's work is done. The squabbles will continue, I have no doubt, but your execution will pacify the Baron enough to keep the peace. But what of Lady Ivy?"

"What about her?" I asked.

"Her father supposedly murdered at the hand of her lover. Her husband will torment her with it every day of her life. Your refusal to speak the truth will taint your name in history. Besides, have you not considered the uppermost factor in all this. The killer is still at large, your punishment will mean they will be unaccused and left free of punishment for their crime."

Flint took in a deep breath. "This I will leave with you to ponder, my friend. For now, back to your cage."

He shut the iron doors, and I gripped hold of the bars. "Is there any news on Carre?"

Flint turned back to face me. "Like you, he still breathes, but for how long, well, this is uncertain."

"I will not shame her," I said.

"Baroness Ivy will always be loved in the eyes of her people," replied Flint, before walking out of the dungeon.

Laying down on the dirty straw that littered my cell floor, I peered up at the ceiling. The frost had encouraged condensation, making the dungeon feel even more clammy and cold. Contemplating whether to take the Detector's advice made my mind restless. He had a point, since Lady Ivy's tribulations would not end on my death, and the more I pondered over the treatment I had received at the hand of my own association, I couldn't help but start to feel bitter. So sour, that Lady Ivy's proposal of escaping this wicked town gave me even more reason to consider abandoning the oath I had sworn to the Blue Swords.

I had battled to appease my peers and meet their expectations, but the truth was I had always felt like nothing more than the runt of the litter. The Governor had grown weary of my troublesome behaviour and speculations, and now that my own senior was willing to sacrifice me only to appease my antagonist, I had little more to offer them.

Amongst all the doubt that lingered in my head, I thought of Fulten and the faith he had once put in me. There was little chance of me avenging his death whilst stuck in this predicament, so I considered my options, should I ever be cleared of Isaak's murder.

It was an unfortunate circumstance, leaving me with only one possibility. The Detector was right, I could not just sit back and allow this conspiracy to be played out. On Flint's return, I would confess to my engagement with the Baroness, leaving me with one last impossible decision to make. I would have to choose to abscond with the woman I loved or leave her disgraced and avenge my late mentor.

Getting to my feet, I was relieved to hear the unlocking of the entrance door and the illumination of light coming from the passage. Ready to relay my account to the Detector, I was surprised to see Sergeant Hock appear before me. Pulling over the stool, he rested the candle on the top, before propping himself against the bars of my cell door.

Expressing his dissatisfaction at my treatment, he asked if there was anything I needed. Declining his offer of hospitality, I was keen to learn of the reason behind his attendance.

Rubbing his hand over his face, he appeared uncomfortable with what he was about to say. "From the time you were appointed, I have snubbed every move you made since, doubting not only your ability, but also your intention. Yet since Fulten's death I have observed your integrity."

Dumbfounded by his unexpected attempt at what I thought was a compliment, I asked him again why he had come to see me.

"You were given strict instructions not to disclose the identity of our representatives and you kept your word. Not only have you kept your word, but you have also gone beyond the capabilities of any Sword at this lock up and delved into the truth of the tragedies that continue to haunt this town."

Looking back at the Sergeant, I frowned before interrupting him. "With all due respect, Sergeant, you speak in riddles."

Watching me intently, he took in a deep breath. "The Cavaliers, Jep. They are the reason this town avoids a substantial revolt, their elegant and discreet influences are all around us, and you have remained true to our institution."

I was aghast. "You're a Cavalier?"

Nodding his head, Sergeant Hock glanced down at the ground.

Gripping the iron bars of my cell, he leaned his face in closer, staring back at me intensely. "We are being hunted, Jep. I fear that I am next. I knew Father Arrend was incapable of taking his own life. Then Carre's attack, orchestrated to make us believe it was all part of a drunken brawl with some outsiders. Once I learnt of Isaak's misfortune, I knew there was only one piece of the puzzle left to fit into place. Me!"

"What is the purpose of telling me this? I am confined to your own dungeon. There is little I can achieve."

"Your relations with the Baroness must not become public knowledge, her purity is needed, now more than ever. There is a change in power coming."

"So, I am to die?"

Hock raised his eyebrows, "You are to guide the Baroness to leadership. This town will prevail. It must. Only Lady Ivy can unite Stanford, once and for all."

"If you wish for me to kill the Baron, this I will gladly do," I said.

Hock seemed Irritated by my brash response, "We are sophisticated men of honour, not barbarians. Leave his demise to his own doing, the people grow tired of his tyranny and ineptitude."

The dwindling light limited my vision, as I stood face to face with the Sergeant, separated by the cage door. Suddenly Hock gasped in horror, as his body was pressed up against the iron bars. A hand covered by a leather glove yanked back the Sergeant's forehead. I attempted to grip the arm of the intruder, but they were too strong.

Hock was dragged back into the darkness, panting, whilst struggling to free himself from his tormentor's grasp. Yelling, I called for help, until I heard the gruesome sound of flesh being hacked, followed by gurgling.

Pushed back up against the door, Hock reappeared, more visible. Blood pulsed from an incision in his throat, causing his eyes to roll to the back of his head. The colour drained from his skin as I pushed my hands through the bars, attempting to apply pressure to the open wound.

Hock's body stiffened, and whoever had committed this savage attack held him tightly pressed against the cell door. Again, I shouted, whilst pushing my face closely against the bars, attempting to get sight of the assailant. The dim light generated by the single candle was not enough to illuminate Hock's attacker, and I was only able to see their silhouette. The intruder remained relaxed and controlled, still forcing the Sergeant against the door, allowing him to bleed out like a hanging pig.

Panicking now, I screamed, determinedly trying to close the incision with my hands. Hock's blood drained from his throat, now covering my forearms and staining the iron bars. His body slowly slumped to the ground, and the attacker briefly stepped forward.

Two eyes watched me from behind the sack that masked their

identity. I froze in dismay at what had just unfolded and my inability to act, before observing the intruder toss down a bloodstained carving knife on to the now gasping Sergeant Hock.

The invader stepped away. I yelled again for help before kneeling beside Hock. Life had left the Sergeant now, leaving him in a pool of blood that seeped into my cell. Observing the door, I saw that his blood coated the iron bars.

Falling back down, I sat on the floor, rotating my hands, examining the blood that now stained my skin and tunic. Noticing the murder weapon and the space between the iron bars, I knew too well that I had been framed with yet another death and this time it was the death of a Blue Sword.

13

THE IRON CHAIR

Sword Lev was the first to answer my cries for help. He knelt desperately beside Sergeant Hock, turning over his bloodied body. Casting his eyes over the laceration in the Sergeant's throat, he anxiously looked across towards me. His eyes widened on seeing the blood that stained my hands and clothing.

Chenchi was next to arrive, his body involuntary frozen by what was presented to him. "May God have mercy," he mumbled.

Stuttering and panicked, I immediately began communicating the events that had unfolded, however Lev and Chenchi observed one another with uneasy expressions, struggling to comprehend what now faced them.

"Stand back, turn and face the cell wall," shouted a stern toned voice from the edge of the passageway.

Sword O'Hara stood poised with his baton drawn, pointing its tip in my direction. "I will break every bone in your body, if you do not obey my order, now stand back," he called for a second time.

I placed my hands out to the side, feeling the blood running down my fingertips and drip onto the floor of my cell. I slowly moved back, staring at Chenchi for reassurance. "He was attacked, the suspect came up from behind, slit his throat, they will not be far."

My words went unheard as all three men dismissed my claim and scrambled around Hock's lifeless body.

The Governor was the fourth to respond to the commotion. He looked down at his friends fatally wounded body, losing his regular stern exterior and replacing it with a look of despair.

"The prisoner is drenched in his blood," said O'Hara.

"I can see that," barked the Governor.

Chenchi stood before the Governor, understanding swiftly the accusation that was coming my way. "Sir, Jep stated the assailant will still be close, allow me to pursue them. The ground is boggy, there must be tracks."

The Governor paused, his eyes flickering between me and Hock. He returned a vacant nod at Chenchi, prompting my friend to sprint towards the passage.

"We must notify the Chief," insisted O'Hara.

The Governor eyed me, unable to hold back a natural grimace, whilst speaking with O'Hara. "Go to the Grand Hall, brief the Chief of the circumstances. All swords are to assist Chenchi in his search."

"Sir, I fear a search will be wasted?" questioned O'Hara.

The Governor growled at O'Hara, "Do I speak in a foreign tongue? You will do as I order."

Relaxing my arms, I moved forward, gripping the iron bars of my cell door. I looked at the Governor in desperation, but he was unwilling to react to the torment displayed on my face. He knelt beside his fallen Sword and began assisting Lev to remove the Sergeant's corpse. No one spoke a word, and the dungeon was the subject of an eerie silence as they carried Hock away.

I spent several moments gawping emptily at the blood trail that now discoloured the ground. Moments later, the Governor returned. His expression remained impassive, making it hard to predict what he was thinking or going to say. Finally he spoke, "We overplayed our bluff, Jep."

"Sir, Sergeant Hock told me the truth."

"The truth?" He grunted.

"He disclosed his association with the Cavaliers."

The Governor glanced down at the smeared blood tarnishing the stone floor. Pausing, he kept silent, reflecting on what I had just disclosed.

Interrupting his stillness, I divulged Hock's theory. "They're being picked off one by one, first Arrend, Carre then Isaak and now our Sergeant."

Still unable to look me in the eye, the Governor shook his head whilst squinting his eyes down at the ground. "I cannot deny your theory. However, the Chief will only look at facts."

"Facts? And what are the facts?" I cried.

"That you stand stained in the blood of a Blue Sword. If Chenchi's search is wasted, and it will be, you will hang for this. What a suitable outcome that will be, not only for Asher, but for our Chief."

The pessimistic words that came from the Governor's mouth echoed in my mind, causing me to take a step back. Slouching down, I slid onto the ground, beaten and demoralized. He looked at me through the iron bars, sympathetically, but just like me he knew what my fate was to be.

"I will have Isa bring food before the Chief's return, I suggest you hide it beneath the straw in your cell. You will need all your strength for what is to come."

He turned and left the dungeon, leaving me sat bleary-eyed and in a daze. The reality of the situation was beginning to take hold. I had been framed, and now left alone to endure the penalties. For the first time I felt like that former peasant boy, replaceable and forgettable. My thoughts spun on who was behind this plot and for once, Hota's name had been replaced. Unfortunately, many others now stood in its place.

I shivered, as my bones chilled from the sharpness of the cold and damp air. My eyes had begun to adjust to the darkness, making each breath visible from the chill. Time became stagnant, leaving me intrigued by every footstep that disturbed the gravel outside the dungeon.

Eventually I heard the entrance being unlocked, followed by a light grunt as my visitor struggled to close the door's solid structure. Blair appeared, but even her energetic features, enlightened by lit flames, was not enough to remove the unpleasant mood that had dampened my feelings.

Leaning her arm through the bars, she offered me cheese and eggs. "Here you go, this will keep you strong for the fight."

Snatching the food from her hand, I moved to the back of my cell, without showing a hint of gratitude.

Blair looked back at me, offended at my dismissive manner. "So that's it then, is it? You're going to roll over and take it?"

Ignoring her remarks, I sat staring blankly at the far corner of the cell, ashamed and unwilling to engage her in conversation.

"I thought you were tougher than this, Jep. We peasants should know what it means to survive and fight."

Her words triggering my irritation, I jumped up, taking hold of the bars and glaring back at her. "What do you know about being a peasant? You are surrounded by nothing but love. Your belly aching and yearning for more grows boring, girl. You really want this? To serve and wear this symbol of corruption? Look at what it has done for me."

Blair turned away, her expression saddened by my harshness.

"Look at me!" I shouted.

Blair peered back at me with tears forming in her eyes.

Seeing her upset, I lowered my voice, but remained just as bitter. "Thrown to the wolves, and for what? The approval of a tyrant, who will forever plague this town and devastate the lives of the people of in it. Blue Swords," I scoffed, "They are nothing more than adherents of this distasteful game."

Blair stepped back, her eyes flickering, unable to meet my stare. I watched as she walked disheartened towards the passageway dragging her feet. She turned back, looking at me with tears now running down her cheeks, "I won't ever give up on you, even if you have."

***

Two nights passed and I remained alone and unvisited. I had anticipated further prisoners being brought to the dungeon, yet none came. All captives must have been diverted to the Baron's lock up to avoid any outside influence on what was heading my way.

Stubble had grown back on my chin and dirt now sat under my nails. My navy tunic was now blackened from the dust and even worse, Sergeant Hock's blood still stained my skin.

I no longer felt remorse for the way in which I had treated Blair, and I was beginning to feel repulsed by the filthy crest that was now unrecognisable on my chest. I remained self-pitiful at the whole situation, unable to justify the lack of empathy shown by my own associates.

My mind often wandered, giving way to Lady Ivy, and for a short moment I felt peace, until I considered the circumstances of my imprisonment. Even Chenchi had stopped hurling the odd reassuring comment from outside.

My mind was brought abruptly back to reality by the sound of heavy footsteps crunching on the gravel outside, followed by the opening of the entrance to the dungeon. The doors slammed shut and the footsteps marched down the passage, causing me to stand, propped against the iron bars, eager to see who came.

Scowling back at me was Sergeant Mosely, stood next to Sword O'Hara, who remained expressionless but whose natural expression was already intimidating enough. "Shackle him to the pillar," ordered Mosely.

I was escorted outside my cell, my legs weak from the confinement meaning I could offer them no resistance even if I wanted to. O'Hara attached my shackles to the chain that ran from the central column of the dungeon, and I stood with my back to both men, the initial silence causing my stomach to knot with apprehension.

Mosely crept closer to me, placing his mouth near to my ear. "Confess," he whispered.

I turned my head to him, so close that he could feel the warmth of my breath. "I offer no confession."

Mosely looked back to O'Hara, before bowing his head.

Stepping forward, O'Hara struck my ribs with his clenched fist. His punch was solid, like a mule kicking out its back legs. I felt bones crack in my side, leaving me squirming and slumping down to my knees, breathless.

"Stand him up," demanded Mosely.

Pulling me back up to my feet, O'Hara gave me a sour look.

"Do you confess?" called Mosely.

Observing my silence for only a short time, the Sergeant gave another nod to O'Hara, who delivered a second blow to my ribs. Grunting, his strike took me off balance, causing me to crash to the ground, and the chains that secured me clattered against the stone floor.

Mosely knelt down by my side, smirking. "His fists are like rocks, are they not? I say he will only need three more before your legs will no longer function. So, let's put an end to this obscenity, and confess."

Stubbornly, I regained my footing, coughing as I brought myself up off the ground. Arching my back, I groaned from the break in my ribs.

I gawked back to Mosely. "He hits the way I visualise you making love, pitifully and feebly."

My tone had angered the Sergeant, and this time it was he himself who delivered my punishment. He punched me on the cheek, which was enough to jolt my head, but had little effect compared to the assault I had received from O'Hara. The impact split the inside of my mouth on a tooth, and I spat the blood in the direction of Mosely's boots insolently.

My ignorance had prompted him to lose composure, and he moved in on me, raining several unrestrained punches to my torso and head, eventually bringing me down to one knee. This time it was Mosely who spat down on me, before delivering a decisive blow to the back of my head, leaving me sprawled out on the floor. I was semi-conscious, feeling only a throb pounding from my temple.

"I will break you. All traitors shall be broken," snarled Mosely, before storming out of the dungeon.

Sword O'Hara remained behind and gently assisted me off the floor. "Your tenacity will not reward you, man."

Removing my shackles, he went on to produce a rag from his pockets and wipe away the fresh blood that covered my face. Lowering me down in my cell, he kicked back the hay, before picking up the remainder of the stale cheese left by Blair.

Holding out the food, he told me to sit upright to ensure my ribs allowed room to heal. My vision had become blurred from the swelling around my eyes, as I watched him lock my cell door and leave the dungeon.

The darkness once again blackened my damp cell when I felt it starting again. Dread, panic and fear all surged through my mind, and I began to lose control of one of my arms. A tingling sensation teased my muscle as my arm dropped. My jugular began pulsing rapidly, whilst sickness took over my stomach. Once again, I was unable to catch my breath as each gasp of air became less fulfilling.

Sergeant Hock's eyes stared back at me through the barred doors and blood trickled from his open neck. I visualised turning Carre's body over in the square, but this time he sat upright cackling back at me, showing no concern for his swollen face. An apparition of Lady Ivy appeared standing opposite me, sobbing relentlessly in the corner of my cell, digging her fingernails into her skin, marking her crisp, white complexion.

The visions all blurred into one and tormented my head, causing the walls of my cell to spin. When it eventually ended, I churned out my insides on to the hay covered floor before steadying my breath and resting on my side. I curled my back, reaching my arms around my knees and laying in the cold blackness.

***

I woke up sore and aching from the previous day's interrogation. Griping, I cupped my ribs, touching the bones damaged by Sword O'Hara's forceful blows. The muscles in my face felt tight; they had been bruised by Sergeant Mosely's knuckles, after my stubbornness had caused him to lose his self-control.

Commotion came from the entrance of the dungeon, followed by the sound of squeaking wheels running down the passage towards me. Then I saw it and trepidation lined my stomach. Its thick wooden arms and back had been plated with iron. Small sharp spikes littered the armrests, as well as along its back and seat. O'Hara noticed me observing its chilling sight, and sighed, before assisting an enthusiastic Mosely in removing the contraption from the wooden, wheeled barrow.

"Let us see if your stubbornness will endure," called Mosely.

My eyes were fixed widely on the iron chair, its haunting appearance matching its sinister reputation. Its sight alone made me consider whether to admit to crimes that I was innocent of, yet somehow, I still could not. They wanted my submission, and under no circumstances was I now willing to give in to them, nor identify Lady Ivy as a key witness to my innocence.

"It looks rather comfy," I said in a sarcastic tone, before coughing.

O'Hara rolled his eyes, unamused by my lack of willingness to comply and confess my guilt.

"Normally we would allow you to observe a fellow criminal become acquainted with the chair, but as you remain here alone, let us move forward," replied Mosely.

The Sergeant demanded my removal from my cell, prompting O'Hara to unlock my barred door. Seeing my struggles as I clutched hold of the wall, he understood I was little threat and gripped my upper arm to help me to my feet.

Hovering me over the spiked seat, he relaxed his hold, allowing me to lower myself, cautiously onto the spikes. Witnessing my reluctance, Mosely stepped forward and pushed me down onto the iron chair.

I yelled, as the metal teeth penetrated my back and buttocks, piercing through the top layer of my skin. The sharpness of the steel spikes was intense, but it was bearable without any further added pressure. I had managed to remain slightly raised, in order to keep the penetration minimal.

Mosely now stood before me, stroking his fingers across his moustache. "Do you confess?"

"You do what you must," I murmured.

Waving his hand at O'Hara, the Sword picked up the ropes used to attach the chair to the wheeled trailer. He began placing them over my body, looping them back around my thighs and chest.

"You are a pig-headed fool," whispered O'Hara.

"I would rather die advocating truth, than die of shame," I said.

O'Hara paused and watched me, before he finished positioning the ropes over my arms.

I could hear Mosely standing behind the iron chair. He leaned down enough that I could smell the stale mead on his breath. "You shall confess."

Agony filled my clenched body. Mosely pulled back on the rope, tightly wedging me against multiple spikes that covered the chair. He held me in place, causing me to scream in distress as the steel stabbed deeper through my skin and into my tendons. I looked to O'Hara who looked away from my sight, showing a hint of pity for what I was being made to endure.

Sergeant Mosely released his hold of the ropes, relieving the tension and giving me the opportunity to inhale deeply in an attempt to numb the discomfort. But the needle like spikes still pierced into my skin, leaving me overcome with pain.

Mosely crept around to face me, clearly bewildered by my lack of confession and unwillingness to cooperate with our Chief's wishes. Looking up at the ceiling, he sighed. I lifted my head up, glaring at him with sunken eyes, displaying my loathing.

"You ready to confess now, Jep?" he asked, this time a little less sure of his tactics.

"Damn you and the Blue Swords," I growled.

Sergeant Mosely leaned forward, brashly tearing the crest from my tunic, still irritated by my stubbornness.

My light-headedness had begun to mask some of the pain, but this was short lived. A surge of adrenaline coursed through my veins as Mosely yanked firmly on the ropes once again, forcing my body even harder into the chair's teeth.

The blood dripped from the open wounds encompassing my body. I yelled out, embracing the sheer volume of torment I was being made to suffer. My eyelids began to feel heavy, and I felt my insides becoming numb as the lighting in the room diminished and my vision faded.

The clattering sounds of armour and raised voices brought me back to consciousness.

"You release him from that chair at once!" bellowed the Governor. "I did not authorise this act of barbarism in my lock up. Now get my Sword to his feet or you will be next to feel its iron."

"With all due respect, Sir, the Chief has given me precise orders to extract the truth from this man using whatever means I feel necessary. You are well aware that his behaviour has indeed fallen short of our honourable standard," retorted Mosely.

The Governor growled, leaning in towards the Sergeant. "We wear the same crest. Your lust for maiming one of your own disgusts me. Now aid him to his feet or it will be you who bleeds."

Mosely nervously looked across to O'Hara, who held back from offering his senior any support.

"You heard the Governor; we will refrain from any further punishment," said O'Hara.

O'Hara and the Governor pulled me up to my feet, and I groaned as the spikes slid out from my flesh, releasing my body. I had no control over my legs and was reliant on being held up by them both.

The Governor examined the blood that oozed out of my skin and leaked from my dishevelled clothing. "Jep will return to his quarters, you will fetch for the surgeon to dress his wounds."

"Sword O'Hara will be placed to guard his chambers and there will be no interference from others," insisted Mosely.

As I was led out of the lock up into the open air, the vividness of the bright sky blinded my eyes, causing me to squint and feel nauseous. The Governor offered me motivation, encouraging me to move my legs to cross the courtyard.

"His muscles are weak," the Governor said to Sword O'Hara, who supported my other arm. My blood leaked from my wounds and trailed behind, staining the loose stones on the ground.

A voice roared from the parade room door. "You savages!" Chenchi came marching towards us.

"Stand down, Chenchi," demanded the Governor.

The Governor gave my friend a second order to yield, but Chenchi disregarded our superior's demand and remained absorbed in a staring conflict with Sword O'Hara.

With neither man willing to look away, Chenchi spat to the ground, dismissing our associate.

"This is how you treat one of your own, you vile bastards?" said Chenchi, now fixating his anger towards Sergeant Mosely.

"Chenchi, you will vacate your chambers and join Lev,"

commanded the Governor.

Refusing to acknowledge our leader's instructions, Chenchi moved in front of me, gently resting his hand on my shoulder, "There will be justice, that I swear."

14

THE INVITATION

Awakening to the sound of chirping birds, I opened my eyes, struggling to adjust my vision to the daylight. I shuddered and groaned whilst attempting to prop myself up against the wall at the head of the bed. Reaching out to the bitter pain that covered my back, I brushed my fingertips over the tightened bandages covering my wounds.

I pictured the steel spikes that were responsible for inflicting my injuries and felt instant dread, as I remembered the circumstances that had placed me there.

Squinting my eyes at the door, I could see the shadow of boots of the guardsman that patrolled outside my chambers. Exhaling, I laid back down. Lady Ivy was not far from my thoughts, and I began to feel distraught at the thought of what lies she had likely been told. To consider that the Baroness felt ill of me was worse than the idea of facing a wrongful execution.

Knowing that what awaited me was a damp cell, I held in my breath, attempting to hold back a cough so not to draw the guard's attention to my conscious state. Unable to conceal the itch in my chest, I began to splutter, prompting the watchman to enter.

A young man stood over me, nervously assessing my condition. His service to the Blue Swords appeared as limited as my own. He was of a similar age, but his face was fresher and his clear skin was much less weathered than mine.

His anxiousness was made clear through his refusal to make eye contact and his hesitation at assessing my wounds.

"You have no need to see me as an enemy," I advised.

The young Sword gulped. "I do not, but you have been detained for murder, so forgive me if I appear a little stand-offish."

I peered up at the ceiling, before sighing. "The irony of all this is that we are the good ones, yet here I find myself on the wrong side, like a senile dog that has bitten its master."

"I have no doubt that truth will prevail," the Sword replied.

"We are at similar stages in our paths, so you may think me condescending saying this, but one thing I know for sure is that being a Blue Sword may give you the right of authority and a sense of righteousness, but it also dangles you much closer to the edge of the chopping block."

Dismissing my cynicism, the guard insisted on calling for his Sergeant, appearing satisfied with my injuries. If ever there was a chance to escape this awful predicament, it was now, but my weakened limbs would not allow it, even if I had sought to abscond.

The door was vigorously opened causing me to involuntarily flinch. Sword O'Hara appeared, frowning as he leaned over, examining me with his fierce glare, behind all the scarring that disfigured his skin. The Governor appeared and stood back, sternly observing O'Hara.

"He can return," said O'Hara.

"He still looks flushed, he clearly has a fever," replied the Governor.

O'Hara scoffed, shaking his head, "Sir, if we do not move him now, he will only be moved on the Sergeant's return, you heard the Chief. This way he can be made comfortable, left fed and watered."

The Governor grumbled whilst nodding his head and accepting the proposal. "Very well."

I had hoped to set eyes on one of my companions, yet the grounds of the lock up seemed quiet that morning; even the horses made little noise. O'Hara gripped hold of my upper arm, moving me along like I was a belligerent drunk. The rodents scurried across the ground, disturbed by the sound of the dungeon door slamming shut behind us.

The Governor kept his message brief, assuring me that Isa would be along shortly to offer me food. O'Hara pulled back my cell door, kicking aside the hay and ensuring the cage was clear of any contraband. A look of shame flowed from his eyes, making it hard to determine whether it was me or his own behaviour that humiliated him.

The cold dampness of the dungeon was quick to take hold, and I was offered limited warmth by the sunlight piercing through, its rays illuminating the abandoned iron chair. The silence loomed, leaving me saddened and empty. I cast my mind back to when I first joined the Blue Swords, a time when I felt triumphant and noble. Yet now I had been left to rot once again in the dungeon I had once filled with true criminals.

***

Over the following days, Isa's visits became less frequent and the food less sufficient. Brushing my hand against my now overgrown, filthy hair, I felt that I had aged, even though my time in imprisonment had been limited. An untidy beard along with a diminishing waist reminded me even more of the predicament I was in. My uniform was now unrecognisable, just like my latest thoughts of the Blue Swords. Loathing the crest I once swore to honour now caused sickness to swirl inside my stomach. I had grown to detest the Swords and my treatment had caused me to forget the admiration I once had for the organisation I served. Now I felt bitter, seeing them as nothing more than another authority which had been riddled with corruption. I felt sick at the thought of knowing that I had added to that injustice, by allowing an innocent merchant to hang.

***

Several days passed and I waited alone and unvisited. On a windy evening an unexpected guest arrived to greet me at my cell door. Her long black hair flowed down her cloak and her blue eyes were enlightened by the flames of a burning torch in her hand. Truda appeared before me, shrewdly dressed with her cleavage pressing up against her corset, peeping out from the inside of her gown.

She grinned, forcing her cheek bones to tighten. "Well, well, how the mighty do fall." My refusal to engage had no effect on her willingness to tease me. "Don't be offended, I have quite the taste for a rugged man filled and energised by revulsion."

"What is it you want?"

Smirking, Truda took her time to answer. "I come with notification. I hereby serve that before the next holy day, you will receive punishment for the murder of our Baroness's father and the murder of your senior. In light of the charges, you will be sentenced to death."

I scoffed, making my contempt known. "Is that all?"

Astonished by my careless reaction, Truda watched me as I leaned back against the rear wall in my cell, clutching hold of my broken ribs.

"They plan to hang you Jep, your lack of anger indicates guilt."

"You do not even offer me a clean death. This conviction comes as no surprise, a swift victory for all," I replied.

Truda struggled to respond, clearly taken aback by my lack of concern and defeatist acceptance. Eventually she settled on my reaction, and returned to her usual, playful self.

Stepping closer and gripping the bars of my cell door, she stared at me. "Does the thought of the Baroness's ill feelings towards you not leave you a tad disturbed?"

Chuckling, I was keen to assure that my true feelings towards Lady Ivy were not demonstrated. So I steered the conversation away from the Baroness. "What unsettles me is that since your arrival, this town has become a victim to further bloodshed and torment. You allow a tyrant to hump you like a common whore, and yet I feel that it is you who is in control."

Truda peered down her nose at me, before raising one side of her mouth. Seductively, she pulled back one side of her robe, revealing her bare shoulder and tightly fitted, purple corset. I stared back at her grave faced, but inside, her provocativeness had got me somewhat aroused.

Tugging at her corset, she exposed both her breasts and continued to make eye contact with me. She gave her bottom lip a pinch with her teeth. "Have me, I am yours for the taking, at least allow yourself to die fulfilled."

The thought of pressing my body against hers, and touching her through the bars of my cell, tempted me to move forward. Fortunately, it was not only my body that had matured and I now was able to act with some self-control, something I had lacked in my youth. Declining her invitation, I laughed and began shaking my head, offering Truda nothing more than a pitiful look.

Truda's seductive expression transformed into a frown as she began to cover herself back up. Huffing, it was apparent my rejection had caused her much dissatisfaction and mortification. "Enjoy your death, peasant."

My resentment had now become my acceptance, leaving my mind closed and unwilling to concoct any consideration to Truda's part in the predicament I found myself in. Even Hota's name had emptied from my thoughts, as sadly did my late tutor, Fulten's. I was blank, empty, I had been beaten and lacked any more fight inside.

***

A day later, the robust opening of the dungeon door startled me. Sword Fawkes appeared, looking flustered and agitated, which made me anxious about his reasons for visiting me. The daylight made him clear and visible, and I couldn't help but notice that his face was pale and his skin clammy.

Immediately Fawkes growled with volume and insistence. "They have taken her."

"Who do you speak of?"

"Blair," he bellowed, "He has kidnapped her."

"Hota?" I asked.

"Who else? I will kill him Jep, even if it takes me a lifetime," roared Fawkes, now pacing by the doors of my cell.

I was unable to look Fawkes in the eye. The servant girl had offered me so much charm over my past few years within the Swords. My initial instinct was to feel saddened for Blair, remembering the way in which I dismissed her childish whines on our last meeting. To know that she was now at the mercy of Hota, was a difficult thought.

Fawkes remained quiet, but continued to pace up and down, impatiently awaiting my response. My mood suddenly shifted as I evaluated my own dilemma, and I felt my sympathy for the girl begin to diminish.

Sighing, I then looked back at Fawkes through the iron bars, squeezing my lips together and raising my eyebrows. "Your news comes as little surprise, once again the Swords have dismissed Hota's capabilities."

Fawkes scrunched up his face as he watched me casually slump down at the rear of my cell. "Your lack of empathy astounds me, Jep."

"Does it? And where was your empathy when I was branded a murderer?" I snapped. "I have been beaten, tied to a chair and sliced like meat and now they cannot even allow me a dignified death. Forgive me if I appear a little uncaring and self-indulgent."

"Blair is one of us, Jep, she is a Sword."

I walked towards the bars and placed my face against the cold iron. "I am no Sword, not anymore."

Fawkes glared back at me, his face a mixture of confusion and resentment. He paused, unsure of how or whether to respond.

"Hota will only return her, should you be offered in her place," Fawkes said.

Grimacing, I stared back at the experienced sword. "So now I am to be traded from one corrupt bastard to another. The question is, which one wants to kill me the most?"

"I have no opinion on your detention, all has been done to clear your name. At least this way your death will not be in vain. Where is the noble man that once stood before me, offering so much potential?"

"He is on the wrong side of this door," I answered.

It was the first time I saw distress appear on the face of one of the most courageous swords in Thear. As his hope drained away, so did the complexion of his skin. Dragging his feet, Fawkes walked to the passageway, before pausing, insisting on the final word.

"She was the only person for whom I begged approval, and yet still, I have let her down."

It took me the night to brush off the sulk I had so often found myself in of recently. One thing about sitting in darkness was that it forced one to reflect. Knowing that Blair's fate rested in the hands of Hota, I began to feel chills through my veins. I knew that his summons was nothing more than a way to trap me and most likely he would kill both me and Blair, but once I dismissed my own self-pity, I began remembering the captivating little girl who had transformed into a fearless woman.

My life hung hopelessly at the edge of a cliff, but Blair had everything ahead of her. It was my duty to help, and if I should fail, at the very least I would give my life trying.

15

BEATING DRUM

Isa expressed her gratitude by attempting to supply me more niceties that she was able to salvage from the nightly feasts. Each time she entered, Isa praised my willingness to help, knowing that my meeting with Hota would most likely result in my own death. I found the ability to drown out my fears; Isa's despair and grief was enough to do that.

On this occasion, Isa entered the dungeon with a hint of satisfaction displayed as she approached the cage door. "They will sit this afternoon and you are to join them, Jep."

Taking hold of the bread she offered me, I respectfully bowed my head, acknowledging her remarks. I understood full well the people with whom I was to have an audience.

Sword O'Hara eventually arrived at the dungeon in the early afternoon, and on unlocking my cell door, he ordered me to rest my palms out on the rear wall. After shackling my wrists, he escorted me outside and to the parade room. I could not help but take a second look at the battle scars that lined his face; he had quite the warrior's appearance. Even though he was robust towards me, I sensed a hint of compassion; the man had morals and was easy to admire.

The room came to an abrupt silence on my arrival, and all who had been awaiting my attendance stared at me, showing alarm at the condition in which I was now presented to them. My hair was collar length and covered with dirt, as was the facial hair that curled around my mouth. My unsteadiness on my feet, a sign of undernourishment, was something else which also appeared to shock my associates.

The Governor was seated at one end of the table and the Chief at the other. Chief Muir gave me a brief, dismissive glance through his narrow eyes, before insisting that I was to be seated. Detector Amir and Detector Flint sat on one side of the table, alongside Sergeant Mosely, who refused to meet my gaze.

The empty seat opposite was left for me, making the surroundings feel like it had been set up for an interrogation. The Governor invited me to eat, but was cut down by the Chief's eagerness to hurry proceedings along.

Detector Flint nuzzled his mouth into his clenched fist, whilst beginning to fidget uncomfortably in his chair.

"Do you have something to add, Detector?" asked Chief Muir.

Flint peered back at our leader, taking in a deep breath. "Are you blind to the condition in which our companion is presented?"

"Steady," muttered Amir in a low voice.

"You will respect your audience, Detector," growled the Chief.

Making my own outspoken remark, I scowled at Chief Muir. "So come on, what is it you want of me?"

My impolite reaction to Chief Muir deflected Flint's previously discourteous comment, and brought a further uneasy silence to the room.

Chief Muir smirked back at me, slumping down into his chair. "I see your spirit is yet to be broken, boy."

"Sir, may I suggest we get on with the matter in hand?" said the Governor.

"Quite right," replied the Chief. "Jep, you are aware that one of our servants has been abducted by your former acquaintance."

"The servant has a name; Blair," I replied.

"How noble of you, so she does," said the Chief sarcastically. "Anyhow, the former Sword, Hota, whom I trust you're familiar with, has taken the girl whilst she was outside the confines of the town, courting with one of the local guards."

"Markus?" I asked.

"I am unfamiliar with the boy's name; he was released without harm and was required to deliver this scroll. I trust you can read?" He handed me the note.

I unravelled the parchment and scanned over its contents. Hota had named me on the scroll, inviting me to attend a village located south of Stanford. He had clearly stated that in exchange for my unaccompanied surrender, Blair would be released.

"As you can see, Jep, we have very little time," said the Governor.

"I say we storm Yaxil. There is one road in and out, the residents will have already been slaughtered," insisted Sword O'Hara, who stood in the corner of the room behind me.

"He will slit her throat before one of your hooves hits the ground of Yaxil," advised Detector Amir.

"Do we have no Swords present there?" asked Chief Muir, with one eyebrow raised.

"Swords have not patrolled the villages for years; I believe this was due to a lack of silver. Well, that is what you once wrote on a deployment order, Sir," replied the Governor.

The Chief sighed and pulled back his head. "This child, is she worth reclaiming?"

The Governor sneered. "May I suggest Sir, that you not repeat that question to Sword Fawkes, or you will have more than a mutiny to contend with. Blair is one of us."

Chief Muir looked at me, "Very well, then we have no choice." Muir placed his elbows onto the table and leaned closer, eyeing me. "I tell you this, boy. Make an attempt to flee and I will consider it a dereliction of duty, and I assure you, there will be an arrow awaiting you."

"But Sir, if I may, sending Jep to Hota is sending him to his death, the man is hell bent on revenge," pleaded Flint.

"He is to face the noose anyway, why not allow him to die with a degree of dignity?" said the Chief. Turning to face me once again, Muir continued. "Do you fear death, Jep?"

"Death shall greet us all, even you," I replied, with a hint of a threat. "All that matters is Blair's return."

"And here was me thinking you were unnoble," said Sergeant

Mosely.

Flint scrunched his lips together and lowered his head, he knew what my outcome was to be, as did the others who sat around the table. The Governor tried to insist on allowing me to shelter in my own quarters, but his request was swiftly denied. However, Chief Muir did agree to permit me to indulge in the riches shared at the evening feast, clearly unaware that this was already being allowed.

Returning to my cell after my first proper meal for weeks, it took a while for the reality of the terms to which I had agreed to set in. The thought of facing Hota while I was unarmed and vulnerable disappointed me. I had longed for a meeting with the killer of my beloved tutor, yet now I was to meet him on his terms and at his mercy. The chances of him honouring the arrangement were slight, but something that I had to gamble on. After all, what choice did I have? I wanted to give Blair a fighting chance, and I was already a walking dead man.

The following afternoon, Flint arrived at the dungeon, appearing surprisingly chipper considering my looming fate. Teasing me with news, he finally blurted out the reason for his visit.

"He has agreed to allow you temporary release. Only for the evening mind, and you will be shackled and in my company, and that of O'Hara's."

"And where is it you suggest I go? I am in no mood to socialise in the company of Swords, unless it is with Chenchi."

"Your ingratitude astounds me, Jep. You have become quite the grouch, a true Blue Sword. A band of bards plays this night at the Playhouse, and their sound is rather dramatic. It's just what you need to infect your mood and prepare you for what tomorrow brings."

"I have little to be grateful for, how did you get the Chief to approve this outing?" I asked.

"Hota is one of Thear's most wanted men, and you are to have an audience with him as a Sword. I have reliably informed our ruler that if the opportunity arises, you will ensure his death is met. This concept has left Chief Muir keen to send you off happy."

Flint felt uncomfortable about applying the shackles, his hands shaking as he secured the cuffs.

Walking through the rear of the compound, I was keen to see Chenchi. "Does anyone know of my release?"

"No, and I think it best we keep it that way. If Mosely sets eyes on you conversing with anyone but me or O'Hara, this night will be short lived."

Sword O'Hara stood awaiting us at the front of the lock up, with a long dark cloak in his hand. Flint took the cloak from O'Hara and began dusting it down. "It's a little dirty, but it will keep you from being recognised."

Pulling the cloak over my shoulders, Flint wrapped it around my front, ensuring that the shackles were well hidden. O'Hara growled, insistent on getting our outing over and done with.

Walking under darkness through the poorly lit estate helped us go unnoticed. Flint took us through a back passage, that meant we cut out the square and arrived directly on Main Street. The track was boggy, and mud flickered up the back of our boots, prompting further grumbles from O'Hara.

"So do tell me, Flint, has the Chief not considered the idea of me fleeing during this release?"

My dry remark caused O'Hara to come to a standstill, and his chilling stare was enough to encourage anyone to comply with his demands. Flint noticed my concerned reaction to O'Hara's expression, and began to laugh.

"Please do try, I would love see this brute of a man tear off your arms. Consider this your test of loyalty," said Flint, whilst patting me on the back. "Anyway, Jep, you are still destined to join me in Alma, I will make a Detector of you yet."

Flint oozed confidence. I would have been lying if his actions this evening had not raised my spirit, but his determination to make me his student gave me a moment of belief. I now regretted not taking him up on his initial offer, for now it was too late and the man whom I had stayed to hunt was now going to have me handed to him on a plate.

The noise from the playhouse ricocheted off the walls of the passage as we drew closer to the venue. The ambience was apparent from outside. The sounds of drums being struck in time with lutes made the music vibrate through my chest.

Diverting away from the queue of people outside the front entrance of the double floored structure, Flint led me down a narrow walkway at the side of the playhouse. Roaring flames from torches illuminated the stone walls, allowing the hanging scrolls advertising the folk bards to quickly catch the eye.

Flint knocked heavily on a low framed, wooden door.

"A secret entrance, I guess they save this for the more illustrious guest," I said.

"No, this is the workers' gate, I guess Fulten did not bring you here on night patrols, such a stickler for the rules was that man. The workers enjoy the presence of Blue Swords, I have seen some of Thear's greats perform here and never paid coin, not once."

The door was pulled back and we were met by an older, rounded woman in an oversized, red dress. She beamed on seeing Flint. "I was told you were coming; it thrills me to see you, and still so handsome," she giggled.

Flint pulled out all the charm, flirtatiously conversing with the willing stewardess. She was lured in, making little of me or O'Hara, and relished in lapping up Flint's banter.

Following Flint down the dingy tunnel, I could feel O'Hara's heavy breath hitting the back of my neck.

Flint turned to face me, giving me a wink. "See, there are many benefits to being a Sword."

I smiled back at Flint before looking up at the falling dust from the vibrations on the low raised ceiling.

Wandering through the workers' chambers, we received several startled looks before finally arriving in a prestigiously presented corridor. Woven thin red carpet lined the floor, and carved wooden patterns were fixed to the stone walls. Gold plated railings ran down the centre of the wall and added to its luxurious setting.

"I am reliably informed that the Witham chambers are unoccupied this evening, top of the stairs, central room," whispered the stewardess conspiratorially.

The corridor opened to the staircase which continued to maintain the extravagant décor. O'Hara stomped up each wooden stair, giving me a firm reminder of his presence.

Once on the landing, Flint came to a standstill at the first room. I glanced above at the inscribed carving above the door. It read, *Stanford suite.*

I started to ask why we had stopped at the wrong room, but Flint gave me a stern look, immediately losing his previous humorous wit. He placed a key into the lock of my shackles and released the cuffs. "You can never speak of this, as we will all lose our heads. Your time is limited, so say what you have to say, then we must leave."

Baffled, I looked around at O'Hara who remained stern faced, and subtly nodded his head towards the door we were stood by.

"We will wait here; remember what I said, time is against us," insisted Flint.

I looked between them both, unsure but somewhat intrigued at who or what awaited me on the other side of the door. Pulling down the handle, I pushed open the heavy oak door, only to be hit by a wave of blaring melody coming from the stage below the Stanford suite.

Lady Ivy stood primed and undeterred by my intrusion. I gasped as I became swamped with nerves at seeing her stood before me. She smiled, indicating I was most welcome to enter. Seeing her dressed in a yellow silk tunic with green stitching and embroidery, I was once again taken aback by her brown, smooth hair. Her green eyes shone back at me, sparkling, allowing me to revel in my delight at seeing her.

Baroness Ivy stood casually, propped up against the wooden balcony, making it apparent that we were alone on the viewing platform. The door closed behind me, and it was then I understood that Flint had gone to tremendous lengths to plan this meeting.

The music continued to captivate the theatre and add ambience to the tension between us. Lady Ivy made the first move, stepping towards me, pushing me back against the door as we kissed with passion. Conscious of my previous abode and the stubble on my face, I felt shy about the condition in which I presented myself to the Baroness.

Lady Ivy made it clear that my current dishevelment was not a factor in her feelings for me. She cupped her hand around my face, grasping at my rugged skin. Sensing my unease, Baroness Ivy pulled away, giving me a rather perplexed expression.

"Do I disappoint you?" she asked, her voice muffled by the sounds of a drum being struck.

"Look at me, I am not fit to be in your company."

"I would long for you no matter your condition."

Her words reassured me and allowed me to forget my current standing. Leaning forward, I kissed her firmly, this time reaching around her back and holding her tightly. I playfully pushed her against the door, pressing my body against her. Lady Ivy exhaled in my mouth as our touch got firmer and our bodies squeezed more tightly together.

Feeling her fingernails dig into my shoulders, I began kissing her neck, longingly. Lady Ivy moved her hands upwards, running her fingers through my hair, prompting me to grab hold of her hips and lift her from the ground.

Now zealously pressing our lips together, Baroness Ivy wrapped her legs around my waist. We met as if it was our last time, savouring every touch, every feel of one another. I wanted to take her, and I felt the feeling was mutual. Our fervour was energised by the dramatic melody that bellowed out below us. My heart raced, pulsating through my chest, louder than the sound of the beating drum.

However unconventional the setting, making love with Lady Ivy was like melting into gold. The moment may have been short lived, but it was the most intimate and exhilarating moment of my life and one that I would never forget.

We lay on the hard floor, giggling and conversing like carefree youths. Our hands wandered comfortably and remained on each other's bodies as if we had been together for years, it was natural and so blissful. I had longed for this moment with her, and for a short time I had forgotten what destiny had planned for me.

As the vibration of the music disturbed the floor, I sat upright beside her, bare chested with my elbow resting on the floor. Leaning my head into my palm, I took time to embrace the moment I was so fortunate to be in.

Unfortunately, Lady Ivy assured me it was time to confront the issue at hand and brought me swiftly back to reality.

"You are to leave tomorrow to face him," she said.

Inhaling, I looked at her intently, refusing to drop my eyes. "I do. Fate is destined for it to end with him."

"I understand why you have to go, but I don't want you to. I have just lost a father; I cannot lose you too. It angers me that they attempt to frame you for his death."

I immediately felt reassured, knowing that Lady Ivy attached no blame to me for the death of her father. Hearing her speak so freely about him gave me the closure I needed.

Baroness Ivy softly stroked my chest, gazing up at me full of thought. "What if we were to leave?" she asked suddenly.

I chuckled back at her, lightly taking in her words.

"I do not pretend. What is there left here for either of us? My husband's demands have mastery over us both. You will die and I will be left to vanish."

I gazed back at her, understanding that her idea was not so outlandish; Lady Ivy was right, my life here had finished. I had been portrayed as the villain not only by the Baron, but also by the Blue Swords.

"And how do you plan we should escape?" I asked.

Lady Ivy sat up right, motivated by my willingness to entertain her suggestion. "Flint has told me that you are to travel alone to meet with Hota and exchange yourself for the child. I would flee and we could travel north, back to our own people."

"I do recall you not finding comfort on our previous expedition," I chuckled, "Besides, you said it yourself; the child, Blair has not asked for this, she deserves the chance to live her own life, I have no doubt he will kill her if I do not attend."

"Are we not deserving of a life?" Baroness Ivy replied.

"The Baroness I fell in love with would not turn her back on anyone in need, especially a child. You speak out of desperation."

"This is what love feels like doesn't it, Jep?"

A tear ran down her face, and she turned towards the balcony, keen for me to not see her upset. I leaned down closer to her, guiding Lady

Ivy's face back to mine and then kissed her. I felt another tear run from her cheek and onto my skin.

I whispered in her ear, "Once Blair is freed, I will return, no matter what it takes. Then we shall have our happy ending."

Clutching her head close to my chest, we remained silent. The melody tone changed, it softened, allowing the lute to expand its sound. Our bodies lay together in peace, however our minds raced back to the reality of what was to come and the likelihood that this would be our final encounter.

A heavy knock shook the door, and I knew my time was up. Fastening up my weathered tunic, I ran my hand through my unkept hair, brushing it back. Once the Baroness had covered herself and dressed, I opened the door. I expected to see Flint smiling back at me, pleased with himself, but the sympathetic expression he wore in reality was much more fitting for the circumstances.

He looked behind me at the Baroness. "Forgive me my Lady, but I am afraid we must be leaving now."

O'Hara stood to the side of Flint, appearing awkward as he looked down at the floor.

Lady Ivy leaped forward giving me a final kiss whilst resting her hands around my jaw. "Come back to me, stay alive," she demanded.

The sound of Sword O'Hara clearing his throat was his way of giving off a polite warning. Pulling away from Lady Ivy left my heart feeling torn, as I stepped out on to the landing. I was unable to look back, feeling my throat swell and my eyes water.

"You heard her Jep, all you have to do is stay alive," muttered Flint.

16

FAREWELL

As we entered the rear courtyard, the raised voices and bickering could be heard from the front of the lock up.

"This is ludicrous, the man will be gone at the first opportunity he gets," argued Sergeant Mosely.

"The Chief has agreed, if Jep plans to run, he will likely do so the moment he leaves the gate," said the Governor.

Mosely smiled, "Not with O'Hara tracking him, any sign of diversion and your Sword will feel the cold head of an arrow in his spine."

On seeing me return with Flint and O'Hara, both our seniors hushed their quarrel, but Mosely sourly fixed his sight on me.

Marching towards me he scowled, scrunching his moustache against his nose, "If it was down to me, you would already have had your neck stretched."

"Lucky for me, no one seems to give a damn about the drivel you speak."

Grumbling, the Sergeant stomped away, leaving the grounds of the lock up. Fawkes and Lev stepped out from the stables.

"Chenchi will be pleased to be having one more night with his lover," said Lev, causing me to smile.

"As will I."

The Governor approached me, "What you are doing is most commendable and one would not judge, should you flee."

"Jep is a man of his word; that is why he wears our crest. I have no doubt he will do what is right," interrupted Fawkes. Turning to face me, Fawkes observed me through ominous eyes. "If the opportunity arises, you kill the bastard, you hear? Not just for Blair, but for Fulten."

Flint took over the conversation, insistent that I was to return straight to my chamber, to avoid giving Mosely any reason to lock me up in the dungeon on my final night.

"You will be guarded by one of the Alma Swords. Chenchi will be with you shortly, I will ensure he brings adequate meat and ale. Come, you must go," said Flint.

"For Fulten," called out Lev, as I turned away and headed towards my quarters.

***

Once inside, Flint briefed my warden on who was allowed in and out, before joining me. "I will return at first light, with a fresh tunic. May I suggest you dip your head in that barrel outside before we leave, she must truly adore you to have put up with that stench," he said, wrinkling his nose.

I laid down on my bed, embracing the comfort of the straw mattress. But the peace and quiet gave way to my forever restless mind. Stupidly, I had allowed myself to overlook the reason for which I was agreeing to meet with Hota in such unequal circumstances, and began pondering Lady Ivy's proposal. I even attempted to justify my considerations of escaping with her, knowing full well if my agreement to meet Hota was not met, Fawkes would surely storm Yaxil, and provide Blair with some hope of survival. My fondness for the girl and my maturity allowed me to conclude that what I had decided to do was right and that I would face Hota and pray that the man still had some compassion left in his soul. I would exchange Blair's life for my own as already agreed. The brief silence was short lived, and the interruption welcomed, as Chenchi flung open the door. The man whom I had considered disloyal in the past had now grown to become my closest of friends.

"Tonight, we drink like kings, but we must eat as dogs. I am afraid my request for a fine last meal was declined, so it is rabbit leg and rotten quail eggs," he laughed.

Chenchi handed me a jug of wine, insisting that I get up from my bed and guzzle down the beverage. "Come, Jep, let us poison our blood, you will be dead by dusk tomorrow, anyway."

"Actually not, as it's at least a day and a half ride from here," I said.

"Well at least it will give you time to clear a befuddled head."

We indulged in wine and spoke recklessly for the best part of the night. I could feel my own intoxication, my speech had become slurred, and my senses jumbled.

"Maybe I should ram a knife in his gullet at the earliest of opportunities," I said.

"Yes, the idea is good, but his followers are sure to not only kill you, but Blair too. Not that it matters to me, I have always found her somewhat of a pest," slurred Chenchi.

"Or I should run away with Ivy? Hide out in the edges of the north, fishing, making love, a life away from all these dramatics."

Chenchi grunted, whilst sucking the last remains of meat from a leg bone. "I have never understood how a man of your size is so easily spoilt by wine. Don't get me wrong, Jep, you're a mere worm compared to me, but you do carry some mass."

Waiting for Chenchi to speak of my internal investigation, I had tried to steer the conversation in an attempt to pluck some answers from him. However unintentionally, he diverted the conversation away from the matter of the crimes of which I had been accused of committing.

I needed to know the truth and understand what Chenchi knew, so this time I decided to ask him directly. "Do you believe I killed Sergeant Hock?"

Chenchi huffed and leaned back in his bed, sighing, as he gazed up at the straw roof. "There were no tracks from the dungeon Jep, no sign of hoof marks nor footprints leading away from the lock up. The ground was muddy from the rain, yet still, there was nothing."

I leapt on to my feet, feeling foul tempered, "So you share wine with a murderer?"

"Easy, you must consider listening ears," replied Chenchi, nodding his head towards the door, where the guard patrolled outside. "No, I do not believe that you are a murderer, but what I do know is you humped the Baron's wife and humiliated him in front of the town, so your death was inevitable."

"So, I am to be made an example of?"

Chenchi stood up pulling a stool closer to where I paced up and down. He insisted that I sat down, and allowed him to speak freely, without risk of my backlash.

"If you know what is good for you, you will run, and run alone. If you flee with the Baroness, you will have every regal guard in Thear hunting you down. If you go alone then you will have a handful of Swords, mostly your allies tracking you. Soon enough the pursuit will become stale, and you will become nothing more than a cold and forgotten case. Take Lady Ivy with you and you will both be chased down and captured."

"And what about Blair?" I asked.

"What about her? The girl is so feral, she will be leading the Crooks herself, by the end of the winter. You are nothing more than a surety, an offering from the Chief to the Baron, in exchange for peace. You have no future here."

It wasn't long before the wine put Chenchi on his back, so I attempted to sleep. I mused on what Chenchi had said. He was right; my future here was tarnished. I had been abandoned by my own, only to be tasked with one final deployment before my sentence of death. I wanted to run, and the thought continuously skimmed through my mind. But there was Blair to consider, and the consequence of my choice no longer only impacted on me.

The grey clouds loomed above but the temperature had risen, indicating winter was nearing its end. Leaving my quarters, my throbbing head only added to my anxieties surrounding the next couple of days.

Chenchi was already awake and outside, telling rambling tales to the watchful Sword, who politely indulged him, intimidated by Chenchi's magnitude and harsh exterior.

Hearing me moving inside, Chenchi came back in and passed me a freshly prepared tunic, "We can't have you meeting the turd looking like that, do you not remember how precious he was?"

We walked towards the stables, and met Lev, Fawkes and the Governor, who were standing awaiting my arrival. I noticed Sergeant Mosely eying me from under the archway of the parade room entrance.

"Has Flint not arrived?" I asked.

"He awaits you at the gate. Yaxil is over a day's ride away and you will need to camp and stay hidden from the main road," said the Governor.

"Why, Sir? I am a Sword, surely my enemies will turn their backs to me."

"You are to go unarmed; these are the orders from the Chief, hence why we are being observed by that swine," said the Governor, glowering at Mosely.

"Spike is prepared and ready for you, but take it easy on him though, he has become a little stubborn of late," Lev advised.

Tilting my head, subdued, I looked over to my loyal companions, offering each of them my hand, and even the Governor embraced me.

Taking in a deep breath, I noticed the desperation displayed on Fawkes's face. Fawkes who had not only defended my honour in the past, but also my life, now needed me more than ever. It was at that point that any selfish ideas of absconding and diverting away from my mission left my mind.

"I will ensure her safe return, you have my word," I said, purposely looking at Fawkes.

Fawkes clasped his hand on my shoulder and offered me a rare smile, "I have no doubt, Jep."

Leading Spike from the stables, it took the horse a while to warm to me again; my absence and neglect appeared to have offended my once loyal stallion. Leaping up on his back, he tossed his head backwards, snorting, whilst stamping one of his rear hooves on the gravel.

Lev crossed in front of me, brushing his hand gently down Spike's neck, "You need to make it up to him. He, like you, is delicate."

Chenchi had been ordered to escort me to the gate and had already directed his horse away from the courtyard. Spike jinked, but eventually his resistance wore off and he finally began to settle. Passing through the estates, I was reminded of my early days on patrol. The panic in the faces that stared back at me, unnerved by my presence, the whispers, the muttering in each other's ears, gossiping and telling tales. Now I posed an even deadlier threat. Not only was I a Blue Sword, but I was now also deemed a lawless Sword, with nothing to lose.

Chenchi started to fidget, insisting we divert from the main path. I peered back at him dismissively, refusing to waste any more time. Looking ahead, I noticed the reason why he had become so uncomfortable.

"Stay on the far side, we have no reason to engage with them," said Chenchi.

"He is our Baron, we are obliged to acknowledge his significance," I grinned.

"You just want to pick a fight, Jep."

In the past the mere sight of Asher had put me on edge, yet now I felt hollow, and with my death looming, I felt little need to pacify the man. On seeing us approach, the Baron arched his back, in a vain attempt to tighten his bulging gut. Sitting upon his horse, he wore a green hunting doublet. He eyed me with revulsion, and I braced myself to endure the foulness of his tongue.

Truda was mounted alongside the Baron, with Eruk, the veteran Blue Sword, on horseback strategically positioned behind them. The ex-Sword appeared rather disinterested in their affairs. Truda dismissed our meeting, looking away, and endeavouring to make idle talk with her hired guardsman.

Riding by, I had no intention of interacting with them and kept my head up and my sight fixed on the Square, but Asher could not resist a chance to snipe or try to start a quarrel.

"You're all bones, boy," called out the Baron, before glancing back to Eruk, seeking applause. However, Eruk did not react but instead looked up at the sky, making it apparent he did not wish to indulge the Baron's futile mockery. Still, I reacted, and couldn't help but respond with a sarcastic remark.

"Judging by the buckling of your horse's legs, you are still overfed," I retorted quickly, prompting a chuckle from Eruk.

Digging his heels into his mount, Asher forced his horse to sidle closer to me. Riled by my ridiculing, he raised his upper lip and refused to withdraw his stare. Seiloff sat on his horse, intently watching our interaction.

Responding to his intrusion, I said, "Be careful, your pet is some distance away. I am a criminal, remember."

Asher moved his horse back, showing alarm at my flippant though threatening comment. He turned to face Seiloff, who was now riding towards us. Upon seeing his henchman narrowing the gap between them, he disguised his apprehension and responded with a snarl. "If Hota doesn't kill you, I will look forward to tearing your limbs off in front of the town. Now go save that little bitch of a servant girl and meet your well-deserved fate," he added, before spitting on the ground near Spike's hoof.

Riding away, I turned back to look at Eruk. He met my eyes with a sympathetic expression on his face, before discreetly nodding his head back at me.

Asher was clearly not content and wanted more. He scoffed and drove his horse swiftly towards me. "Remember this as you die; your whore will be forever my wife. Mine to hump, mine to torment and mine to kill, whenever I see fit."

Chenchi shook his head, knowing my temper and likely reaction to the Baron's vile tone. Unsettled by his wicked and tormenting statements, I gulped, before ensuring I had the final word. I was keen that my threat would be overheard by onlookers, "Sword or not, when I return, I will end you, that I swear."

Asher was taken aback by my menacing reply and looked at Seiloff for assurance. Tapping my heels into Spike, I moved forward, leaving the Baron to mull over and stew on my words.

Chenchi laughed, "I am glad I am no longer your enemy, Jep."

***

Flint was already awaiting my arrival at the gate. I jumped down from my horse, greeting the loyal Detector.

"You kept the beard and curls?" commented Flint.

"If I am to run amongst Crooks, I may as well look the part."

Flint glanced down to my waist, "You are wearing your scabbard;

good. Here, take my blade."

Flint withdrew his sword and handed it over to me. "Secure it swiftly."

"Why do you give me your sword? I will be disarmed on my arrival at Yaxil."

Flint gave Chenchi a suspicious look, triggering Chenchi to speak. "You do not have to go to Yaxil, Flint's blade will keep you safe on your journey, wherever it is you wish."

Shaking my head, I eyed the hilt of the sword Flint had given me, before looking between my two companions. "Blair came to the dungeon. She wanted to give me encouragement, comfort. She told me, she would never give up, even if I had. I dismissed her, sending her away saddened. That was the last time I set eyes upon her. I have licked my wounds, and now I refuse to cast her aside. If the chance presents, I will plunge this sword into Hota's heart, for Fulten."

Mounting Spike, I looked across to see Chenchi grinning back at me. "See you on the other side, brother."

Flint called for the gate to be opened, and on his order, the guard began hammering the inner timber board, loosening it from its iron joints. Directing Spike forward, I rode outside the walls, before bringing him to a halt on the path which led to the vast woodland. Taking a final look at Flint and Chenchi, I bowed my head towards them as the gate closed.

***

Once at the edge of the woods, I paused, observing the divided pathway before me. My options were to either travel clear of the main road and take the woodland path adjacent to the southern road, or continue on ahead and stay on northern paths.

Rustling came from the undergrowth, causing me to grip the hilt of my sword. Sword O'Hara appeared, walking boldly and undeterred by our meeting.

"This is not so inconspicuous, are you not meant to be tracking me? I feel you have rather failed at remaining hidden."

"Bugger that! A guilty man would not have taken the punishment which you wilfully endured. I will ride alongside you until tomorrow and then I shall follow from a distance."

"I have no intention of running," I said.

"Honourable, but still foolish. Nevertheless, I am thrilled to be getting away from that shitty town."

***

One thing any Sword could not resist was to tell proud tales of their time in service. I learnt this tactic while being tutored by Fulten. If ever he was displeased with my actions, and offered me silence, I would ask him about stories of his time as a Blue Sword. This worked like a charm and always made him forget his annoyance at me. He would often repeat the same accounts he had previously spoken of, and I would pretend to listen along intently, even though I was well aware of the ending.

O'Hara was an unsocial man and tended to grunt more than he spoke. But pressing him for stories of his past times as a Sword allowed the conversation to flow. Not only was my method working to keep him engaging with me on our ride, but I was still keen to learn more about the city of Alma.

"Picture your town but on a much grander scale. Slums, brothels, taverns and much more depravity all mixed in with lavish gardens, expensive churches and a grand palace, overlooking its people," said O'Hara.

"Palace?" I asked.

"Yes, high walls, political houses, thrones and grounds richer than heaven."

"And what about the Swords, where do they sit?"

"Our Lock up is north of the city, and the dungeon houses many prisoners. We are joined to a great tower, a school."

"You have children learning close by?"

"The school is for the Detectors, a place where Flint believes he can get you to come and train, should you survive."

I pondered on what O'Hara had described, and for a few moments found some excitement deep in my stomach once again for the Blue Swords. But sadly, this spontaneous exhilaration was short lived when I remembered where I was headed.

"You will find it very different in the city, because respect for the Swords is a thing of the past there. You are not only fighting the criminals, but even the honest folk have learnt to detest our ways. Organised bands rule the slums these days."

Pressing Spike up the hill towards the forest's opening, he became agitated by the jagged undergrowth. However, once inside the woodland, the narrow path forced us to ride singly. O'Hara took the lead, and I began to dawdle and fall back, mesmerised by the tall, lush trees, that ran as tall and far as the eye could see.

Deer ran freely amongst the shrubs, darting away on our approach. O'Hara was too slow to react with his bow, giving me reason to mock him, which was not well received at this stage of our friendship. The daylight began to fade, and the grey clouds darkened the night sky prematurely.

"Over there, we will camp for the night," said O'Hara.

As we drew closer to the clearing in the forest, I noticed Sword O'Hara raise his hand quickly. Voices could be heard laughing from a break in the trees, further along the path we were travelling. The narrow path meant we would be unable to pass by unnoticed.

17

THE MERCHANT'S SWORD

Tethering our horses, I gently stroked my hand down Spike's nose in order to settle him. One of the strangers' voices spoke over the top of the others, his tone pious and arrogant but also familiar.

Crawling on our bellies over the hard soil, I was able to observe the camp. Six men sat together, seated around a fire, all engrossed in light conversation and drinking. Three were unfamiliar, although their rugged exterior and animal furs, along with their painted faces indicated they were Shadow Crooks. The remaining three men I had met before.

My stomach began to knot, and my blood simmered in anticipation. The sharply featured merchant and his two followers sat, telling tales of their time in Stanford, bragging of the distress they had caused on their recent visit.

Recognising Carre's attackers, I quietly drew my blade from its scabbard. O'Hara grabbed hold of my sword arm, holding me back and scrunching his face in dissatisfaction.

"You may watch if it pleases you, but I have a promise to keep," I muttered.

Ducking down my head, I shook away his hand from my arm and crept forward, watching and listening to the merchants engaging in merriment with the Shadow Crooks. I wanted to keep the element of surprise as an advantage, as I was unconvinced I would be backed by

O'Hara. I was now a Blue Sword on trial, so he had no accountability nor reason to join me in the fight.

Hidden behind the final shrub before I would become visible, I waited for the right moment to pounce. Drawing in a deep breath, I allowed my emotions and longing for vengeance to consume me. I knew I would gain an even further advantage attacking at night, but I was being impulsive and not thinking rationally. I wanted blood and I wanted it now.

Recklessly I emerged from the bushes, bellowing out a war cry with my sword held out horizontally from my side. As I charged forward, all six men jumped up from the fallen tree trunk, startled by my aggressive intrusion.

Two of the three Shadow Crooks reacted swiftly, indicating they were seasoned warriors. The heavier built of the two Crooks charged at me with a short-handled axe in his hand. Undeterred and reacting to my infringement, he mirrored my own growls.

I had been caged, contained like a wild wolf in captivity and now I was loose. I wanted this battle and I wanted redemption. The muscular Crook raised his axe and salivated down his beard as he brought it down angrily towards my skull. I relaxed my shoulder, loosening my arm in order to avoid his axe shattering my bones on impact. Bringing up my sword, I blocked his axe and stepped sideways away from his fighting arc.

Keen not to lose sight of his companion who was approaching speedily from behind the burly Crook, I jabbed the tip of my blade into his abdomen just above his hip. Pulling free my sword, its steel now stained in blood, I left the large, bearded Crook grounded and bleeding out on the dirt.

His companion was much less erratic. After witnessing his associate fall to the blade of my sword, he slowed down his charge. Pulling out a second sword, he now awaited my next move, standing poised, armed with a weapon in each hand. His slenderer physique meant he would be faster and less predictable than the previous, hot headed Crook.

We eyeballed each other for a while, until I briefly was forced to remove my stare away to locate the position of the other men. The Crook saw his opportunity and pounced on my inattention, lunging towards me, forcing me to block his strike unsteadily. Using his second sword, he hooked the blade around with the intention of slicing my lower body. After defending the second hit, I was left alternating my defence, as he rapidly swung both his swords at me. Our speed was matched, leaving me little time to offer a counter.

An arrow hissed through the air, thumping into its intended target and causing both me and the Crook to divert our attention away. O'Hara had fired an arrow from the hedges, taking out the third Crook who was only a few feet away from engaging me, armed with a mace. My adversary was now stunned at seeing his companion face down with an arrow standing out from his forehead, gouging the dirt.

This gave me the time to gain the advantage and drive my blade down onto one of his swords, relieving him of his second weapon. Countering, he swung his remaining sword across the front of my torso forcing me to step back. Placing both my hands on the hilt of my weapon, I raised my blade high before powerfully slamming the steel edge into the crown of his head. Stunned, he gave me a final desperate look as the blood poured down his face from the incision in his skull. Once he had fallen to his knees, I prised my sword out from his head leaving him to tumble lifeless to the ground.

Turning my attention to the three merchants, I saw the plumpest of the three had managed to escape, however the other two had been cornered by O'Hara. They stood in front of the battle-scarred Sword, trembling at the sight of the arrow aimed in their direction.

Walking behind the cowering merchants, I yelled for them to turn and face me. With the Crooks' blood now staining my blade and splattered over my skin, they looked back at me in horror. Seeing the snide, sharply featured merchant with the spiteful tongue, I squeezed the hilt of my weapon more firmly, remembering the condition in which he had left my friend, Carre.

Observing their terror, I lunged forward, remaining silent and mercilessly sliced the throat of the first merchant. Scowling across at the skinny, pointed nosed trader, I grunted, witnessing his bottom lip begin to tremble.

"Remember me?"

Looking to O'Hara for assertion, he stuttered, now without his arrogant tone, "You're a Sword, surely you will not execute me without trial."

"You beat a local man within an inch of his life, not to mention the household guard's throat you slashed. This makes you undeserving of a trial. Unfortunately for you, as it stands, I am no longer a Blue Sword, just a man lusting for revenge. I am not surprised at finding you conversing with the Shadow Crooks. But before I run you through, I want to know why, instead of robbing you, they sit and allow you to entertain them?"

The merchant took another look at O'Hara, expressing his distress, but all that he saw directed back at him was a cold, hard stare.

"I will show you, the item is by the camp," he faltered.

Leading the way, I made little of the bodies that littered the ground. The merchant quivered after taking a glimpse at the bloodied men, before leaning down beside the fire and pulling loose a package that was wedged under the log.

Sword O'Hara demanded that he uncover the item from the cloth in which it had been wrapped. The merchant's hands trembled as he carefully folded back the fabric.

My eyes widened at its content. Seeing the item laid out before me, neatly preserved for the Crooks, momentarily stunned me. All the pieces of the broken puzzle began fitting together in my mind.

The bronze hilt with three curved edges either side, added to the sword's exquisitely crafted presentation. Its perfection was finished with the heavy glistening steel that had been affixed so elegantly to its blade.

"A fine sword," said O'Hara.

I stared over at him, bewildered upon recognising the sword that I had recently seen affixed above the entrance to the Baron's guards' quarters. Ricard's sword, proudly left on display like a shrine.

Watching the cowering and now kneeling merchant, my aggression had converted into disbelief, and now it was I, who stuttered. "Who gave you this sword?"

"I was paid to collect it, paid well I must add. I was to receive even more coin, once it was in the hands of its rightful owner."

I stomped closer to the merchant with my teeth clenched and recognising his danger he shivered and raised his hands, begging not to be harmed. I gripped the collar of his tunic, pinning him to the ground, resting the edge of my blade against his throat, "Who paid you? Tell me."

Weeping, the merchant gasped "A Shadow Crook, he is the one in charge. Hota, his name is Hota."

"And who did you collect this from?" I growled.

"It was one of his men, he was an official, war-torn. He was staying in the town. We met by the river to the west of Stanford."

"His name?" demanded O'Hara.

"He gave me no name, but I remember he was well dressed, he didn't resemble the look of a Crook," stuttered the merchant.

Releasing my grip on his collar, I left him lying in the mud. I stared down at the grass, mulling over what the merchant had disclosed. Eventually I came back around and took another look at the cowering trader who lay shaking at my feet. Rage overcame my thoughts, and I glared at him, remembering how he had left Carre beaten and dying on the cold stone cobbles.

Raising my sword, I had every intention of running him through, until Sword O'Hara grabbed hold of my forearm. "You have had your blood, justice has prevailed. You still bare the crest of a Sword; we are not executioners. Now I think it's time you brought me up to speed with your knowledge."

Staring back down at the relieved merchant, I noticed the swelling in his pointed nose, where I had previously caused him injury. Lifting my boot, I kicked the bottom of my foot into his nose, once again causing it to crack. He clutched at his nose, writhing on the floor, gasping with the pain. O'Hara chuckled, before leaning down to pick up Ricard's sword.

***

Back on the woodland path, I looked over to O'Hara. "He or his associate will inform Hota of our interception."

"Who cares, it will be you that takes his father's sword to him. He may see it as a peace offering and spare your life."

"Or consider it an insult. After all, I did kill his father and returning his father's sword could appear like a kick in the balls," I replied.

"There is that," grinned O'Hara.

Settling for the night, O'Hara was keen to camp away from the woodland path. I cared little for being disturbed by bandits, knowing that by noon tomorrow, my fate would be in my enemy's hands and my hope of survival bleak. O'Hara found a spot deep in the undergrowth, keeping us hidden from any travellers that passed by.

Sword O'Hara was kind enough to offer me some wine from his bota bag.

"You will take Ricard's sword back to Stanford, hand it only to the Governor, and disclose the description of the man that handed it to the merchants. This will allow the investigation to be opened and finally reveal some truth," I demanded.

"I will not be taking the sword."

I sat up, surprised by his lack of willingness to return it and present it as evidence to our fellow Swords.

"You must, it will help them identify the Crook within our walls."

Yawning, O'Hara replied in an uncaring tone, "The Chief will care little about a stolen sword of a dead guardsman. You will do better to take it to this Hota, then may you discover truth."

"I will turn back, return it myself," I said.

"Then the girl will die, for time is against you."

Grunting, O'Hara rolled onto his side and closed his eyes. For a few moments I remained silent just staring at him in disgust before snapping. "You couldn't give a rat's arse about me, Blair or the truth, could you?"

O'Hara opened his eyes and leaned up, laughing as he answered, "No I could not give a damn about you or the girl. I do not condone your mistreatment, but you have joined an organisation whose leader cares more for politics than truth. By summer, I shall retire and take my coin, then finally, I shall get some peace. My advice to you, if you survive, is to harness your whimpering."

Watching the Sword thoughtlessly drift off to sleep, I couldn't help but think he was right. Without a name for the inside Crook, the matter would be overlooked in order to keep the reconciliation that had been brought about by my wrongful imprisonment. I had been given my part to play, which was to ensure Blair was returned alive.

***

No longer shielded by the forest, we followed a rocky track that ran parallel to the main road. Sword O'Hara insisted on our separation at this point in the journey. He made it clear that his plan was to track me from afar, and stringently reminded me of the consequences should I divert from the task in hand. Offering me his hand, we said our farewells, before I rode Spike through a brook and re-joined the main path south to Yaxil.

Southern Thear's landscape was much easier on the eye than the endless forest. I passed through valleys, overlooked by steep, green hills. The tranquil and undisturbed settings presented flourishing vegetation and pleasant terrain. Water trickled through the rocks of the adjacent stream, flowing gently alongside the road.

The cry from a red kite above caused me to look up and admire the creature's impressive wings as it soared under the dark clouds. I was drawing close to my destination now; on the other side of the meadow was the village that housed Hota and his followers.

The trail inside the pasture was boggy; its soil had been disturbed often by the heavy passage of wagons. My spine tingled and the skin on my arms developed bumps from knowing that I would imminently come face to face with Hota. Somehow sensing my unease, Spike became irritable, rearing and pulling away from the path. Patting his neck, I tried to settle the both of us, but my heart continued to pound, and I felt breathless. This was not the right time to start panicking, I needed to stay composed and not show any weakness.

The sudden whistling of arrows gliding through the air dispelled my fright and my body flooded with adrenaline, preparing itself for combat.

Two arrows thudded into the ground, just short of Spike's front hooves, causing him to rear up on his hind legs.

A female voice called from the trees that surrounded the meadow, "Dismount, and place your weapons by the arrows."

Leaping down from Spike, I looked in the direction from which the authoritative voice had called, but no one appeared.

I pulled my sword free and stabbed the tip of the blade into the soil, before letting go of its hilt.

"And the weapon that rests on your horse's rump," called out the person, who I assumed must be a scout.

"This is a gift for your leader, one that I think he will be enthused to receive," I shouted.

"Do as I command or I will fill you with arrows."

Unfastening the straps, I yanked it from Spike's saddle. Unwrapping its cloth cover, I placed the sword horizontally next to my own, before raising my hands out to the side. "That is all I have."

Rustling came from the undergrowth and the scout appeared on the path. She stood, poised, with her fingers pinning back her bow string, pointing the attached arrow towards me. Her tanned skin was covered in dye, and her thick animal furs rested on her shoulders. She wore a brown gown that had been cut short and the remaining cloth had been used to cover her waist, leaving the skin of her thighs exposed.

The Crook glared at me unforgivingly, eyeing me up and down, before ordering me to avert my gaze from her.

I looked down to the dirt. "I need to know whether the girl is still alive."

"You're in no position to make demands, you will soon find out. Put your hands on your head and face your horse."

Complying with her instructions, I interlocked my fingers, resting my hands on the crown of my head. The Crook fixed a rope around my wrists, tugging to ensure I was suitably restrained. Pulling my sword from out of the ground, she examined its steel, scoffing, before throwing it into the bushes at the side of the track.

She approached Spike, prompting me to react, "He doesn't take well to strangers."

Whispering in his ear, the scout gently ran her hands down his cheek, settling my stallion. "I thought Swords only cared for themselves, it surprises me to hear you being so passionate about the beast."

"I owe him, he is the only one who listens to my troubles."

"Well then he is much deserving of a rest," said the Crook.

Mounting Spike, she brushed her fingers gently down his neck, soothing him. Her gentle movements prompted Spike to respond calmly to her direction.

She faced me, and I did not receive the same niceties. "Walk." Leaving the rags that covered Ricard's sword, she pointed the tip of the blade towards me. "Try to run and this time, it will be you who feels steel in your back."

Hearing the Crook's comment reminded me of the tormenting I had previously received from Seiloff, the Baron's head guard. He had also shown his displeasure over my actions concerning Hota's father. Everything was starting to make sense to me now. Seiloff worshipped Ricard and was unable to mask his bitterness towards me. Seiloff was the link between Hota and Stanford, the inside Crook.

18

HOTA

Yaxil was a modest village, the boundaries were marked by log walling. The gate securing the entrance had been modified, and sharp, pointed stakes now surmounted the top wooden panels.

Two severed heads had been impaled on to the end of the outer barricade, their ligaments and windpipes dangled loosely and stained the posts with blood, a warning sign to those who dared to attack. The outline of a hawk had been engraved on to the helmets of the dead guards, making a clear statement of the Crooks' thoughts and intentions towards the Crown.

The gate was dragged back on our approach, allowing me a quick glimpse beyond the entrance. I was taken aback by the sight of villagers who had been allowed to continue to go about their business, uninterrupted. The Crooks were easy to spot, with their hefty furs and painted faces. My father used to tell me tales of pagan warriors that roamed the land freely, stealing and ransacking towns. The Shadow Crooks were just like those savages in my father's stories, Godless and unforgiving.

Local people began lining the only path that ran through the village, some showing distress at witnessing the capture of a Blue Sword. The Crooks stared back at me with venomous expressions on their faces, and it was clear that my name had been vilified amongst them.

Even the offspring of the Crooks stood out from the other village children, as they played robustly and dressed similar to their elders' attire.

Walking between the rows of huts, I still couldn't quite apprehend how at peace the local people appeared. I had expected to see a slaughter, yet they walked amongst the Shadow Crooks, without suffering torment or fear.

One Crook leered at me with much more malice than his associates. He grimaced as I met his eyes and began panting and puffing up his shoulders, before stomping closer to meet me.

A gasp came from the onlookers, observing him grunting and marching towards me like an angered bear. His obvious aggression and hatred of me made him predictable, he was surely going to showboat his anger and attempt to strike me down hard, with one decisive blow.

He swung his fist at my head and I ducked, leaving his fist to hit nothing but air. I leapt to the side of him, aware that my hands were still constrained. Kicking my foot into his calf, I took away his legs, causing him to lose his balance.

A further intake of breath came from the spectators, whilst I had allowed my own irritability to vent. Straddling over him, I drove my entwined fists, rapidly and repeatedly into his face, having no consideration of the consequences.

A voice called my name, its familiarity bringing my actions to a halt and leaving the bloodied Crook barely conscious. "Now that is the spirited peasant boy that I remember."

Tilting back my head and breathing heavily, I sat beside the grounded man. Hota stood before me, smirking and clapping his hands together. His appearance was much different to the one I remembered. His well-groomed, wavy hair had been cut short to his scalp and he had allowed his beard to grow, so that it now finished at the top of his chest. He was much more intimidating and had lost the boyish features that I remembered.

"When you have finished whipping my man, do feel free to join me," he said.

Squinting across at my sworn enemy, I felt stunned by his lack of enmity, but this was Hota, he was shrewd and as I had learnt in the past, an expert at keeping his true intentions hidden.

Standing above the pounded Crook, I turned back to the scout who nudged up her chin, indicating for me to follow Hota.

Hota smiled at the villagers, holding out his hands in a comforting manner. "Nothing to see, all is calm, go in peace."

The local people showed him warmth and appeared reassured by his presence. I was not fooled; I had seen the true side of this wicked Crook. Following him, I stared at the back of his head, engulfed with animosity and loathing towards him. I even visualised lashing out at him, but realism held me back.

The road ran all the way through the village, which was occupied by rows of trading stalls and living huts. The fruit on sale had been freshly picked and the meat was vibrantly coloured with no signs of decay. The scent of ginger lingered in the air; it appeared that the people lived well here.

Another barricade had sealed off the back entrance to Yaxil, patrolled by three Crooks. Logs mirroring those of the village walls had been fastened together to erect a church, its rectangular shape thatched with straw.

Hota looked up at the elegantly crafted crucifix attached to the ridge of the church's roof. He marked the sign of the cross on his forehead, causing me to snigger.

"Do I amuse you, Jep?"

"I fear God may have turned his back on you a long time ago." I replied.

"Not just me," he smiled.

***

Inside, Hota had transformed the church into his own Great Hall. The pews had been piled up, making way for a vast feasting table, placed centrally in the room. Hota's men and women relished the banquet on offer, they laughed and exchanged gossip between one another, unaware of my arrival. A priest stood at the altar, lighting candlesticks, undeterred by the intrusion that had been forced upon him.

Hota called out, demanding the room's attention. "Fellow Crooks, may I introduce to you Sword Jep. Some of you may feel hostility towards him, even vengeful, but he is here as my guest, under my protection and he is to come to no harm."

My eyes scanned the hall to read the reaction. The Crooks offered no niceties, sneering back at me with nothing but repugnance and disgust at my presence. The female scout entered the church hall, and brushed past me dismissively. "Hota, he was in possession of this."

Taking the sword, Hota took hold of it with both hands, assessing its weight. He held out the exquisitely crafted blade, admiring its glistening steel and bronze plated hilt. Hota beamed with delight at being reunited with his father's weapon.

Swinging the sword in a figure of eight, he boasted his abilities to the room and passionately showed off his blade's magnitude.

Turning back, he looked at me, giving me a baffled expression. "You weren't supposed to deliver me this."

"I thought it would be rude, arriving without a gift," I said sarcastically.

Hota glanced back to his sword in awe. "Jep, we have much to discuss."

"Where is Blair?" I demanded.

"All in good time, my impatient friend," Hota replied, still transfixed by the sight of his father's sword.

Snubbing the scowling Crooks, I felt ravenous and greedily picked at the vegetables and cheese on offer. Hota watched me, still appearing enthused at our reunion. His reaction made me uncomfortable, as if he was admiring a pig he had fattened for slaughter.

Pouring wine into my beaker, he smiled at me. "When you are refreshed, we will talk."

"I will not talk until I see that Blair is alive."

Hota waved his hand, calling over one of his followers. The Crook swaggered across the hall with confidence, flexing his enormous shoulders.

"Bring me the girl," ordered Hota.

"She hunts," replied the brute.

"How that girl does appreciate the outdoors," Hota chuckled.

"Blair is out hunting?" I asked, astonished by the revelation.

"Yes, we are not as Godless as you assume we are," said Hota.

Hota raised his arm in the air and demanded that all but me should leave the church. The Crooks began to depart from the hall, a couple insisting on growling back at me as they walked by. Hota called to his well-built follower and requested for him to bring more wine to the table.

"You can take the first sip," I said.

"Dak will not poison you, his story is not dissimilar to your own. He sought me out after his village was exploited by regal guards, they were the cause of his family's death; starvation is wicked and a slow way to die. Not the kind of tales your Blue Swords wish to boast about."

"We are not regals."

"No, you are not, but you do serve the same Crown, Jep."

Dak returned and began pouring the wine, after which he sat opposite me and offered no animosity, unlike his associates. Hota inhaled, holding his breath, before guzzling back the wine. Placing down his goblet, he belched and stared at me intently.

"You must be wondering why I have abstained from taking your head. Well in truth I have longed to avenge my father's murder, that was until lately, when I accepted the advice from someone who shares my grief. You and I were companions once, my father saw potential in you, I took your tutor, and you took mine. But now there is a much larger quarrel to be had, much greater than our own vendetta."

"And that is?" I asked.

"You shield a town that has turned its back on you, a town that is inundated with lies and betrayal. The Swords have dangled you to the lions, not even allowing you the goodwill of a trial." Standing, Hota continued, slightly more animated, "For what, to appease an oppressor, who himself is at the very heart of the immorality? You see Jep, I fight for those people, people like you, the deprived and unprivileged. Why do you think I pressed so hard for you to become a Sword? It started with me, remember?"

Pondering on what Hota was explaining to me, he summarised it too perfectly, copying what had already been my own conclusion.

Something was niggling in the back of my mind, prompting me to respond. "Blair has told you of my recent mishaps?"

"The girl has too much loyalty to you to repeat idle gossip," said Hota.

"Markus, the young gate keeper. It was you that scarred his face."

"After watching the merchants go in, we disguised ourselves as traders, and marked the boy. I knew you would accept the easy decision, yet in your heart, you knew the boy's assault was my doing. In doing so you condemned an innocent man to die. I watched you that afternoon, Jep, examining the scene, peering across to the woodland. I knew you sensed my presence."

"You left the necklace, knowing that we would retrieve it and link it back to the merchants. What purpose did any of this serve?" I growled.

Hota responded, raising his voice. "Oh, do come on Jep, I needed to expose you to the truth. The Swords are as corrupt as the rest of this pig ignorant civilization. I say again, you allowed an innocent man to hang for a crime you knew very well he did not commit, and I will gamble all my silver that you pleaded his case with the illustrious Governor, and your belly aching fell on deaf ears. I know you. I am certain that the old merchant's execution is something that haunts you to this day."

"What of the rest? Hock, Isaak and Carre. Your way of settling your grudge, I suppose, wiping out the Cavaliers, the ones who exposed your father for the traitor he was."

Hota replied, tutting at my accusation, "You believe it was I who murdered Sergeant Hock? I wouldn't have wasted my efforts on the cantankerous old arse."

"You lie," I yelled, crashing my fist into the table.

Hota raised his hand towards Dak, who was now poised and ready to respond to my aggression. Casually, Hota then spread his hands out on the table and leaned over its edge towards me. Shaking his head, he eyed me, before scoffing, "These insinuations that you concoct baffle me, Jep. I had you down as much wiser. The merchants who were tasked with bringing me my father's sword bragged of their assault on a loud-mouthed farmer, and as for Hock, the priest and Isaak, I think you need to search much closer to home."

"Closer to home?" I repeated, "You were the snake that slithered through the grass before kidnapping Blair, bartering her life in exchange for my own. This has your foul stench all over it."

Hota boorishly marched to the front of the church, forcefully yanking open the doors. "Leave, you are not my captive, the only ones that imprison you are the Swords, so go, return to them."

Even though he had invited me to leave of my own free will, something had struck a chord inside my mind. His manner, his explanation, it was all ringing too true and matching my own thought processes. I wanted to hate him, to kill him, yet now I found myself beginning to agree with the man I detested.

"You haven't answered my question. Who murdered the Cavaliers?" I asked.

Hota snorted. "Jep, you never asked me, you only accused me," he said, in a much less angry tone. "My own ambition goes much further than the removal of Cavaliers. I still want Baron Asher's life and to give Stanford back to the people, to fulfil my father's ambition."

"And how do you plan to do that?"

"With you."

Rubbing my hands over my face, I looked across to Dak, who stared back at me, eagerly awaiting my response. Tiring of my silence, he attempted to reiterate what his leader had said, "You and me are from the same stock, always kicked to the dirt, whilst these rich bastards choke us with the mud. There is no democracy, only control."

"What you're suggesting is a revolt. Why would you need me?"

Hota intervened. "Because I know how much you want to kill the Baron and my plan will give you that opportunity."

The doors to the church opened and Blair entered, breathless and alone. She stood, cheerful and ecstatic to see me. Hota watched my eyes as I looked her up and down, surprised at seeing her dressed similarly to that of a Shadow Crook.

Blair had embraced the traditions of a Shadow Crook. Her face was decorated with dye and her hair plaited. She raced over, keen to embrace me and I was just as delighted to return the greeting.

Holding her face with one hand either side, I asked, "Have they harmed you?"

Hota chuckled, causing a reaction from Blair, who pulled away from me. "They treat me well and with respect."

Blair engaged with Hota politely and with esteem. The feisty girl had never hidden her feelings of revenge after the death of Sword Fulten, yet now she appeared to have accepted Hota.

"Were you successful?" asked Hota.

"Very much so, a stag the size of Chenchi," she replied.

"Go, meet the others at the Nobleman's kitchen, they will help you prepare the animal for supper. Tonight, you have allowed us to feast well, Blair," said Hota.

Blair smiled back at me, before running out of the church hall, filled with enthusiasm.

"There is a Nobleman in the village? Why not acquire their lodgings?" I quizzed.

"We are guests here; it would be impolite to kick the Nobleman from his own Great Hall. When you come to terms with the fact that we are not as cruel as you assume, then you may allow your ears to listen," said Hota.

***

The intensity of my arrival was soon expelled by the hearty consumption of mead at the evening's festivities. The church hall was crammed with Crooks, all merry and joyous from the entertainment provided by a local musician. His fingertips flicked lightly over the strings of his instrument. Linking arms, the Crooks danced around the outside of the room, as onlookers cheered and stamped their feet.

Some of the more enthusiastic men eyed up the women as they twirled. The bolder ones leaned out, attempting to grope the girls, only to receive a firm stare or a swipe from the feisty, fearless Crook women.

The environment was unfamiliar, and refreshingly lacked any supremacy. All the men and women appeared equal, something that was clearly attractive to Blair. I caught the eye of the scout who had escorted me to the village, but she stared back at me hard faced and uninviting. I could not help but feel attracted to her narrow eyes and chiselled cheek bones.

Suddenly I felt a light punch to my ribs. Blair looked back at me, giggling. "You have no chance."

Bashfully, I coughed, clearing my throat, "What garbage do you speak now?"

"Sheron is one of the Crooks' most feared warriors. She would cut out your heart before you even had a chance to wink at her. Stick to your usual kind."

"And what is my usual kind?" I asked, feeling slightly inept.

"The needy, feeble ones, that always require saving," smiled Blair.

Blair grabbed hold of the arm of the last dancer in the line, and skipping off, she excitedly joined in with the Crooks prancing around. I took a second glimpse at Sheron from across the hall, and she met my gaze with a chortle.

Dak placed a horn of ale in my hand, insisting I drink and enjoy the celebrations.

Resting his hand on my shoulder, he raised his voice and leaned towards my ear, enabling his words to be heard over the music. "This is how it feels to be free. No one should claim ownership over another."

"You should quiz your leader on your thoughts, he didn't hesitate to take away the rights from my mentor," I said.

Gracefully, Dak inclined his head, unwilling to debate my response, "Hota has never forgotten his actions that day in the church, but ask yourself this Jep, if your father expected you to follow on with his beliefs, would you not?"

Leaving me to contemplate his reply, Dak bellowed out to one of his companions in elation, before meeting the other Crook and lifting him off his feet boisterously. Watching their joyously hearty greeting, I witnessed a sense of fellowship and could not help but slightly admire the inclusive manner in which the Shadow Crooks regarded one another.

19

DEVIL'S BLOSSOM

Hota allowed me to walk freely around the village, which added to my quandary of what his true and untrustworthy intentions really were. The man was ingenious, and he knew how to manipulate to a great degree.

At first impressions of the Crooks' incursion, all appeared ideal; the villagers seemed undeterred by the meddling of outsiders and the majority of the Crooks now offered me limited antagonism. Even though my tunic resembled the mark of the oppression they fought against, they seemed accepting of Hota's orders to refrain from inflicting harm on me.

But something felt amiss, when I thought back to Hota's serpent eyes staring back at me from across the church hall in Stanford, having just taken the life of Fulten. Back then, Hota was demonised and foul, and it all seemed too convenient to suggest he had forgotten our feud.

The Crooks had allowed me shelter for the night at the Keeper's lodge, just outside the Great Hall, which also housed my friend, Blair. She was the greatest mystery; despite knowing of the enmity between me and Hota after Fulten's murder, she had still embraced her time here amongst the savages. What Blair didn't understand was that Hota's plans to overthrow her hometown would result in harm to her mother's partner, her own mentor. I kept his plans from her, keen to use it as leverage at a later point, should it be needed.

***

Walking between the rows of huts, the path was barren underneath the moonlight. My shack was now in sight, and I was looking forward to laying on a bed, rather than the damp ground.

I could hear footsteps approaching from a passageway between two of the huts, but I paid little attention and continued walking in the middle of the road towards my lodgings.

"Not all are as forgiving, Sword," called a gruffly toned voice, from the entrance of the passage.

I turned around, and rolled my eyes at the person who taunted me. Feeling tired, I was in no mood for further conflict. The Shadow Crook who had charged at me on my arrival now glared back at me, his eyes reddened, with his chest puffed out.

Shaking my head, I showed him my back and stepped away, offering him nothing but disregard.

"You dare turn your back on me? I will tear off your limbs."

I tilted my head to the side. "Then what? You will tell your leader that I was maimed by wolves? Go to bed, you are drunk, I am weary and have already put you on your arse once today."

Hearing his boots crunching on the ground, I span around to see the enraged Crook sprinting towards me. For a second time, his temper gave away his thoughtless and anger-ridden intentions. I braced my body, ready to engage him, only to be saved the effort by a passer-by.

She appeared from behind me, and swiftly intercepted my attacker. Skilfully, she moved with precision, lunging her body towards the hot-headed Crook.

Sheron looped her arm around his bulging neck, pulling him down to the ground like an eagle taking down its prey. The Crook crashed down onto the sodden path and Sheron limberly rolled away from his side. Rapidly she jumped up and rammed her boot on to his throat. The man gasped as he stared up at her wide-eyed, clutching at her foot.

She growled down at my floored attacker, "Your defiance is noted, Oskar. You dare challenge this man again, and it will be you who I hunt."

Watching on, I felt awestruck by this bold Crook who had come to my aid. She was truly remarkable, and observing her abilities made me even more attracted to her valour.

Scowling across at me, Sheron made it apparent that my feelings were not reciprocated. "It would serve you well to understand that not all are pleased to see a Blue Sword in our camp. I suggest you retire to your quarters, before another one of my mead-fuelled companions tests their manhood against you."

Shyly, I moved away, but I could not help but take another look back at Sheron, who assisted the sulking Crook to his feet. She caught my gaze and remained harsh faced.

***

Nearing the end of winter, the humidity had begun to rise. Bleary eyed, I wandered through Yaxil, observing the local people preparing their morning stalls. I was ushered to the side to make way for livestock being herded through the street. The children played freely, chasing and giggling with one another and getting under their elders' feet. It felt peaceful, and with no sign of Oskar, I was yet to receive any new hostilities.

On entering the church hall, Dak stood smiling, clapping his hands together. "You're still here."

"What can I say, you people intrigue me," I replied.

"You think far too much, my friend. Today we hunt, will you join us?" asked Dak.

Initially the idea of hunting sounded rather appealing; that was until I saw Hota enter the hall from the far side of the alter. His smugness made me feel tense and irritable. "I will stay behind and explore the village, if it is all the same to you."

"Come Jep, stop being petulant, the forest will give you time to clear your mind," insisted Hota.

Blair came hurrying from out of the passage behind where Hota had appeared. Her face was painted with mud and she had a bow slung across her back. Sheron joined her from the walkway, holding in her hands a leather quiver filled with arrows.

"Come Jep, we are tracking boar," called Blair.

I scrunched my mouth and huffed through my nose. Sheron noticed my hesitation and triggered conversation, "Are you familiar with a bow?"

Blair chuckled, "Are you joking? Jep can scarcely wield a sword."

"That is not true, be assured I know first-hand of Jep's proficiencies with a blade," corrected Hota.

I looked back at Sheron, feeling momentarily drawn to her, forgetting everything I knew of Stanford and of Lady Ivy. Agreeing to the invitation, I noticed the Shadow Crook subtly raise one corner of her mouth, showing satisfaction at my acceptance to attend the hunt.

***

The sunlight splintered through the trees in the forest, situated east of Yaxil. Dak had gone ahead, tracking the movements of a boar, leaving us to casually saunter along behind. As usual Blair chattered, and like most people, Sheron had warmed to her brazen humour. Attempting to join in their conversation, Sheron was quick to dismiss my input.

Suddenly, Sheron raised her arm with her fist clenched, instructing us to halt. Hushing Blair, she scanned the tree line, before pointing and directing our attention towards the sound of breaking twigs in the undergrowth.

Following her lead, we crouched down, staying low, closing in on the bushes. Sheron gently removed the bow from her back and offered it to me. Abruptly jerking her chin forward, she directed my gaze to the rattling thorn bush in the distance. There, a black, tusked hog munched on the berries from the shrubs.

Propping against me, she whispered, telling me to take aim. Holding out her hand, Sheron muttered in a low voice for me to follow her finger to line up on the boar. "Inhale on your pull back and breathe out on release, smoothly, allow the string to encourage the arrow."

The rustling from the undergrowth became much louder, and the noise did not indicate the movement of a pig. Heavy panting followed, causing Sheron to take a nervous look back at Hota. Placing her hand over the arrow, she guided me to lower the bow.

Dak appeared, red faced and with a stranger detained. As he dragged the man along, I was quick to recognise the black shirt which Dak held on to. Dak threw the terrified merchant on to the path before Hota, and he peered up at me, horrified by my presence.

Looking back at Hota, displaying his pointed, beak like nose, he began to beg for his mercy. "Forgive me Sir, I was on my way to inform you of the ambush, I swear."

Hota chuckled, undeterred by the merchant's capture. "You cause me no offence; I have possession of the sword. Who delivered it was neither here nor there. What does disturb me, on the other hand, is learning of your violent attack on the farmer in Stanford."

The merchant looked across at me, his eyes widened and filled with dread. "Your merciful companion has already offered me my pardon, Sir."

Turning to me and frowning, Hota raised his shoulders in query "Is that true, Jep? You allowed this man to walk free after he left Carre beaten and fighting for life? This I find astonishing."

"My tracker gave me little choice," I said.

Hota scoffed, "Now why I am not surprised, a stalker? The Swords really have turned their back on you, my friend. Well, they are not here now, or are they?" Hota cupped his hand against his mouth and shouted into the wilderness, "Do you watch on, stalker? it will please you to know that Blair is alive and well!" Looking back at me, Hota continued. "As for you Jep, I am certain your follower intends to escort you straight to the chopping block on your return."

Looking over at Blair, she watched on, unsure of Hota's meaning.

Hota exhaled, whilst staring down at the submissive merchant. Removing a dagger from his belt, he walked in front of me and held out its handle. "Take it, you will decide his punishment. Carre is your friend, it is only right that you cast judgement."

Blair stared at me anxiously, awaiting my decision. Looking to Sheron, I wanted to be guided by her reaction to the circumstances, but as always, she remained stern-faced and poised.

The merchant stared up at me through terror filled eyes. Begging for my compassion, he whimpered like an animal caught in a trap, his long hair sticking and smudged across his face.

Muting his cries in my head, I stepped closer to the merchant, gripping the knife's handle firmly in my grasp. I visualised Dam sobbing as she observed her battered husband, lifeless on the table. My chest started to pound, filling with rage, and I briefly considered all the wrongs that I had recently experienced. The torture at the hands of my own organisation, the hanging of the innocent trader and finally of Lady Ivy weeping as I left her isolated in Stanford.

I clutched hold of the merchant's greasy hair and he gasped before his bottom lip began to quiver at my stare. Jerking back his head, I glared down at the man, before pushing away his head and throwing Hota's knife on to the dirt.

Blair sighed in relief, whilst Hota casually stepped forward to collect his knife from the ground. Turning, he plunged the blade upward into the merchant's chin. Smirking, Hota watched as the man gasped, before dropping over on to his side.

"Sometimes we are required to seek our own justice, Carre is a good man. I feel we have hunted enough today, now we shall drink. We have much to discuss."

Taking a final inspection of the man whom Hota had just slaughtered, I finally thought outside my own self-pity. I realised that my old self had not evaporated, and I still had a sense of duty.

***

Once back at the church hall, Hota was quick to bring forward the evening's festivities. I was seated at the end of the table and had already indulged in my fair share of ale.

Although my tongue had loosened, I remained coherent. Hota told Dak and the rest of the seated Crooks to leave the table and enjoy their spoils elsewhere. I raised my beaker towards Dak as he left us alone, for I had taken a liking to his company.

"He admires you, Jep," said Hota.

"As you said before, we are not too dissimilar," I replied, after guzzling down the remainder of my drink.

Hota looked at me, clearly concocting in his mind the best way to relay what it was he wanted to disclose.

"You belong here, with us," he said eventually, prompting me to chuckle,

"As of recent times, I longed for your death, yet now I appear to be able to tolerate your presence."

Raising his beaker, Hota smiled, "As did I, but we shall put this quarrel behind us, and move forward with our vision."

"Your vision, not mine," I insisted.

Hota scoffed, before continuing, "What do you think will happen on your return? Yes, there will be rejoicing at the safe return of Blair, but then what? The Chief and Baron Asher will not allow you to walk freely within the town, you will be executed, or if fortune is on your side, banished."

"That is the risk I must take."

"What about Lady Ivy?" asked Hota.

"What about her?"

"If what you say is true and the Cavaliers have been eliminated, then I fear she is in grave danger. When the Chief is gone and you are dead, who do you think will protect her? Who will stop Asher from tormenting her further, and inevitably killing her? My sources have reliably informed me that the Baron already poses a grave threat to her."

"Yet you are unwilling to tell the identity of these sources," I replied.

"I am forgiving, not foolish."

Hota turned away from me, observing his companions competing to see who could finish their drinks the quickest.

"These are your people Jep, and I offer you the chance to lead them to freedom and prosperity. You have the opportunity to achieve your dream of walking freely with Lady Ivy. For neither one of you to be judged or heckled. You can taste normality, family, to live in peace and luxury."

"You wish to offer all this to the man who slayed your father?"

Clenching his lips together, it was clear that I had hit a nerve and that not all was forgiven, yet Hota remained composed and honest in sharing his disgruntlement over the circumstances of his father's death.

"Like I said, someone has guided me away from vengeance."

"So, what is it you propose?" I asked.

Hota leaned forward, interlocking his fingers and nuzzling his mouth into his thumbs. "I have at least fifty able fighters here and a further one hundred making their way down from the north. Breaching the walls alone will cost me at least half of my warriors. I have no concern about our capabilities at overpowering Asher's men, but the Swords on the other hand, they will prove difficult, especially with the added band of men who protect the Chief."

"Well then, you have your answer, and you understand there shall be no fairy tale ending," I replied.

"Unless you will join us, and then I promise that I will see all your desires met."

Tightening my lips, I glared back at him in disgust, knowing what task he wanted me to partake. "You want me to kill my own?"

Hota rolled his eyes, before gently placing his hand on my shoulder. "What have they ever offered you, my friend? The Governor has never taken much of a liking to you, Lev ridicules you at every opportunity and as for Fawkes…"

"Fawkes has saved my life on more than one occasion," I interrupted.

"Yes, this is true, but I am sure it was he who begged you to come to me and exchange your life for Blair's." Standing up, Hota raised his voice and became more animated. "Tell me, which one of your so-called loyal Swords comes to your aid now? Which one of them has tried to put an end to your imprisonment?"

I stared down at the table, thinking of how to argue against his statements, but once again the man I had sworn to bring to justice was speaking the truth. The only two men who had really fought my injustice were Chenchi and Detector Flint.

Tilting back my head, I looked up at Hota through sullen eyes. I felt repulsed by the picture his words conjured in my head, yet still I expressed my desire to learn more. "What is your plan?"

Hota smiled, his insides clearly teeming with joy at my willingness to listen to his scheme.

"You will poison them and therefore remove our greatest obstacle."

"I refuse to take the life of the ones who fed me."

Hota accepted my negative response to his plans. I sat silently, concerned that my refusal to assist him with his scheme had most likely secured my death. However, once again my old foe wished to toy with me further, and he permitted me to retire to my quarters.

***

Standing on the hilltop overlooking the village, I watched the trees swaying under the moonlight. Contemplating Hota's proposal made my stomach gripe, yet his suggestion was the only chance of giving me the outcome I had longed for. My mind battled between my loyalty to my fellow Swords and the love I had for Lady Ivy. If I were to refuse Hota's plans, and he allowed Blair and I to return to Stanford, I would surely die, or at the very least, be banished from the town.

Hota had convinced me enough that he was not responsible for the deaths of the Cavaliers, which left the culprits still disguised within the town. With that in mind, I knew Lady Ivy's life was in real jeopardy.

My turmoil was disturbed by Sheron, who walked up the hill towards me. She trod delicately around me, knowing that Hota had divulged his intentions and that my mood was unsettled.

Standing by my side, mirroring my gaze into the woodland, she spoke softly. "He has told you of his aims."

"And you have come to assist me in coming to a decision, I suppose?"

Sheron stepped forward, turning around to face me and raising her upper lip. "I have come to offer you companionship, you are big enough to come to your own conclusions."

She turned to walk away, leaving me at the top of the hill. I called out to her, "Wait, your company is very welcome."

Sheron refrained from trying to persuade me into deciding what I should do. I changed the direction of the conversation by asking her about her own childhood. At first the fearless warrior was evasive about her past, but eventually she elaborated on what had persuaded her to join the Crooks.

"My father headed one of the organised gangs in the city. He never brought his dealings home or allowed us to witness his chosen profession. He was protective like a father should be, and he gave me and my sibling's all the love and attention we required. After his execution, my mother and I were enslaved by the Crown, and my brothers were made to join the regal guards. Like Blair, I was assigned to the lock up, to serve the city's Blue Swords. One of your honourable associates took a liking to me and would ask me to join him in his quarters. After a while he became tired of enjoying my youthfulness and got his thrills from being, shall we say, more robust."

Noticing a tear running down the hardened Crook's cheek, I remained silent and listened to her intently.

"One evening I limped into his quarters after the previous night's beating had been inflicted on me but this time, I hid a kitchen knife under my dress. He threw me down on his bed, I submitted at first, losing breath to his heavy weight as he laid upon me. Timing my attack perfectly, I thrust the knife at the side of his temple. My slender hand was unable to penetrate the bone, and my inexperience had made me act rashly. The assault on the Sword didn't even leave him with a scar, yet my mother was burnt to death for my crimes and feral ways against the Crown."

Facing her, I felt dismay at hearing her story. "Did you ever disclose this to another Sword?"

"Of course I did, I pleaded with them, but being a child, my accusations were promptly dismissed."

"Why do you tell me this?" I asked.

"I tell you so you know that there is good and bad in all; even heroes can be villains and villains, heroes. It is not always as straightforward as we assume," replied Sheron, before turning and leaving me on the hilltop.

***

Getting dressed the next morning, I heard the sound of children's laughter coming from outside my quarters. Stepping out to the walkway of my lodge, I stared into the distance at the same hilltop where I had conversed with Sheron the previous evening.

Three of the local youngsters from the village played under the morning sun, beaming with joy and excitement. Dak stood with them, playfully wrestling the hyperactive children to the ground. After allowing them to wriggle free, he acted wounded and begged for mercy, giving them a sense of victory.

It was warming to see the gentle giant of a man interacting with the villagers. But witnessing Dak's sensitivity only clouded my mind further.

I strode to the church hall, keen to seek an audience with Hota. My arrival caused Hota to clear the room, and insist I joined him at the banquet table.

"I suppose now you plan to leave? If this is your will, then take Blair and return to Stanford."

Tossing back a cup of wine, I sighed and momentarily paused. "I am with you, but I do have terms."

Hota leaned back in his chair, beaming across the table at me. "Go on, speak freely."

"At any cost, Chenchi and Flint are to be spared."

"That can be arranged," said Hota.

Digging my elbows to the table I leaned forward, "I am doing this for Lady Ivy. Once Asher is defeated, she must be given rule over the town, as Baroness."

"And you, Jep, will be by her side?"

Ripping apart a loaf of bread, I frowned back at him. "I care little for my fate, I am doing this for Lady Ivy."

Hota insisted that we discussed tactics later in the day, to give me time to reflect on my decision, but I was resolute on getting the plan discussed and finalised.

"Hemlock will offer a comfortable death. With numbness they will simply slip away," said Hota.

"The devil's blossom," I replied.

"There are worse ways to die. It is vital that you hide the poison within the lining of your trousers, you're still a prisoner and are guaranteed to be searched on your return."

"It will be discovered," I argued.

"And how many waist cords did you pat down my friend? Only the most seasoned of Swords would carry out such a thorough inspection. Besides, you are still one of their own, your search will only be cursory," said Hota.

I looked back at Hota grimly, asking him when I was to leave.

"There is no reason to hang around, I will attack on the next holy day,"

"That is the day I am to be executed," I said.

"Well then justice will prevail. You must not speak a word of this to Blair, she may have enjoyed our customs, but her heart will always remain with the Swords," insisted Hota.

"What about her mother?"

"She will be cared for, and you have my word, no harm will come to the men and women who submit to our invasion. Just like the people of Yaxil, they will be allowed to remain dignified."

20

HERO OR VILLAIN

Coming to the end of the meadow path, Blair turned to hug Sheron, and they both held one another.

"You can always stay, your life is your own," I said.

"And miss your hanging, now what kind of friend would that make me?" said Blair, smiling.

Sheron gave me an intense look and handed me a sword. "Do remember Jep, that no person should be handed privilege, it must be earned."

Once free of the woodland and out of sight of Sheron, I began scanning my eyes across the stone walls that barricaded the green fields, in search of Sword O'Hara. Blair rode on Spike's back, appearing rather sullen and unwilling to make any conversation.

"Does it not please you to be going home?" I asked.

"What am I returning to? A life of serving others, waiting on Swords and listening to their boastful tales."

Taking hold of Spike's reins, I brought him to a halt. "If you are to continue in this defeatist tone, then you may as well return to Yaxil, see out your time with the free folk. Or you can stop this brooding and go and take what is yours. You are loved by all you meet; you fight harder than any man and you take direction from the most formidable Blue Sword in the land. But what is it that really troubles you?"

Blairs eyes became watery, "They're going to kill you Jep, what reasons have you to return?"

Placing my hand gently on her knee, I looked up at the servant girl, mounted upon my horse. "Because, like you, I will have to fight to get what I want."

***

Waking to rain pouring from the sky, we had arrived at the forest cold and drenched. The rain came pattering down against the leaves, bringing the woodland to life. Blair remained upright on Spike, giving her the vantage point of the road ahead. Whistling down to me, Blair jerked her head back, indicating the approach of another on the path. Resting my fingertips against the hilt of my sword, I poised myself for the impending meet.

Sword O'Hara casually rode towards us. On seeing Blair, O'Hara squinted, before laughing at my success.

"You took your time," I called.

O'Hara brought his horse to a standstill, "I had no choice but to retreat, my tracks were being picked up by one of their scouts, so it pleases me to learn that you kept your word."

"If I had known you had fled, then maybe I would have carried on south."

"Fawkes will be pleased to see you, Blair," said O'Hara.

"Maybe now that pig-headed Chief will appreciate that Jep is no traitor," replied Blair.

***

The walls of Stanford were now visible from the path as we emerged from the woodland. With only grassland separating us from the gate, O'Hara called out to me, "Now is your chance."

I slowly turned around to face him, emulating Blair's puzzlement.

"There is no future for you behind those gates. You have fulfilled your promise and ensured that the girl is safe. How the rest of the story plays out, I will leave up to you. Besides, you are young, I am an old man, my legs grow tired and I have little chance of capturing such a youthful Sword."

Staring back at the town walls, I momentarily considered O'Hara's proposal, but I had to see out my word, others now depended on it. "I am grateful for your suggestion, but there is still much to be done."

Chuckling, O'Hara looked across to Blair, "Well then, we had best be getting this stubborn bastard to his death."

***

Lev was the first to greet us in the courtyard behind the lock up. Focusing all his attention on Blair, he rejoiced at seeing her alive and well. He yelled out to attract Fawkes' attention, and it wasn't long before the seasoned Sword appeared from his quarters.

Glancing up at the sky from his decking, Fawkes breathed a sigh of relief before banging his fist against the door of his hut. Isa opened the door, startled by the commotion. On seeing her daughter, she sprinted across the grass, to be met halfway by Blair. Grasping her child firmly in her arms, she sobbed with joy at being reunited with the happy girl.

Fawkes strutted towards me, ruffling Blair's hair with his hand as he passed her. Holding out his arm, he embraced me with a firm grip.

He clenched his lips together and firmed his chiselled jaw line. "Now it is you who has saved my life."

The warm greeting was short lived however, interrupted by a loud thud caused by the hasty slamming of the parade room door.

"I trust this man has been searched?" called Sergeant Mosely.

"He has," replied O'Hara, knowing very well he had not carried out an inspection.

"Place your arms out on the wall and spread your feet. We can never be too careful," demanded Mosely.

"Is this necessary?" argued Fawkes, "he has returned willingly."

Ignoring Fawkes's question, Mosely kicked my feet apart and began vigorously patting his hands over my arms and torso. I felt my chest beating harder than usual and my breathing became more erratic as his hands approached my hips, but just as Hota had said, only the most competent Swords searched the waistline and Mosely had proven his worth, failing to locate the devil's blossom tied to the string of my linens.

Taking my sword from its scabbard, Mosely handed it over to Fawkes. "A sword! I feel my men have treated you with leniency. Return this to the armoury at once, Lev. Sword O'Hara, escort the prisoner to the dungeon."

Reluctantly, O'Hara gripped his hand under my arm and began to usher me across the courtyard. Blair and Isa looked on in desolation, as I was returned to incarceration.

Closing the cell door, O'Hara scoffed, "You should have fled."

Once again, I was enclosed by darkness, the bitterness of the surroundings reflecting the feelings in my heart. I found myself mulling over the potential ways in which the pouch of poison would be best served.

Inhaling its contents myself would give neither one of my adversaries the satisfaction of claiming my death, and in turn would remove me from the equation and the troubles that were looming over the town.

To contemplate killing my own was a concept that I had never thought would ever cross my mind. Yet now it was all I thought about. Without Hota's interference, Lady Ivy was as good as dead, as was I. So here I was torn between the woman I loved and the brothers I served.

***

The sound of footsteps coming and going across the courtyard continued throughout the night. Raised voices, one being Chenchi's, continued to protest against my imprisonment. I believe none of them had prepared themselves for my safe return and had only assumed that Hota would have dealt with me on their behalf.

It took me a while to rouse and recognise the person who had joined me in the dungeon that morning. Squinting from the daylight that shone down the passageway, I was eventually able to see her staring back at me from behind the barred doors.

Seeing Lady Ivy alone, I raced forward, placing my hands between the iron bars and gently caressed both sides of her face. However, I quickly sensed that something was wrong. The purple staining and damaged skin under her eyes made me pull down her hood and confirm the horror that looked back at me.

The swelling on her lower lip and misplacement of her nose made me understand that, yet again, Lady Ivy had been a victim to the Baron's cruel and brutal ways.

Attempting to mask the rage that plunged deep in my gut, I delicately ran my thumb across her lip, before tenderly placing my palm against her cheek.

"It brings me much warmth to see you alive," whispered the Baroness.

I paused fleetingly, examining the wounds which had been inflicted on Lady Ivy. I reflected on the time when she was humiliated and had been paraded appallingly before her people in the Square.

"It ends now," I said.

Lady Ivy looked back at me in despair. "They will offer you no pardon. My face is the consequence of my arguing for your innocence."

I had no choice but to disclose Hota's plan of attacking the town. Lady Ivy was just as baffled as I by the Crook's reasons for not vengefully killing me. I refused to tell her of my agreement in aiding his assault, as I knew all too well that the Baroness would refuse to leave me in a position of choosing between her and the Swords.

"When the fighting starts you must stay within the Grand Hall. If Hota is victorious, you will be spared."

"The question I have for you Jep, is which side will you be fighting for?"

"I feel ashamed to say this, but that is something I am yet to decide."

Flint appeared from the passageway, calling out to Lady Ivy in a low tone, "Forgive me my Lady, but the Chief will be here soon, I must ask that you depart."

The Baroness gazed intently at me; her eyes became tearful and her face expressed her sorrow. "Whatever your fate may be, my heart will be forever yours," she said quietly, before bowing her head and leaving.

***

The arrival of the Governor, inviting me to supper, made me feel nauseous. Knowing what I had in my possession filled me with distress, but like a cornered rat, vigorous action was required, and this would be my one and only opportunity.

Entering the parade room, I was greeted by a loud cheer from my companions. Lev, Fawkes and Chenchi all remained seated, encouraging me to over-indulge in the evening's festivities. The spoils were not sparse; duck, wine and cheese littered the table making the banquet setting feel more like a celebratory meal.

The mood remained light and free of current predicaments. After toasting our fallen brothers, the Governor ordered Chenchi to relieve Blair as lookout for any of our unwanted associates. Grasping at my shoulder on his exit, he smiled down at me, showing his pleasure at my safe return.

Once the parade room door closed, the Governor stood to his feet, giving me a severe look.

"Leave us," he called to Isa.

Once Isa had departed, our leader wandered to the edge of the table, displaying nothing but grief on his face.

"The Chief has accepted your success in returning Blair to our home. However, he refuses to stand up to the political barrier that would see you freed. He has concluded and brought forward his ruling. You are to be beheaded at noon tomorrow."

"Well, it is more graceful than being hanged, I suppose," sighed Lev, before receiving a bitter expression from Fawkes.

"And you thought it best to relay this without Chenchi present?" I asked.

"He does not know of the verdict and I feel he will not take the outcome lightly. I would be grateful for it to remain that way, at least until you are clear of the town walls," replied the Governor.

"You are going to set me free?"

"We are going to turn a blind eye, it's the least we can do."

Exhaling, I rubbed my hand against my forehead. "What about the Baroness?"

"Flint has organised her departure, she will be awaiting you at the cross-roads. There, Sword O'Hara will meet you with horses. You will be pursued, and the best chance you have is to get to the border and turn your back on these lands," said the Governor.

Tilting back the empty jug of wine, I insisted on going to the kitchens to refill our beverages. The kitchen was more of a pantry, kept out of sight of the parade room.

Relieving Isa, she appeared startled by my arrival and bewildered by my offer to take over her chores.

"As this will be our final evening dining together, it is only fitting that I wait on you for a change, Isa. You have always been kind to me."

Once alone, I began filling the jug with wine. I then removed the leather pouch from my trousers. The herbal contents remained securely sealed inside. It was time to play my hand and reveal all to my companions.

21

THE BETRAYAL

Startling my fellow Swords, I banged the jug of wine down on the banquet table. I threw the leather pouch of Devil's Blossom before them, and they glanced at each another, bewildered by my sharpness.

"This is poison, intended for you. All courtesy of our previous associate, Hota. He planned for me to use it to end your lives."

Fawkes stood from his chair, growling, "And did you agree to this plan?"

"Of course I did, but no, my intention was not to harm you, I would never turn my back on my brothers. I am afraid the poison is a much lesser threat to that which now faces us. Hota, along with one hundred and fifty armed men and woman march on this town, all intent on overthrowing not only Asher, but also to eradicate the Blue Swords in Stanford."

"May God have mercy," said Lev soberly.

The stillness in the room identified the thoughts that now raced through my friends' minds. I looked to the Governor, awaiting, in anticipation, his reaction to the potential chaos that now threatened our town.

He stared down at the table in a daze, with his fist clenched under his nose. Eventually he reacted, demanding that we were all to attend a meeting with the Chief as a matter of urgency.

"What about Jep? I do not feel his presence at the Grand Hall will be well received," said Fawkes.

The Governor sighed, "There are more pressing issues that must be addressed at once. I fear that it is not only Jep's life that is in jeopardy."

***

Our late and unsolicited arrival at the gates of the Grand Hall alarmed the nervous guard who patrolled. He was insistent that he was to declare our arrival, but the Governor glared down at him from his horse, demanding immediate entry into the grounds. "I come with news of a grave threat that will impact us all. Now don't be foolish, and step aside."

The stammering guard cast his eyes over the five of us, all mounted and with little patience for niceties. He finally allowed us through the gate and into the courtyard, and another guard promptly appeared at the top of the steps leading to the main door.

Fawkes swaggered towards him ordering him to tether the horses, causing the guardsman to look to his previous associate, Chenchi, for reassurance.

"Trust me, the Baron needs to hear what we have to say, all our fates depend on it," assured Chenchi.

The Governor had already paraded up the steps and pulled open the heavy wooden doors. He then proceeded heavy-footed down the hallway, making his way to the Great Hall. Two further guards took a fleeting look between each other, panicked by our sudden and intense intrusion.

"Move!" snapped the Governor to the doormen.

The guards hesitated, frightened to make eye contact, before one of them scrambled through the doors of the hall.

Lev reached out to grasp the closing door and said sweetly, "After you Sir, it is only polite to give way to our elders."

The laughter that echoed throughout the hall came to a dramatic halt on our entrance. Following our leader through the hall, I couldn't help but notice the guests giving me uncertain looks and whispering amongst themselves. Lev nodded his head, confidently meeting the sight of Asher's guests. Smiling, he impolitely picked at the leftover food whilst passing the banquet tables.

The Baron was seated on a platform, overlooking the room. His stout rear was wedged between the arms of the oak Baronial throne.

His face dropped on seeing us walking towards him and once he caught a glimpse of me freely moving amongst my companions, he dropped his chin to his chest and narrowed his eyes.

Chief Muir was stood on the corner of the platform with his back to the guests, conversing with Truda. On observing us, Truda cleared her throat, ending the conversation and bringing our attendance to the attention of the Chief.

Wide eyed, he stepped down from the stand and stomped forward to meet the Governor. "Explain to me why this man is not in chains?"

"We come with grim and sensitive news, Sir," the Governor replied.

Baron Asher plucked himself from his chair and got to his feet, "Speak clearly, and answer your superior. Why do you allow a murderer to walk freely within my hall?"

Raising one side of his mouth, the Governor, glowered back at the Baron, before stepping around the Chief, and insolently turning his back to the podium, dismissing both his senior and the Baron. Addressing the audience, he watched as the privileged stared back at him, unsettled by his disrespect and lack of obedience.

"We are on the brink of an invasion," he announced, prompting a terrified gasp back from the guests.

"Chief Muir, I demand you take control of your men and refute these foul claims!" shouted Baron Asher.

Looking perplexed, the Chief ignored the Baron's orders and invited our Governor to continue.

"Sword Jep has confirmed that Hota moves on our town; with him comes over one hundred warriors. They are intent on taking Stanford."

"And why are we to believe him? The man is a traitor, no better than Hota himself," argued the Baron.

Grunting, the Governor turned and frowned at Asher, throwing the leather pouch of Devil's Blossom at his feet. "This poison was intended for my Swords and I, in order to leave you weaker during their proposed attack. Baron, it is you they come for, with the intention of removing you from power."

Asher looked over to Truda in horror, and his drink-flushed cheeks began to drain of colour. Slumping back into his chair, his eyes flickered down to the ground, an expression of despair passing over his face. Truda hurried over to the Baron to offer her support. She too had lost her usual expression of condescension and haughtiness.

Nervously she peered back to the Governor, spluttering her words. "Noble Sword, when is this attack due to commence?"

"On the next holy day," I interrupted.

Truda closed her eyes despondently, knowing there was no time to call on reinforcements from the city.

Chief Muir called for silence. "Hear me. Your town is protected by Swords. My men are the most able in this land. Combine this with the Baron's guards, and we will meet their confrontation with honour and fury. Shadow Crooks!" he scoffed, spitting on the ground, "Nothing more than lawless peasants, and they will learn the ways of order. As Chief, I will lead our defence against these Godless creatures. Baron Asher, how many men do you have at your disposal?"

Asher leaned his forehead into the palm of his hand. Eventually he managed to answer, but in a defeatist tone, "I fear not enough."

"Speak up man," demanded the Chief.

The Baron squinted back at Truda, keen to seek her assurance and guidance. Truda walked towards the Chief, playing with her fingers, "My Lord, at least half the infantry has been dispatched to escort the new Bishop and his treasures back to Stanford."

"Half? What riches does this Bishop carry?" asked Chief Muir.

"These are brutal times, my Lord, and bandits prey on travellers. This town has never housed a Bishop. We wanted to ensure that we were well regarded through the eyes of the Church. Respectfully, as you have pointed out, we are fortunate enough to have you and your band as guests, and with the town's appointed Swords on our side, we are sure to be victorious. My own guardian, Eruk, served with the Blue Swords for many years and is a formidable combatant."

The Chief frowned, studying the Baron, unimpressed by his self-pity and recklessness. He demanded that all guests were to depart, and to spread word of the impending assault planned against the town.

It was refreshing to see our Chief taking command and showing his authority; no longer did he appear like an appeasing puppet, dancing to the tune of the Baron. The situation gave him the opportunity to flex his muscles and offer his followers true leadership.

The circumstances had allowed me to approach the Baron unchallenged. I eyeballed him with malice, causing Truda to step aside with unease.

Looking back at me, he appeared fearful.

"If Hota does not end you, I most certainly will. Never again will I allow you to torment her," I whispered.

The Chief stepped forward, realising that I was not exchanging pleasantries with the man I detested, "We shall reconvene at the lock up."

***

We were only two days away from Hota's planned arrival, and the talk of battle now flurried around the local people. Some had gone as far as to flee and head for sanctuary in the forest; however, the majority had placed their faith in not only the Swords, but the remaining guardsmen, loyal to the Baron's household.

Baron Asher had provided the town with more evidence of his feeble nature, confining himself to the sanctuary of the Grand Hall, and refusing to engage with his people. Lady Ivy had been sent to do his bidding, wandering the Market Place, offering hope and reassurance to her townsfolk.

Chief Muir excelled in his preparations. His ongoing inspection of the walls, fortifications and structure made him restless. He would often be seen walking the ramparts with the Governor, ensuring that all walkways and parapets were reinforced and able to sustain an attack. Seeing him there gave the people optimism and a guarantee that they were well protected.

Tactics were often discussed within the parade room, offering debates on our defence strategies and battle plans. All calculated plotting was led by the Blue Swords and a small cadre of the Baron's guardsmen.

We all knew that our paucity in numbers already put us at a disadvantage. Chenchi and Lev were tasked with recruiting able-bodied men and women to join us in our fight against the Shadow Crooks. However, with limited weapons and armour, we were offering the Crooks a resistance of nothing more than farmers and peasants.

***

Knocking on the door of Western Farm, I could not help but feel somewhat anxious about the condition in which I would find my old friend Carre. Rye answered the door, and clearly enthused by my visit, welcomed me inside the family home. Carre's twin boys raced around the house teasing one another. A grunt came from the rear chambers and Carre appeared, limping, with his back hunched. He looked somewhat decrepit but I was relieved and delighted to see that he still lived.

One side of Carre's mouth had drooped, and his left arm now hung loosely down his side. He was able to raise a slight smile from the unaffected side of his mouth. He grumbled at his sons' boisterousness, but they ignored his impatience and irritability, continuing to charge around full of excitement.

Dam stepped out from behind her husband, reprimanding the boys and ordering them to play outside. Grimacing, Carre grumbled, lifting his capable arm and pointing through to the other room.

"It is too early for ale, my love," insisted Dam.

Carre replied with a growl, triggering Rye to chuckle.

I grinned back at the hot-headed farmer. "It is never too early for ale."

Carre shuffled over towards me, slapping his hand on my back, expressing his joy at our reunion and my eagerness to indulge in a morning beverage. Once seated at the table, Dam gave me an awkward glance, however Rye was less shy in asking the question that remained unsettled in their minds, "You have been freed, so have they acquitted you of Isaak's death?"

Carre reacted with a grunt and scowled across the table at Rye.

"Not that I believed you were guilty, Jep," stuttered Rye.

I turned my face to Carre who sat beside me on the bench, "As you know, the Crooks will arrive the day after tomorrow. Once again, I have refused the proposal of an alliance with Hota. He will come with wrath and in truth we are outnumbered. If you wish to leave, you should do so now."

"I shall not run and hide like a coward, I will fight beside you," announced Rye.

Carre nodded at his gallant farmhand, proud to hear him offer his hand in battle. Struggling to his feet, Carre stubbornly refused the assistance of his wife and limped over to the back wall of the farmhouse.

Unhooking a long-handled axe from its place upon the wall, he turned to us, raising it in his strong hand and proceeding to growl, vociferously. His refusal to submit gave me the spur and motivation I needed in preparing for combat with the Shadow Crooks.

Approaching the door, I looked back at the table. "Justice has been served on the ones responsible for your assault."

Dam sighed with relief and Carre bowed his head at me, before lifting his beaker and draining his ale. I was unwilling to disclose the truth, that it was Hota who executed one of Carre's attackers.

***

Chenchi ran to catch me up whilst I was making my way back through the Burn Oak estate.

"It pleases me to see you walking without restrictions, you could at least appear pleased by your freedom."

"I fear we have little chance of defeating Hota and his Crooks?" I said.

"Only God knows our fate. I think it will be enjoyable finding out, I am more than blood thirsty."

Detector Amir greeted us at the front of the lock up. "Good day, your attendance at the armoury is needed."

"And so it begins," cheered Chenchi.

Stepping away from Amir, he called to me. "Jep, the half-moon indicates that this will be an even battle; it is not just armour that you must prepare, your mind must be free of doubt."

The line of men outside the armoury consisted of the Chief's band of Blue Swords. O'Hara stepped out, already dressed in chain mail.

Lev was at the front of the line smirking. "Is your skin resistant to steel? Or are your aging bones too weathered to carry plated armour?"

Sword O'Hara glared back at the brazen Sword from behind the previous war markings on his skin. "Heavy armour does not go with this pretty face; besides, if I need a shield, you will be adequate enough."

Lev turned back to the two younger Swords behind him. "Most enemies would flee at first sight of that face."

Passing, Sword O'Hara acknowledged me standing in the line and raised the long handled, broad axe in his hand, whilst grinning.

Sergeant Mosely gave me an unfriendly expression as I stepped into the armoury. Chenchi was stood beside me, having his torso eyed by Fawkes.

Shaking his head and tutting, Fawkes directed his attention over to the shelves filled with armour.

Sighing, he rubbed his chin, speaking with his back to us. "I always knew it would be difficult to meet your sizing requirements Chenchi. Maybe you should remain clear of the fighting and help Isa with the cooking."

Chenchi strutted forward, reaching out for a hauberk. "Like O'Hara, I will leave the plated armour for the more precious and needy amongst us." His comments sparked a smile from Fawkes.

Chenchi turned to the rear walk, inspecting the rows of hanging weapons. His eyes lit up at the sight of all the axes, long swords and maces. Plucking a long sword from its harness on the wall, he then reached down, picking up a small, rounded buckler shield.

"Do you not think it wiser to carry a larger one?" I asked, pointing to the row of kite shaped, heavier shields.

"I only plan on attacking, not blocking," replied Chenchi.

"Jep, take what you need," insisted Fawkes.

"And sparingly, there are others in need of equipment," called Mosely.

I examined the armour, feeling the weight of the gauntlets and the thickness of the pauldrons. Reaching my arm through the grooves of a silver chest plate, I looked down at the Blue Sword initials, engraved in the top corner of the steel. "This will suffice."

"If you are not planning on occupying one of your hands with a shield, may I suggest you take a long sword, it will save on repeated blows," advised Fawkes.

Resting my chest plate against the wall, and duplicating Chenchi, I removed a long sword from the wall. Its weight took some getting used to and required me to adjust my hold from my short sword. It took both my hands to hold its hilt steady, catching Fawkes' attention. "Familiarise yourself to its needs. Mastering the blade will make you formidable."

Scoffing, Mosely called for the next Sword.

Exiting the armoury, Blair was stood proudly alongside the Governor.

"You will stand against them?" I asked.

"They plotted to kill my brothers, I will not hide and allow this to go unpunished."

Smiling down at the girl, I felt privileged to be serving alongside her. Blair's character and competency had already fated her to become a remarkable Blue Sword.

***

Positioning the wagon in the centre of the market square, I saw that the usual lively atmosphere had been replaced by empty stalls and rattled locals. The people scurried around making their final preparations.

Less than twenty men and women had attended, offering their services to fight alongside us. Rye was amongst those few brave men and women. One attendee's appearance had surprised me. The old, cantankerous inn keeper from the Viking Invader had arrived, keen to defend his town.

Over the years the town had suffered at the hands of rival bands that tormented the residents within their rival estates. They incited violence as a way of marking their territories and met their pointless adversaries with brutality. Yet now the town needed these thugs to divert their hatred away from one another and towards a real enemy, an enemy that posed the greatest threat to their lands, yet they had hidden themselves away and maintained their cowardice.

The handful of brave men and women had begun arming themselves with the weapons and armour from our wagon. Rye placed his head through the grooves of a chest plate, grinning back at me, proudly.

"It complements you, Rye. Your valour will be remembered at the Spring Trials," I said.

Lady Ivy appeared from Main Street, accompanied by one of the Baron's guards. I began to approach, causing her to dismiss her protector.

"They're courageous," said Lady Ivy, observing the townsfolk who mingled, showing off their new weapons and armour to each other.

"I had hoped for more," I replied.

"With the joining of our people, my household guards and your Swords, I have no doubt in my mind that we will be triumphant."

Observing her discoloured skin, I felt saddened by the thought of failure and knowing that her fate could be potentially left in the hands of my enemies. "You should leave."

Lady Ivy turned back to me and gave me a sour look.

"Head north; once the fighting is over, I will join you and we can continue, seeking adventure and fulfilment elsewhere."

The Baroness stared back to the Market Place and took in a deep breath. "You are no longer a prisoner here Jep, and your willingness to stay and defend our town is noble. But this impending incursion met by the reaction of my pitiful husband has finally mapped out my destiny."

"I don't understand."

Placing her hand onto my cheek, she gazed back at me, but this time there was no hint of sadness, only that of strength. "I am no longer satisfied with being the troubled maiden in the tale. Stanford needs me, my people need me. If you are to stay and fight, you must do so with clear thought."

Walking away, Lady Ivy sternly called over to her guard. Watching her leave, it felt as if something had changed, her determination had shone through and she was no longer willing to be overshadowed by her merciless husband. Whatever the outcome of the battle, Lady Ivy was poised and ready to lead.

22

THE CROOK AT THE GATE

It was the eve of the next holy day, so we ensured that we dined like kings and queens. Chief Muir knew it was in his own interest to see his warriors well fed before going into battle; spirits needed to be high. Duck and fresh vegetables had been delivered to the lock up, along with some of the most fruitful and spiced wines I had ever consumed.

The Governor refused to allow Isa to wait on us, especially as her daughter Blair had volunteered to fight, even though it was very much against her mother's wishes. Fawkes could see the despair in his lover's eyes and declared his loyalty to her by giving Blair strict and potentially, controversial orders. "You are to stay and assist in the defence of the Great Hall, that is where your mother will be."

Blair frowned. "And you are not my father, so your say will not be considered. I will be with the rest of you, on the front ranks."

Rubbing his hands together, Fawkes grunted. "No, I am not your father, but I am a Sword at this table and unless my senior wishes to object, you will do as I command."

The Governor presented no objection to the seasoned Sword's demands. Blair huffed, only to be quickly reprimanded by her reassured mother. Fawkes had no desires of denying the girl her moment, but despite her stubbornness, he adored her and loved her mother.

He rested his hand on Blair's forearm. "You may sulk all you wish, child, but before you act the brat, listen to what I have to say. Your mother is the most precious thing in this land to me. If I were to fall and it is possible I might, I want to know that she has your sword protecting her. Now take my words as condescending if you so choose, but the truth is, there is no one else at this table who I trust more than you to watch over the woman I love."

Lev laughed and slammed his beaker down onto the table. "Have you quite finished with this feeble talk? You're making my bones weak. Blair, if I had my way, I would send you in first, you peck like a crow and that alone would scare off those seeking to do us harm."

The room erupted with laughter, and even Fawkes grinned at his companion's humour.

Chenchi was keen to add to the careless satire, "I say we place bets on which side of the wall Jep will throw his blade. Let's be honest, he is more erratic than a ferret in a rabbit hole."

"It is Jep's loose trousers that have caused this mess. But do not fear, if our womaniser is to fall tomorrow, I will be happy to oblige with the Baroness' needs," said Lev.

Lev's cheerful indulgences were always guaranteed to unstiffen any mood; however, the Governor was ready to deliver his own words of inspiration, and in doing so, civilised the atmosphere.

Banging his palm onto the table, he ordered for calm, before staggering to his feet with a goblet of wine in his hand. "It is true, some of us may fall tomorrow. All I ask is that you have one another's back's and once this ordeal has drawn to an end, make sure someone brings me Hota's head!"

It was unfeasible to rest, even though the wine had tried to numb my overactive mind. Opening the door to my quarters, I saw that Chenchi was already inside. "Are they here?" he asked.

"I am yet to hear word of their arrival."

"Where are you going with your armour?" he asked.

"I am going to the wall. I want to see them as they emerge from the forest. Are you coming?"

Chenchi sat upright in his bed. "And risk not picking out the ones I am going to kill? Of course I am coming."

***

Our footsteps against the wooden walkway caught the attention of the Baron's watchmen who were keeping observation atop the front wall. Chenchi dismissed the patrolmen, before resting his forearms on to the curtain wall.

The red morning sky and the settled weather made it almost feel tranquil. The birds could be heard from the trees and rabbits ran freely and undisturbed on the grass that separated the town from the woodland.

Sniffing, Chenchi took in a deep breath. "And to think that field will be stained with blood by dusk."

"Do you think he will still fight, when he learns that I have not kept my word?" I asked.

Chenchi scoffed, "Hota is even more tenacious than you. He will challenge us, even if he believes he will not be victorious. He is a man of principle and will be sure to attempt to secure his father's legacy, at any cost. Once he knows you have not carried out his request and have gone back on your word, he will be even more eager to taste your blood."

"This is why it must end now, on this day," I said.

Chenchi held out his arm for me to grasp. "We rise together, and we will fall together."

The wildlife began to scurry away from the field, and within moments the mood changed as the first few of the Shadow Crooks began to emerge from the opening at the edge of the forest.

"And so it begins," mumbled Chenchi.

Leaving me alone, Chenchi sprinted away, keen to warn the others of the Crooks' arrival. I remained poised, staring across the grass at our enemy, watching as they began to line themselves in front of the trees.

The wooden beam below me began to vibrate, and I was joined by the Chief. He stood beside me, silently observing the men and women who had come to invade our town.

Hota was the last to appear, his followers clearing the way, allowing him and Dak to lead them. Truda and Eruk were the next to arrive and took position on the other side of me. Truda drew in a sharp breath, in dread at the force now arrayed before her.

Eruk turned to the Chief. "There is no more than sixty, this is a mob, not an army."

The Chief nodded his head. "They will not attempt to penetrate our walls with that pitiful number, but we must not grow idle; more may come. Jep, gather the Swords and meet me in the square, I must be swift in holding a briefing." Having to regain my attention the Chief raised his voice, "Focus man, and quickly assemble the Swords!"

Pulling away from my daze, I did as requested, and reported the arrival of the Crooks to my companions.

***

As we rode through the estate kitted out in heavy armour, the local people lined the paths to cheer us, offering their backing and blessings. The Governor led us to the market square, with Chenchi and I on one side and Lev and Fawkes on the other. Blair followed on foot, dressed in a black quilted jacket, armed, with her sword hanging neatly from her waist.

Boisterous voices could be heard from the Square. The joint gathering of Swords, townsfolk and guards had generated inspiration and excitement.

The twenty locals showed off their armour and weapons proudly to their families, yet behind their parading, fear and apprehension haunted their eyes. The Baron's guardsmen snubbed the volunteers and only spoke amongst each other. They stood pompously to one side, smartly dressed in claret tunics primed and protected by chain mail.

O'Hara looked masterful with his long handled, broad axe fastened across his back. The novice city Swords, Victor and Glan inspected each other. Like me, they were yet to experience a full scaled battle, and clearly struggled to contain their anxieties.

The Chief arrived on horseback, accompanied by Sergeant Mosely. They confidently entered the square, parading in glistening, heavy armour. Mosely was the only Sword to wear a great bassinet, but had unpinned his visor, displaying his beak like nose and moustache.

Flint and Amir followed, wearing their prestigious black Detector gambesons. Detector Flint rode towards me, before dismounting from his horse. "Is it true? No more than sixty Crooks have arrived?"

"Yes, but I will not be surprised if Hota has a scheme hidden behind the poor show," I replied.

"Indeed. Still, what Crook stands a chance against us Blue Swords?" said Flint.

Last to arrive was Baron Asher, alongside his advisor, Truda. Unarmed and unprepared for confrontation, his smart grey tunic indicated that he was not planning to fight. Lady Ivy followed, her shoulders covered by animal fur in the chilly morning air.

The Chief demanded silence, insisting we present ourselves before him. Manoeuvring his horse in front of us, he began issuing his battle orders. "Hear me! The ruffians that come for our blood stand on the other side of these walls. They have no army, just a wretched number of lawless and Godless men and women who need reminding of the values of democracy. I am your gold command, Baron Asher will act as silver and your Governor, bronze. If any of us are to fall, you will take leadership from the lesser. We will deploy in sections; Sergeant Mosely will direct half of the Baron's infantry to the ramparts and offer long range cover with their bows. The rest of us will meet the enemy head on. I will front the charge with my Swords. Being on horseback will give us the advantage and the opportunity to crush this rebellion swiftly. As for the citizens, you will be my infantry and join me on my signal."

The Chief looked back to the Baron, who was staring emptily at the ground. Muir coughed, gathering Asher's attention, indicating for him to deliver his speech of inspiration.

Uncomfortably, Asher peered down at the rows of people who were stood and prepared to fight for him and for the defence of Stanford. His voice was disjointed and muffled. "May I offer my gratitude in your willingness to fight the enemy that threatens us at our doors. May you be successful in the campaign to preserve this prominent town, that you are all privileged to reside in."

Chenchi tutted, turning to me and shaking his head in disbelief. Even our Chief was unable to disguise his annoyance at the Baron's woeful speech.

Lady Ivy steered her horse forward, disregarding her husband as she passed him by. Addressing us, she spoke with sincerity and clarification in a clear loud voice. "Local combatants of Stanford, you have stepped up in our time of need and for that I applaud you. With the spirit of our own fighters and the skill of the Blue Swords, we are most certainly going to be victorious. These Crooks have orchestrated trouble and despair in our town for too long, and now they come to our walls, intent on taking what is yours, and I say we do not let them in. We shall rise together and show them that it is the people of Stanford who shall decide their own fate. Many may fall on this day but be sure to remember that they will fall defending our own families and the principles that bind us together, that make us all equal. May God bless you all."

We roared on hearing the Baroness' words. The townsfolk who witnessed her address came alive, cheering and chanting her name. The applause became deafening and was sure to have been heard by the Crooks, sending an indication of our passion and determination to prevail.

The Baron glanced back at Truda, before frowning across at his wife. Lady Ivy remained in tune with her people, oblivious and careless of Asher's venomous expression towards her.

"Archers to the walls, the rest of you, with me!" yelled Chief Muir.

***

The gates gradually opened, allowing me to look out onto the field. Chief Muir led, pressing his horse forward, before halting and facing our enemy, with the Governor beside him. Eruk positioned himself on the left flank, behind our seniors, with me by his side. Chenchi was next to me, followed by Fawkes and Lev. Sword O'Hara placed himself on the right flank next to the two novice Swords, Victor and Glan.

Detectors Flint and Amir rode around our horizontal line, moving a few paces in between us and our leaders.

Lev called out, so all could hear. "What makes them so special? It amazes me that they even remembered which hole the sword fits into. They're far too pretty for battle."

Amir was not as humoured as the rest of us, and turned around to give Lev a rather severe look.

The brave townsfolk followed the Baron's guards on foot and staggered themselves behind our row of horses. Rye was stood at the front, his chest heaving and his breath panting. Meeting my eyes, he nodded back at me with his sword gripped firmly in his hand.

Hota sat mounted, a short distance ahead of his Crooks. He scanned his eyes across the lines of our defence, stopping when he noticed me. With his head positioned in my direction, we watched each other across the battlefield.

Deliberately I remained stern faced, unwilling to allow him to learn my true feelings of apprehension. Inside, my heart raced as if it was going to burst out from my chest, but I forced myself to display nothing but composure. I began thinking about the episodes of panic that had become frequent in my life recently, which made the thought of losing my self-control even more unbearable in this situation.

Chenchi observed me, well aware of the dread that lurked inside me. I felt the colour drain from my face as my head became light and my vision blurred. Arguing with myself, I attempted to dispel the feeling of trepidation, "For Stanford, the Baroness and for Fulten." I yelled at the top of my voice.

My outrageous cry caused my fellow Swords to give me a surprised look. But it worked. I had channelled the fear into rage and now felt ready to fight in the name of my late mentor.

Hota displayed a menacing grin and raised his father's sword in the air, before pointing its tip in my direction. Bellowing to his fellow Crooks, he began galloping towards our lines, followed by his roaring warriors.

"Hold!" shouted the Chief, with his fist clenched in the air.

Hota closed in, his eyes narrowed as he fixed his sight on me. With his mouth widened he growled, his father's sword still pointing towards me.

Spike became irritable, digging and stamping his front hooves into the ground. Once again Muir ordered us to hold. I yanked my sword free of its scabbard, squeezing the hilt, feeling the muscles tighten in my forearm.

Chenchi rumbled from the back of his throat, with his eyes

broadened and his teeth clenched. Flint had noticed Hota's intentions, and turned back to me, tilting his head, to ensure I was poised and ready to meet Hota's attack.

Now within seconds of combat, I steadied my breath, readying myself to meet my adversary on the battlefield. Waving his hand forward, Chief Muir yelled for our archers to release their arrows from the curtain walls. "Archers loose."

Arrows soared, hissing through the sky above our heads before plummeting down on to our enemy. Hota continued to charge forward, undeterred by the assault that flew from the ramparts. Members of the Crooks began falling to the ground, as the arrows penetrated their skin.

After a second round of arrows had been fired, Muir gave the order for us to engage.

Flint galloped around me, heading towards Hota with his weapon drawn. Their swords clashed together and as their blades collided, both growled, each showing their eagerness to dismount the other. Flint pulled back on his horse's reins, forcing Hota to engage him a second time. They stabbed towards one another, meeting each other's attack.

The Shadow Crooks had now reached our line and pressed us to meet their assault. My attention had been diverted away from Hota, and I found myself occupied by the relentless swarms of aggressive men and women. They hastily attacked, motivated by their hatred of our crest.

Chopping down my blade, I hacked away at the hurried Crooks; one after another they fell to the ground, instantly released in death from their heightened state. One of the more energetic Crooks caught me off guard. Charging at me from the rear, he gave away his intent with his howling voice.

Swinging his long-handled mace furiously, he narrowly missed Spike's neck. Steering my horse away, I put distance between us and the angered Crook. Regaining my composure, I squared up to the combatant, before digging my heel into Spike's sides.

Closing in on him, I leaned my torso out to the side and pulled back my sword. Lining up my opponent, we roared at each other, bracing for the impact of our weapons clashing together. At the last moment I tilted upright, giving myself an even higher advantage.

Swinging my blade, I sliced it through his neck, decapitating the Crook with one swipe. His head rolled away from his body, before he slumped to the ground, adding more blood to the reddening grass.

Fawkes and Lev were already in the centre of the horde of Crooks, chopping and cutting their way through our adversaries. On the far side of the fighting, I noticed Sword O'Hara dismounted and his horse laying on the ground, with a spear piercing its chest.

O'Hara circled around his enemies, sweeping his axe from above his head, carving away at the limbs of the Crooks who dared challenge him. He was in a rage and appeared in a berserker's daze as the blood of his foes sprayed onto his clothing.

The Governor continued to cover Chief Muir, as together, both our battle-hardened seniors made short work of the conflict that met them. Boasting their skill and abilities, they rapidly decreased our enemies' numbers.

Flint continued his gruelling exchange of blows with Hota. Dak emerged from the gathering of Shadow Crooks, his face covered in black dye and his shoulders bulging as he clenched one axe in either hand.

Intent on aiding his leader, Dak threw one of the axes towards Flint, which embedded in the rump of Flint's horse, causing it to rear. Flint was flung from the back of his horse, and his body was hurled to the ground. I yelled out, attempting to distract both Hota and Dak away from my floored companion.

Chenchi turned his attention to me on hearing my cry, following my line of sight to learn what had caused my outburst. Being closer to Flint, Chenchi charged his horse towards both the Crooks. Hota looked across, to see his burly former associate closing in on him, and quickly steered away his horse, retreating from the conflict.

"Coward," roared Chenchi, who was unknowingly being watched closely by Dak.

Jumping down from his horse, Chenchi swiftly lifted the wounded Detector, and placed him over his saddle.

"Get him to the Grand Hall," I bellowed to Chenchi, catching Dak's attention.

Dak narrowed his eyes, turning his interest to me. Leaning down, I pulled my sword free from the chest of a Crook I had just slain. Shaking his head, Dak gave me a disheartened look, disappointed at witnessing me killing and betraying his people.

Reluctantly, I rode Spike towards Dak, who turned away and continued to engage, slicing his axe into members of our own infantry.

Detector Amir appeared in my line of sight, charging on horseback, closing in on Dak. Spinning his body around, Dak managed to brace his axe and block the Detector's blow. Dak reacted speedily, and before Amir had a chance to bring his horse back around, Dak had released the axe from his hand, hurling it towards the Detector.

Amir's body jolted, before losing grip of his horse's reins as he tumbled to the ground. Revulsion struck me on realising that my hesitation in engaging Dak had cost the life of one of my own.

Dak withdrew his long sword from his back scabbard as I raced towards him, causing our blades to collide. His superior size and strength were enough to topple me from my saddle.

Winded from the fall, I was momentarily stunned before desperately looking around to locate Dak. He came towards me with fury, slamming his sword at me. I left it late to block his strike, twisting to one side, however it allowed me to get back up onto my feet. We circled, watching each other keenly, forgetting our previous niceties.

Making the first move, I lunged forward, slashing my sword towards him. Dak was quick to react and tilted his blade, effortlessly fending off my attack.

We struck at each other in a melee of blows, but Dak's magnitude gave him the upper hand. He scowled back at me, showing his intent to end my life. As he drove his sword downwards at my head, I met his strike. Grunting, he used all his weight to push his blade down towards my face.

I used every ounce of grit I could muster to keep his steel edge from carving into my skin. Knowing I had no chance of matching his power, I slipped backwards and promptly side stepped, placing one knee on the ground. Now with my head in line with his waist, I swung my heavy sword with both hands, slicing it through the backs of his legs, severing his hamstrings and separating his calves from the rest of his legs.

His cries lessened as his complexion became pale, from the blood that pulsed from his wounds. Hovering the tip of my sword over him, I plunged it downwards into his chest, abruptly ending his suffering.

Panting heavily, I looked around, noticing for the first time the bloodshed that now covered the battlefield. We had gained the advantage. Crooks began retreating to the woodlands, some being pursued by Fawkes, Lev and our seniors. But two Shadow Crooks had not given up on their fight and now stalked me, one on each side.

Leaping across at the one on my right, I drove my sword into his sternum, before pulling his body around while skewered on my blade. I used his torso to shield myself from his associate, and the second Crook hacked his axe inadvertently into to his companion's back.

Withdrawing my sword, I dodged around the men, positioning myself behind the second Crook. Thrusting forward my blade, it pierced his spine, severing it and causing his collapse.

Wiping the blood that soaked my hands on my trews, I heard a cheer come from our rear infantry. Rye stood before his fellow surviving men and women, shouting, with his sword raised high in the air.

The blood-stained grass was now home to countless men and women who lay squealing and calling for help, injured in the confrontation.

Victor knelt beside the corpse of his companion, Glan, who had sadly made the ultimate sacrifice. I rested my hand down on his shoulder, and he looked up at me through his tearful eyes.

"Do not weep for him, avenge him," I said.

O'Hara wandered the battlefield, swinging his axe down into any injured Crooks he could find. Chief Muir galloped back, analysing the aftermath of the fight. "Gather the wounded, I am satisfied."

Chenchi had returned and had already begun aiding our survivors back to the town. Spike ignored my calls and continued to graze on the patches of green grass. All were accounted for except Eruk who was nowhere to be seen. I nervously began inspecting the corpses, eager to locate him and ensure he had not been forgotten or missed.

Approaching Chenchi, I asked him if he knew of Eruk's fate.

Lev overheard my question and answered in a bitter tone, "The coward retreated, almost instantly. A legend, my arse."

Fawkes shoulder barged Lev in the back, "You have no idea of the man's suffering, and will do well to respect his past achievement."

Chenchi sniffed, "Do you smell that?"

Inhaling, I replied, "Smoke."

Fawkes's eyes widened as he stared back at the town. Black smoke was rising into the air from inside the walls.

An arrow soared down from the ramparts, triggering us to desperately seek where it had been released from. O'Hara turned, confronting us in disbelief, before the colour began to drain from his face. Opening his hand, he released the handle of his axe, dropping it onto the ground.

As he folded over from his waist, I saw the arrow which had embedded in his back. As we cried out and ran towards him, O'Hara fell over on to the grass, dead.

Fawkes pointed to the town. "To the walls."

Staring up at the curtain wall I saw Sheron, the Shadow Crook scout, standing above and watching us, with at least ten Crooks armed with bows. Sergeant Mosely was held squirming, and looked down on us in dismay. Hota had our Sergeant's arm grasped in one hand, and with his other hand, held a knife against Mosely's neck.

Slicing the edge of his blade across Mosely's throat, Hota caused the Sergeant to gasp, before his body was pushed over the long drop of the wall's edge, plummeting down onto the path leading to the gate.

A flurry of arrows rained down upon us from Hota's warriors.

"Shields!" yelled the Chief.

Sprinting towards Spike, I unhooked my shield from his saddle.

"Hurry, get to the gate, the gate," insisted Fawkes.

Arrows began hitting our infantry, forcing them to rush towards the wall, abandoning their horses. Dashing through the gate, the Governor watched in horror as more arrows struck the men and women who continued to struggle to make it inside the town's boundaries.

"Halt!" shouted the Governor, keen to use the overhead archway as cover. "The bastards have somehow infiltrated the town. Lev, Chenchi and Jep, you will come with me and take out their archers. The rest of you to the Square. Remain in formation, you are likely to meet hostility. May God be with us all."

23

RISE AND FALL

Racing up the spiralling, stone steps towards the platform on the ramparts, I took a momentary look back in the direction of the town. The smoke was being generated by the flames that now engulfed the lock up.

The Governor sprinted away from us, shouting at the archers, diverting their attention away from our ground infantry.

Fearless and consumed by rage, he charged at the men and women lining the wall, using his buckler shield to protect his body from arrows. The Governor attacked, exuding a sense of invincibility, showing no fear of death. Following our leader, Lev and I covered Chenchi with our shields, moving in a trilateral formation, closing in on our adversaries.

"Stay low," called Lev.

Looking over my shield, I scanned the platform in search of Hota. Unfortunately, he was nowhere to be seen and had surely left to carry out more of his planned tactics. Arrows struck our shields which covered our bodies, allowing Chenchi free use of his sword.

The Governor had reached the first bowman, chopping his blade mercilessly down onto the man's skull, before moving to the next one. Slicing open the stomach of another Crook, he carved through our opponents, with ease and ferocity.

We had closed in quickly, leaving the Crooks with no choice but to rely on their close-range weapons. Lev and I broke away, crossing a wooden beam, that placed us on the far side of the platform, allowing us to corner our enemies.

Sheron led two of her followers to meet both Lev and I. A scream from the far side of the platform caught all our attention. Chenchi had hold of a bowman by his arms and lifted him up, effortlessly throwing him over the curtain wall.

Lev had engaged Sheron, and they began striking at one another, equally matched and both delivering a combination of blows. I could see the Governor and Chenchi approaching out of the corner of my eye, but impatiently I began tackling the two Crooks who faced me.

Growling, I swung my sword, decapitating my first challenger. His associate stepped back, terrified at what he had witnessed. He cowered, desperately looking for an escape route. Thinking of O'Hara, I twisted my mouth angrily at the Crook, ready to avenge the fallen Sword. Struggling, the bowman's eyes widened as he stared down at the blade that protruded from his stomach. Chenchi had attacked from behind, thrusting his sword into the Crook's back, penetrating right through his torso. Wheezing, he slumped to the floor as Chenchi withdrew the long sword from his body.

Lev had been overcome by Sheron's abilities and she had gained the upper hand. Propped against the stone wall, Lev panted, struggling to catch his breath. Unarmed, he now watched as Sheron stalked closer towards him.

"Enough," I called, catching her attention.

Sheron glanced between me and my companions, aware that she was outnumbered and there was no hope of achieving escape. She looked back at Lev, her eyes filled with hatred.

"He is not the same," I called, referring to the Sword that had abused her in the past.

A tear ran down her cheek and she peered back at me. I urged her to drop her weapon, understanding her inner argument of whether or not to take Lev's life.

"Come with us, I swear I will make sure no harm will ever come to you. I will show you that we are not all the same," I pleaded.

Sheron released her grip of the sword in her hand, allowing it to clatter onto the ground. Turning around, she stared back towards the Square, witnessing the carnage and mayhem that was unfolding.

Sheron looked down at the offer of my hand, before clenching her lips together.

"Never forget who you are, act with principle and offer everyone dignity," she said.

Sheron sprinted towards Lev, causing him to flinch, before leaping onto the stone wall and jumping off its edge.

Firmly shutting my eyes, I groaned, attempting to drown out the sound of her body impacting the ground.

"Come, we are needed in the Square," said the Governor.

Dropping my shield, I squeezed both my hands tightly around my long sword and took in a steady breath. I felt even more determined to fight and give Hota his death.

***

The chaotic scenes that had taken place outside our walls now continued in the Square. Our infantry was vastly outnumbered and was struggling to overcome the surprising number of Crooks who had found their way into the town. It disturbed me to see all the bloodied men and women crawling on the ground, desperately attempting to escape from the slaughter. The Chief gallantly slashed away at their warriors, but their numbers continued to grow.

Fawkes had encountered his own adversary, a man who equalled his expertise in combat. Eruk had revealed his true motive and now circled our most able swordsman. The former Blue Sword had unmasked his true allegiance and expressed his intent by vigorously lashing out his blade towards Fawkes in this standoff between the two dexterous fighters.

The Governor observed his old acquaintance's treachery and deceit. Grimacing, he led us into the battle, ordering our charge upon the Square. Death was almost certain, but still we attacked our enemies, slashing away at their flesh, ensuring we took as many as we could with us to the afterlife.

Rye still stood, heroically holding his own against the invaders and refusing to cower away. Witnessing the bravery displayed by our people, who continued to fight relentlessly in our quest to overcome these vile savages, gave me a sudden outpouring of wrath. I became overcome with emotion, which gave me the feeling of invincibility, as I thrashed my blade towards any Crook in range, feeling their blood splash onto my face and splatter on my chest plate. Finally, I had become liberated, amongst the terrors of war.

On the brink of defeat, blood dripping from the edges of our swords, Lev glided through our enemies beside me. Neatly and effortlessly, he ploughed his steel into the bodies of whoever dared challenge him.

On the far side of the market square, Fawkes battled persistently with Eruk, the veteran Sword. Fawkes retained ownership of the fight, whilst at the same time seeing away more Crooks who raced forward to aid their companion.

Dread plagued Eruk's eyes. He knew too well that Fawkes' sword skills had been revealed to clearly outmatch his own during their gruelling combat. Crashing down his sword repeatedly and furiously upon the traitor, Fawkes forced Eruk down on one knee.

Fawkes lined up his finishing blow, lifting his sword above his head, sealing the conspirator's fate. But before he had chance to drive down his blade, our heroic Sword shuddered as steel burst from out of his chest. Clenching his teeth, Fawkes stared down at the blade piercing his chest. Raising his eyebrows, he grunted as blood trickled from the corner of his mouth.

Lev let out an almighty cry, whilst sprinting to assist his old friend. The sword was hastily withdrawn from Fawkes' body, leaving him to collapse to his knees. Dazed, his eyes wandered, taking an empty look at the spilled blood that stained the cobbles, resulting in death and anguish all around. Gasping, he attempted to catch his breath, before slumping to his side in death.

Hota hovered over our fallen companion. He glared back at me proudly, holding out his father's blade, tarnished with the blood of the most courageous Sword known to our lands. His chilling smile loaded with cunning malice reminded me of the manner in which he had killed Sword Fulten.

Lev frantically charged towards him, overcome by fury. Hota strode back, concealing himself amongst the crowd of fighters behind him. Once again, he had initiated devastation and evaded the consequences. He had toyed with us, and in doing so, achieved his aim of eradicating more members of the Blue Swords.

While we were distracted by Fawkes' slaying, Eruk had gathered his composure and regained his dropped weapon. Standing poised, he eagerly awaited Lev's heedless engagement. The Governor emerged and rushed towards his previous associate, driving his shield into Eruk's shoulder, knocking him back down to the ground. Standing over the stunned veteran Sword, the Governor firmly raised his upper lip, staring down at the incapacitated traitor.

Pressing the tip of his blade into Eruk's sternum, he leaned down on to his sword slowly, ensuring that the turncoat felt the sharp coldness of his steel slowly sliding into his chest. Eruk retched, before tilting his head and peering up at the Governor. His eyes expanded as he took a final look back down at the sword plunging deeper into his body.

The Governor spat on the corpse of the once noble Sword, who had gone on to dishonour our crest. Lev gathered Fawkes' sword and placed it gently upon his torso. Sombrely, he gazed down at our fallen companion, showing despondency. The sight of Lev's misery confirmed my fears, that all hope of victory was lost.

The end felt close now; cries echoed around the Square from the maimed men and women who had fought so valiantly in our bid to defend Stanford. It was now a slaughter, with the Crooks confidently regathering their formation. All that remained of our defence was a handful of downtrodden townsfolk and a dwindling group of Swords.

Chief Muir inspected the devastation with a cold and barren stare. Tipping back his head, he drew in a deep breath. Looking back at his remaining Swords, he squeezed his lips together and then relayed his final orders. "Regroup! Let us give these Godless heathens a final dance."

We were destined for defeat, but in the true nature of the Blue Swords, we would rise together and fall together. Looking between each other, we lined the edge of the square, Chenchi, Lev, Victor and I. Rye still stood, leading the small remainder of surviving locals.

Chief Muir turned to our Governor and bowed his head, elegantly. Letting out an almighty battle cry, we raised our weapons in the air, venting our ire and offering our enemy one final and deadly clash.

Charging forward into the square for the last time, we engaged the Shadow Crooks. Impelled by pride, we stood our ground and were accepting of a glorious death.

Our swords collided and our foes began to feel the repercussions of their uninvited arrival. Pushed by determination, our grit ensured the death of many of their infantry.

The cobbles rumbled, caused by the sound of fast approaching hooves that pounded the ground. The thunderous noise temporarily brought a halt to the fight, diverting everyone's attention to the path that led towards the Square. Blurry eyed, I twisted around to observe who rode upon us.

Seiloff, the Baron's guardsman, watched back, enraged, scanning his eyes over the bloodbath that met him. With at least thirty of the Baron's guards mounted behind him, and swords drawn at the ready, an eerie silence overcame the Square. Their apparent hesitation to engage in battle caused my heart to beat heavily.

However, moments later Seiloff yelled, readying his men, before closing the visor of his helmet and pointing his blade in the direction of the Crooks. Rushing towards us, Seiloff began chopping his sword down upon any rallying Crook he could reach. His infantry followed, pouring on to the cobbles and slaying our invaders.

The balance of power had changed, and we watched, catching our breath, as Crooks fled from the battle. Some panicked and sprinted in the direction of the gate, only to meet Seiloff's forces. The Governor bellowed, bringing our attention to a handful of Crooks fleeing onto Main Street. "Jep, Chenchi, with me."

***

We sped after the absconding Crooks, who ran towards the Grand Hall. Closing in on our adversaries, they suddenly veered away from the hall, dispersed at the riverbank and began leaping into the river that flowed adjacent to the Baron's estate.

"Halt," demanded the Governor, "they are cornered."

We strode alongside the riverbank, observing the panic in their faces at our presence.

Chenchi pointed to the raised portcullis. "In all my time in this town, that gate has never been opened, yet now it aids their escape. Jep, get me some arrows."

"It is too late, their remaining numbers offer us little threat," said the Governor.

The fleeing Crooks allowed the river's current to flush them out through the elevated portcullis.

"Eruk," muttered the Governor, realising why the portcullis was open.

Catching sight of the Grand Hall, I was eager to check on Lady Ivy and make certain she and all in the Hall were safe. Chenchi also informed us that Flint had been carried there to have his wounds examined by the surgeon. The Governor insisted that we return to the Square and confirm our victory with the Chief.

***

The screams reverberated around the Market Place. The once grey cobbles now flowed with blood that ran through the rutted ground. The only Crooks to remain were incapacitated, and clutched at their wounds, anticipating imminent execution.

The townsfolk had suffered a great loss. Loved ones sobbed, attending to the bodies of their fallen family members that lay strewn throughout the Square. Lev knelt beside Fawkes's corpse, weeping at the loss of our brother Sword. To see our normally good-humoured companion in such a state of anguish amplified the loss we had suffered. My heart wept for Blair and the thought of her learning of her adoptive father's fate.

The Governor wandered towards Lev, gently resting his hand on his shoulder. It was the first time any of us had witnessed a tear fall from our irascible leader's eyes.

Reaching out, I gently took hold of Rye's arm, startling him. "You fought well today. Your valour will be taken into consideration at the trials."

Rye glared back at me through his bloodshot eyes, before nodding his head and leaning closer to embrace me. I gripped the back of his head, holding him tightly. It was our first battle, and one that would live with us for the rest of our lives.

"I need you to assist Lev in taking Fawkes to the church," I asked of him gently.

Rye looked back at me, puzzled. "Why not the lock up?"

I nudged my head, indicating the smoke still rising from the other side of the estate. "I fear the lock up will require much restoration."

Seiloff strutted towards us, engaging in a debrief with Chief Muir.

The Chief began to immediately discuss the town's recovery from the battle, whilst Chenchi approached Seiloff, prompting them to meet one another with a firm arm grip.

"It is not often I am pleased to see you, Seiloff," smiled Chenchi.

"And it is not the first time I have had to save you." Looking to me, Seiloff smiled and offered out his hand. "Take it as a sign of goodwill."

I accepted his greeting before Chief Muir interrupted. "What a welcome this is for our new Bishop, his services will be very much needed."

Seiloff raised his eyebrows, "Bishop, Sir?"

"You heard me, man, the Bishop whom you were directed to escort back to the town."

Seiloff looked between us, appearing bewildered and nervous at answering the Chief. "Sir, we have not been tasked with chaperoning anyone, Baron Asher sent us out on reconnoitring duties in the wilderness. He was keen for us to test ourselves under the last few winter skies."

The Chief closed his eyes and sighed before giving me a swift and knowing look.

"He knew his infantry would be at a reduced capacity," grumbled Chenchi.

Chief Muir raised his hand. "Let us not act in haste, we are Swords; it is vital that we digest the information before we act upon it."

Anger sparked inside me, triggering me to stare back at the Chief with ill-contained fury. Stepping away from my companions, I began making my way towards Main Street, with nothing on my mind but retribution.

"Stand down, Jep, do not be foolish," ordered Chief Muir, only to be harshly silenced by our Governor. "We are past your orders of appeasement now, Chief. Come, Chenchi, let us join Jep and put an end to this treachery for good."

24

TRIALS AND TRIBULATION

With blood tarnishing my chest plate and dirt coating my skin, I walked towards the Grand Hall, consumed by wrath. Everything had fallen into place and now swirled around in my mind. It was time to end this once and for all; the lies, the deception and the murder.

Local people parted ways for me, seeing that I was in a state of rage. Crossing the bridge to the courtyard, I looked back to see Chenchi and the Governor moving towards me, both equally vexed. Chief Muir followed closely behind, walking briskly and unable to drop his uneasy expression.

The guard at the gate initially challenged my arrival, only to be stood down by Seiloff, who had also arrived seeking answers.

"What are you going to do?" asked Chenchi.

Twisting my mouth, I looked at the Grand Hall. "I will seek justice for all those who have died today."

Kicking my foot into the dining hall door, I startled the affluent townsmen and women who had hidden away from the fight and instead cowered within the comfort of the Baron's residence. The Baron stood from his chair, concerned by my contentious arrival. "We are victorious. Now is not the time to dwell on our ongoing resentments."

I scanned around the room, showing my disgust towards the

wealthy and privileged who had refused to engage in battle. Asher peered behind me, relieved to see the Chief and Seiloff entering the hall.

Approaching the base of his podium, I walked with slow yet heavy feet up the steps to face him.

Lady Ivy called from the far end of the alter, attempting to question the reasons behind my angry demeanour. "Jep, what is it you have learnt?"

Unintentionally, I looked over to her through sunken, battle hardened eyes.

Asher raised his hands, grinning reassuringly at his guests. "This man is feeling the effects of war, so I will excuse his insolence on this occasion."

I tightly grabbed hold of a chunk of his hair, prompting gasps from the onlookers who witnessed their ruler squirming at my hand. Plunging my fist into his face, I felt his nose crack.

The Baron stumbled back against his chair, clutching his bloodied and misshapen nose. He peered up at me, his complexion turning pale, before ordering his head guard to intervene.

Seiloff shook his head, and remained beside Chenchi.

Asher spat out the blood that leaked down into his mouth. "I will have your head, you wretched boy. Guards! Guards!"

Seiloff raised his hand, ensuring that the two guards who appeared from the side door stood down.

"Tell them, tell them what you have done," I cried.

Baroness Ivy walked closer, glancing between me and her husband in confusion.

Baron Asher paused, witnessing the bewildered faces that watched us, and eagerly awaited his clarification.

He shook his head, irritably coming to terms with my revealing announcement of his treachery. "What did you expect? You and your Swords, undermining me at every chance. How was I expected to rule? Your Governor refused to align himself to me, your Chief meddling in our affairs."

I took a step back, allowing him to stand to his feet. "But why Hota? Why associate yourself with the very person who had planned to overthrow you?"

Asher stared at me hatefully, before answering, "because he swore to get rid of you and your grating brotherhood. You have all been an ache in my gut for years, vermin that could not be culled. As for you, I offered you refuge, and in return you fornicate with my wife. Hota promised me retribution and control, all without encroaching on my rule."

Keen to see the reaction from the room, I looked for Truda, to observe her response to the exposed plot. Discovering she was not present, I continued to publicly interrogate the Baron. "It was Eruk who opened the river gate for the Crooks, on the orders of Truda, your so-called advisor."

Asher smirked, whilst deliriously gazing up at the ceiling within the hall. "She was a breath of unfouled air. Women have their ways of making a man believe in ambition well beyond their capabilities."

"So, it was Truda who orchestrated your betrayal?"

"I am no woman's puppet," he barked, "Truda arrived with an agenda, and that was to unite our town with the Crooks."

"It was Truda who murdered the Cavaliers?" I asked.

The Baron perched against his throne and began chuckling hysterically, before bitterly speaking through his gritted teeth. "You fool, it was I who had them murdered and I had every right; their secrecy and whispers were not only treacherous, but also corrupting my town. Having the expertise of a veteran Blue Sword at my disposal, hanging a priest and hacking open your Sergeant's throat was a simple task."

I raised my voice, so all could hear my claim. "You accuse them of treason, yet you offered them no trial. It was Eruk who murdered Hock, that night in the dungeon."

Asher paused, taking a moment to observe the expressions of shock that looked back at him. "As I said, their conspiring was treacherous. Blue Sword or not, his death was needed to re-establish order."

Lady Ivy approached her husband, "What about my father?"

"Nature took your father, but learning that Jep was the last to see him alive and was witnessed aiding him to his bed by one of my guards, his arrest was necessary."

"Guards don't patrol those chambers, you had him murdered," I replied.

"Jep speaks the truth. It was I who agreed to set him up and relayed my evidence to the Chief. I wanted him to pay for the way in which he killed Ricard, I had no idea that the Baron conspired with Hota," announced Seiloff.

Heckles began to echo throughout the room, calling for the Baron's imprisonment. Asher stared back at his people, flustered before pleading bitterly, "I am your ruler, I demand order."

Looking at the Chief for reassurance, he was met with silence. Asher began hissing back at the crowd.

Lady Ivy moved closer towards him. "Did you order my father's death?"

The Baron tilted his head forward and leered at his wife, "You were occupied entertaining the peasant. My only regret is that he died so peacefully." Asher turned his attention back to me. "You should have accepted Hota's offer, for your fate will follow my own."

"His offer was to allow me to kill you," I replied.

"Well, then it appears we have both been deceived."

The doors behind the guards opened and Isa entered the dining hall, with her arm around Blair's waist. Blair cast her eyes around the room, in search of Fawkes, which triggered me to act.

I slid my blade loose from its scabbard, eliciting an influx of gasps from the audience behind me. Asher guffawed ecstatically, displaying evidence of his maddened condition.

"He will be tried and punished accordingly," bellowed the Chief.

Looking across to Blair, I understood the devastating news that I was about to tell her. Holding out my blood-stained sword to my side, I began panting heavily, the sour memories this man had inflicted upon me rushing to the forefront of my mind. They all tracked back to the woman I loved, and the pain and suffering he had visited upon Lady Ivy. It was no longer tolerable to endure his wickedness.

My mind was satisfied with the justification and accepting of the consequences. He had as much of a part to play in this tragedy as Hota. Spurred on by hatred, he had allowed himself to become guided by greed and a lust for control. This man had orchestrated the killing of people most dear to me. Now it was his turn to suffer, and my turn to bask in the fulfilment of revenge.

Drawing back my sword, I stared at the Baron unforgivingly, readying myself to thrust my steel into his heart. He refused to look away and growled back at me, ensuring that his expression would remain imprinted in my memories.

Asher suddenly jolted and began gasping for breath, before staring blankly at the floor. He shook for a second time and stumbled forward, wheezing as he tried to steady himself. Stunned, he turned his body around, displaying a puncture wound in his back that was leaking blood.

Dropping to one knee, the Baron reached out, attempting to stabilise himself by clutching on to his attacker. Lady Ivy stared down at him, furious and unforgiving. She watched as her husband met her eyes, in desolation. It was now Asher who was made to kneel before his wife.

Slumping on his side, the Baron rolled on to the ground with Lady Ivy now standing over him, holding the blood-stained knife that had finally given her revenge for all the suffering he had subjected her to. Asher laid open eyed and dead, slain at the hands of the person he had tormented and intimidated for far too long.

Voices muttered and whispered throughout the Great Hall. I looked at the Chief, who appeared aghast by the events. The Governor strolled up to the altar, poised and uncompromised. He took the knife from Lady Ivy's hand and looked down at Asher's corpse.

Addressing the townsfolk, he demanded silence. "Asher is dead; however, I fear his name will forever plague this town. He has been appropriately punished for his confession of conspiring to murder and committing treason against the Crown. You will be our jury; do I hear any objections in this implementation?"

Met by stillness, the Governor turned to our Chief. "Sir, it is custom that the offspring of the ruler should succeed. As the Baron has none, the Baroness will be obliged to take on the duty."

Chief Muir looked around the room, witnessing the reaction and lack of objection from the local people. "You will hear no dispute from me. The Crown must be made aware of the way in which circumstances have proceeded here, so until you have received their confirmation and blessing, this will only be a provisional solution."

***

The spectators aligned themselves before the altar, thrilled to show their dedication to their latest potentate. Lady Ivy gazed back at me, showing her overwhelming emotions, through teary eyes. I bowed my head, offering my allegiance to our new Baroness.

The commotion and excitement in the hall intensified as more people arrived to celebrate the change in power. The transition would be simple; the people adored Lady Ivy and loathed the oppressor that was Baron Asher. With the townsfolk behind her and with the endorsement of the Blue Swords, Lady Ivy was certain to reign with honour.

Her story would be spoken throughout the years to come. She had rebelled against a life of brutality and coercion and with the blessing of the Crown, she would provide Stanford with democracy and stamp out the corruption that had overshadowed the town for too long.

The Governor pointed to the door, giving us the perfect opportunity to leave unnoticed. I approached Seiloff and gave him a stern glare, before reaching out my arm to embrace him for a second time.

"It seems we have better times ahead. Lady Ivy has my oath, and I will guard her with my life," pledged Seiloff.

I nodded my head in thanks, before staggering away, my vision hazy and my body exhausted. Momentarily things appeared serene and at peace, but there was still the dead to bury and a town to rebuild from the devastation that would haunt us all for some time to come.

***

I went to the guards' barracks when I learned that Flint was resting there after being examined by the town surgeon. The beds were all occupied by brave men and women who had valiantly fought against our invaders.

My boots squelched in the puddles of blood that soaked the floor of the barracks. Groaning came from the wounded, some of whom had cloth wrapped around their severed limbs. The stench of blood and guts made me want to retch. Staring between the beds, I began muttering prayers, horrified by the sight of such suffering.

Flint was on a bed towards the back of the room, sat upright displaying a half-hearted grin. As I stood over him, he exhaled before gazing up at the ceiling. "Once again that serpent leaves us mourning our fellow Swords."

I mirrored his sombre expression. "We have paid a heavy price for victory."

Flint turned his head, observing the maimed woman that lay beside him on the next bed, before speaking. "The Baroness murdered her husband; it is not often you hear of such a justified murder. The town will see a significant change, the question is do you see yourself as part of that change, Jep?"

"That is something I no longer know, nor can answer."

"Your name has been cleared, and my offer of a scholarship still stands. Return to the city with me, become a Detector and allow Alma to open your eyes."

Placing my hand on his shoulder, I insisted he should rest, without giving him an answer.

***

The young gate keeper approached me outside the barrack doors. Dragging his feet, he walked with his shoulders slouched.

"Where is she?" I asked.

Markus pointed to the river on the other side of the gate. "Blair is distraught, I have never seen her like this. She told me to leave her be."

"Blair will need you now more than ever, she has suffered a tragic loss, we all have. Give her time to mourn."

Leaving the gates to the Grand Hall, I wandered over to the riverbank. Blair was sat amongst the long grass hugging her knees. Isa remained a few paces behind her, weeping, whilst she observed her grieving daughter.

Seeing me approach, Isa glanced at me in despair. A lump lingered in my throat and my eyes became tear filled. Reaching out, I hugged her, holding the back of her hair and kissing the crown of her head.

Blair turned around, squinting at me. Isa pulled away, advising me to be delicate with her daughter. I stood behind Blair and she returned her sight to the river, silently watching the flowing water separating between the rocks.

"Without Fawkes, we would not have prevailed," I whispered.

"Without you, he would still be here."

Reaching down to embrace her, Blair pushed away my hand and leapt to her feet to face me. "It is always you who survives to tell the tale, yet it is your actions and behaviour that has led to all this."

I gulped and my heart thumped at seeing her resentment. "I had no control over Hota's intentions."

"Since you arrived, what have you brought? Nothing but pain and death. Fulten, Hock and now Fawkes. The one person who has ever treated me as an equal, believed in me, and now he is gone. Hota's blade has always been intended for you, yet once again you manage to dodge the fight. You're a coward and have no right to share the Sword's crest."

Blair dashed away, tears streaming down her face. I called out to her, but was silenced by Isa who shook her head, insisting that I gave her time. I stared back at the smoke that filtered into the air from the lock up. The blackness of the fumes matched the vile taste in my mouth.

***

Blair's misery reflected the tragedy that lingered throughout the town. However, the new Baroness was not shy of greeting her people and getting her hands dirty. Her presence in the Market Place over the following days was gratefully received.

The arrival of the new priest, Father Alek, gave the grieving families hope. The church had been restored, and even though Father Arrend was never far from our thoughts, the youthful priest brought a sense of rejuvenation to the town.

Things had begun to settle as the spring days took hold. Blair had remained distant, not only from me, but she had also dissociated herself from the rest of the Swords. She refused to serve under her mother and wait on us at the Grand Hall.

The Governor rightfully turned a blind eye to her dereliction of duties, for Blair was still seen as a servant girl, although we all knew that she had earned the right to decide her own destiny. I would often consult with Markus to ensure that she was safe, and he would inform me of her time spent hunting on the Baroness' grounds.

Lady Ivy ordered that memorial stones were to head the graves of all the fallen, regardless of their standing in society. Some of the more advantaged residents turned their nose up at the thought, however it was the Baroness' first step in narrowing the divide between the classes in Stanford. She wanted the brave remembered, and refused to allow their families to bury them beyond the town limits.

***

The final day of processions had been left for my companions. A buzzard soared through the blue skies above the rubble that marked where our lock up had once stood. The fire had been relentless; the flames had roared through its main structure, leaving only our living quarters and the dungeon standing.

Staring at its wreckage, Chenchi called to me, advising it was time to pay our respects. Abiding by our traditions, each fallen Sword had been lined up outside the front of the lock up, in individual wagons, awaiting their final journey to the church.

Five white horses stood, each harnessed to a wagon. Their yokes had been wrapped in woven leaves and the wagons decorated in garlands. The flower arrangements had been prepared on the advice of our new priest, Father Alek.

Amir was in the far-left hand cart with Flint seated on his horse, riding next to the late Detector. Flint had dressed himself in a white doublet, honouring the customs of his dead associate. Next to Detector Amir, O'Hara was laid in the second wagon, his vast size taking up most the cart.

Sword Fawkes rested in the middle, with his great helm propped up against his shoulder. Lev positioned himself behind the wagon, sitting on his horse, staring sombrely at our friend.

Sergeant Mosely was in the fourth cart, his body covered neatly by petals. Mosely had shown me little kindness in the past, but he died doing his duty and deserved my respect. Sword Glan was on the far right, with the Governor positioned next to his cart.

Father Alek appeared, dressed in a black robe. Well-groomed and clean shaven, the blond-haired priest was not much older than I. Chenchi and Victor stood beside me, all three of us on foot behind Lev.

As the hearses made their way towards the square, local people lined the streets of the estates, weeping and muttering prayers as we passed by. Turning my head around, I looked at Blair and Isa who walked closely behind us. Isa was dressed in a faded black gown. Consumed by grief, she remained with her head bowed, gazing down at the ground. Blair stared straight ahead, stern faced, wearing a black doublet and grey trousers. She firmly and proudly gripped the hilt of Fawkes' sword that she had attached to her leather belt.

Once in the Square, the procession came to a halt. Flint nodded at the Chief and diverted away towards Main Street following Amir's wagon.

"Why does he leave?" asked Sword Victor.

"Detector Amir will be cremated, and his ashes offered to the river. Amir will meet the others in the afterlife, he is just taking a different path," I replied.

The Chief had insisted that all Swords were to accompany him to the altar and address the congregation together. I gave Lady Ivy a swift glance as we made our way down the nave. She had refused to be seated away from the rest of the townsfolk. Wearing a grey satin dress and displaying a glimmering silver necklace, she glowed and had changed in her demeanour. No longer was Lady Ivy shadowed by her husband, she now appeared self-assured as the newly appointed figurehead of Stanford.

The Governor stood before the local people, raising his hand to request silence throughout the church. "The bodies of our Swords lay to rest outside this hall, but their legacy will live on within our walls. They led the charge and bled for our town, for you. Loath them or admire them, they fought so you could remain free. For those amongst you that mutter and gossip about prosperity under the ownership of our enemy, who claims he fights for freedom, I say you are nothing but fools. For too long has this town been plagued by injustice and tyranny. The Crooks who howled at our doors wanted to add to that oppression. It was my Swords who challenged them head on and gave their lives for your tranquillity. A new beginning dawns before us, and the way has been carved by the men who we are about to put into the ground, may they live on in our songs."

The Chief observed the anxious reaction from the congregation and stepped up, lightening the mood with a tribute to our newly instated Baroness. "Amongst the dark, shines light. May Baroness Ivy reign with fortune and devotion."

As the people applauded and showed their respects, I observed Blair, who was seated at the far end of the front pew. Frowning, she stared straight ahead, refusing to react. The implacable look in her eye was hateful. Blair could picture only one thing, and that was retribution.

25

THE SWORD AND THE CROOK

The dead had been buried and the streets cleansed. With the new season came a revitalised town. The people continued to work together, avoiding tiresome and unnecessary disputes. Even the nightly disorder had diminished, and there was a sense of unification throughout Stanford. Unfortunately, time's natural way of healing would not last forever and once the fallen had been forgotten and the weapons stored away, the problematic individuals would soon venture back out and subject the town to further tension.

The Chief had waited for reinforcements before returning to the city. He claimed that his extended visit was to ensure the town had sufficient Swords to deter a secondary attack from the Shadow Crooks, but we all knew that he was keen to observe Lady Ivy in her new title role. Detector Flint had also offered his services in restoring the town and lightened our burdens by picking up his own share of patrols. Flint had volunteered to help out until the next recruitment of Blue Swords.

The Blue Sword trials were on the horizon and I had nominated Rye to attend. Carre did not take kindly to me attempting to poach his most competent farm hand, but nevertheless, with some persuasion from Dam, he soon backed down.

Carre was able to talk again, though his speech remained disjointed and slurred. But he was pleased to be able to get his arguments across once more. With the aid of a stick, Carre was back to performing his duties on the farm.

In the days that followed Fawkes' burial, Lady Ivy had kept her distance from me. On the occasions when our paths had crossed within the grounds of the Grand Hall, our meetings were somewhat blunt and fleeting.

Though my feelings for the Baroness had not changed, I understood that her priorities had very much altered. Her commitment to the people came first and I had come to terms with the fact that our previous ambitions were no more than reminiscence and a missed opportunity.

***

The storm illuminated the sky and the rain hammered down on top of the barracks. The fire pit roared in the centre of the room, giving us a place to congregate. The mead flowed that evening and Lev indulged us with past stories of Fawkes' mishaps. "He would place the face of the shield into the snow, perch himself on his knees and ride down the hill. Once, he gained so much momentum that he ploughed straight into Carre's gate. The belligerent farmer went bonkers, especially waking up to find a dishevelled Blue Sword, arse up in his field."

"I just couldn't see Fawkes engaging in such a recreational act. He was always so mysterious and well, severe," said Flint.

Lev smiled. "It was all a façade. Fawkes was a puppy deep down. He loved nothing more than to wind up Hock in his younger days."

The door banged open unexpectedly and Chenchi entered, soaked from the rain.

He approached us frantically, and we all looked back at him, startled by his theatrical entrance. "Jep, you must come to the Great Hall at once."

Lev and Flint followed my reaction and stood from their stools.

"Not you two, just Jep," insisted Chenchi.

I anxiously followed Chenchi to the Great Hall, demanding to know what was going on and what troubled him so much.

Panting, he looked back at me, unable to meet my eyes. "You need to see for yourself, be assured this is no trick."

Opening the door, I raced into the hall to see one of the banquet tables prepared and covered with food and beverages. Baroness Ivy faced me, sitting at the end of the table. On seeing me enter, she stood from her chair, giving me a nervous stare.

Leaning my head around the pillar that blocked my vision from the rest of the diners, I felt thrilled to see my old friend, Gibbon. Behind him, seated on the opposite side of the table were my sister Emil, and her partner Abbot.

Emil watched me in silence, her skin pale, and her gaze numb. Like Gibbon her face was marked and swollen. Seeing the rest of the benches empty, I frowned, asking for the whereabouts of our mother. Emil dropped her forehead into the palms of her hands and began sobbing, prompting Abbot to wrap his arm around her, keen to show my sister comfort.

Gibbon towered over me, reaching out his hand, however I rejected his embrace and again ordered to know my mother's fate.

"Somerby was attacked," said Gibbon.

"And it pleases me to see that you have managed to escape, but where is my mother?"

"Your mother is being held at Hota's mercy," intervened Baroness Ivy.

My heart pounded and my stomach began to churn. I paused, flicking my sight down to the ground, whilst pondering on what I had been told.

"They came at night, catching us all by surprise with fire in their hands. Skinner and his band of pitiful guards didn't stand a chance, it was us villagers who saw off as many as we could. I went back for her, I swear, but the village was abandoned, with nothing but embers drifting in the air."

Clenching my teeth together, I began breathing vigorously through my nose to gain control before strutting towards the door.

"This is what he wants Jep, he is luring you back," called Baroness Ivy.

Turning around I growled, "Tell me, my Lady, should I patiently wait here and pray that she appears? You may have your happy ending, but I am far from mine."

"Easy brother," said Chenchi.

I looked over to my saddened sister. "Chenchi, care for them, ensure that they are provided for."

"I am coming with you," he replied.

"No, not this time. He will be expecting that. I go alone; I started this and now it is time I end it for good, too many have given their lives for my feud."

"He will kill you," cried out Baroness Ivy.

"At least then this will all be over."

I marched purposefully to the stables, ignoring Lady Ivy's request to sit down and think rationally.

As I guided Spike from the stables, Baroness Ivy followed me with Chenchi, still pleading with me to settle and consider my strategy. But rage had clouded my mind, I visualised my mother at his mercy, Fulten murdered by his arrow, and Blair's disappointment in my lack of nobility.

Lev and Flint raced to the stables, to investigate the commotion.

On learning my intentions, Flint pulled at Spike's reins. "You do not think clearly, you are motivated only by hatred and vengeance and that will get you killed."

"Let him go," called the Governor from across the courtyard, "Jep knows what is required."

"Well then we all go," demanded Flint.

"No, if this is a ploy, I am not willing to weaken our defences. If Jep wishes to obtain retribution, he will do so alone."

Lev took hold of Flint's arm. "How can we know whether Hota will be waiting for us to ride out, so he can swoop in on the town?"

Sullenly Flint nodded his head, knowing too well Hota's previous scheming.

I looked over to the Grand Hall entrance, taking a final view of Emil, Gibbon and Abbot, before digging my heels into Spike's sides and riding out of the courtyard. As I crossed the bridge into town, Blair sat on the edge of the stone wall, overlooking the river.

"Maybe now you will end this for good," she said.

"If I do, will you stop stalking these walls like a ghost and fulfil your ambitions?"

Sniggering, Blair looked away, dismissively placing her cloak over her head.

***

I hastily left Stanford under a night sky, energised by the downpour of rain. I stopped only to rest and refused to conceal myself away from the main path. Pressing Spike to exhaustion, his hoofs churned the soggy ground, flicking mud on to my back.

After crossing the great river that divided the north and the south, I knew I was only a day's ride away from Somerby. My mind grew heavier, filling with resentment and ferocity.

***

The dusk sky was blackened by bleak, grey clouds that hovered over my home. Somerby was in sight, and taking a final sip of water from my bota, I examined my village from a distance. At no point had I considered a plan; my vengeful thoughts had drowned out any idea of practicality.

The animosity that had fuelled our ongoing quarrel had now amplified. We had both taken the lives of one another's mentors, yet I was now energised by a darker bitterness, a resentment and lust for retaliation that lined the pit of my stomach.

The stench of smoke still lingered in the air, and my home was now nothing more than black debris, overshadowed by death. Hota had caused me the kind of pain that I never knew existed until now. I had fallen for his wicked ploys for a second time and now left myself open to my own demise, once again.

This would be the final chapter in our conflict and only one of us would survive to speak its tale. I had learnt the truth of justice the hard way, and now I was not here to offer him a trial, I was here to provide him with judgement and avenge my fallen brothers who had died defending the crest of the Blue Swords.

The horror that met me was unbearable to witness. Villagers I had known since childhood now stared back at me, impaled on stakes, lining the border of Somerby.

The slums were now ash, my home nothing more than black ruins that blended in with other burnt down huts. Bodies of all ages cluttered the ground; there had been no mercy offered here.

As I looked upon the massacre that was now all that remained of my home, I felt guilt and desperation. It was me who had brought this evil upon my people. Being so caught up in defending a town that I was still a stranger to, I hadn't stopped to consider the implications of my actions.

Hota had slaughtered anyone with a heartbeat, and as I saw a lifeless child, reaching out for her dog, I felt even more anguish and motivation to end this reign of cruel totalitarianism.

The buzzards circled above the village, excited by the reek of rotting flesh. Seeing the wrecks of the Bull Horn tavern, my memories of joyful evenings scattered like the fragments that blew away in the wind.

Nobleman Skinner's corpse hung from the tired looking stone of the loggia above the main entrance. We had not always seen eye to eye in the past and at times I had found him rather pious and feeble, yet now it was clear that he had stood firm with his people to the very end, which showed his true devotion.

Jumping down from Spike, my limbs began to shake involuntarily. I was fearful of learning my mother's fate. My anxiety was warranted as I approached the church from the Square.

Horror was displayed before me. I had found my mother. Her body was pinned to the church door, with thick steel bolts that had been driven through her palms. The blood had dried around her wounds, and her skin was bruised from the incisions. My vision blurred at the sight of her flaccid head and pale skin, and I screamed out in anguish. She had been drained of life in the most savage and inhumane way imaginable.

I involuntarily fell to my knees before her bare feet. Weeping, I attempted to reach up to touch her, yet was unable to move my arms.

Keeling over, my hand inadvertently pressed into the congealment of dirt and blood below her body. My attempt to scream again was prevented by my shortness of breath.

Misery had suppressed my desire for retribution. I felt empty and unable to move from the muddy ground. Hota had ruthlessly defeated me, knowing that his callous actions would consume me in our final conflict, engulfing me in rage and sorrow, giving him advantage over me.

The gate to the churchyard creaked. Catching my breath, I slowly hauled myself off the ground, pulling free my sword and turning to see whoever approached.

"I do not come to quarrel, I yield, I yield," called Steffen, with arms out to the side.

"Why were you spared? Or did you submit like a coward?" I growled.

"They watch you, Jep, I have been sent down to see how many of you have come."

Steffen looked back at me uneasily, his hands shaking and his lower jaw quivering. Judging by the appearance of his dishevelled tunic and soiled, bloodied skin, he told the truth. I marched forward, taking hold of his collar. He screeched as I kicked open the gate, yanking him into the Square.

Tossing him down on the ground, I raised my sword, squeezing my lips rigidly together.

With wild eyes, I yelled, "I am here, you whoreson. Come to me, let us finish this. Or will you coil in the grass, like the serpent you are?"

Steffen stared across to the embankment behind the burnt down tavern, unconsciously giving away the place where Hota probably hid. His breathing was erratic, and his inability to blink gave away his fear.

Following his gaze, I also observed the embankment before calling Hota out for a second time. "Are you afraid? If so, make it quick and strike me down with the bow you hide behind. You want to avenge your immoral father? I am here."

Only silence and stillness came from the horizon. I stood over the frightened guard. "Flee, and let us hope our paths never cross again."

Steffen looked up at me, astonished by my compassion at granting his escape.

"Now go!" I bellowed, causing him to whimper.

Scrambling to his feet, Steffen lowered his quaking head, before sprinting in the opposite direction of the hill.

Within a few paces of his running, an arrow whistled through the air and embedded itself in the back of his skull, driving him back down into the dirt.

From atop the grass slope, Hota emerged, accompanied by four Shadow Crooks, all mounted and positioned either side of him. They stalked forward towards me, carefully steering their horses down the hill. The Crook to the right of Hota held a crossbow in her hand, with its barrel pointing up to the sky.

Hota surprisingly stared back at me with numbness, his eyes empty, just as they had been when he murdered Fulten. Raising his fist, he ordered his followers to halt and remain by the village boundary before he proceeded alone to the Square.

Leaping down from his horse, he refused to interact with me and began to casually untie his father's sword from the horse's saddle.

Strolling up to me, he took in a deep breath through his nose. "They stink. This village housed such vile and repulsive inhabitants, you should be applauding me for bringing an end to its suffering and deprivation."

"It is true what they say, you Crooks really are Godless, nothing more than gutless heathens."

Hota smirked. "Coincidentally, that is just what your mother said, before I had her nailed to the door. The woman showed not an ounce of dignity, she wailed like an animal caught in thorns. I offered you salvation, Jep, and now all I offer you is death."

His plan to fuel me with abhorrence worked, and I sprinted forward, grunting, with my sword held out to my side, keen to end the engagement swiftly. Hota snarled back at me, drawing his sword and tossing its scabbard to the floor.

Sweeping my sword around I roared with might, leaving Hota to stumble, after barely defending my furious assault. Quickly, I pulled my sword across my waist and then sliced it backwards at his stomach, however Hota speedily tilted his sword and blocked my second attack.

Hota leaned back, digging his heels in the damp ground, and meticulously absorbed my reckless blows, blocking and deflecting each one calmly. Groaning with each thrust, I found myself faltering.

Once again, Hota had effortlessly outwitted me. He had allowed for me to vent out my fury, leaving me exhausted and struggling to hold up my weapon. It was then he countered, his blade soaring from left to right, delivering a flurry of precise blows. I strained to keep up, blocking the fast strikes, retreating and taking steps back, unable to retaliate.

Miscalculating my defence allowed Hota's blade to rip through the upper sleeve of my gambeson, slicing my arm. He grinned at the first sight of spilt blood in our encounter; he knew too well that I was beginning to struggle.

Trapped in between my adversary and the church gate, I was unable to raise my sword to gather momentum for a sufficient swing. Hota rashly drew back his sword, foolishly leaving himself open. Lunging forward, I slammed my forehead into his face, crunching the bridge of his nose and causing a stream of blood to flow down his face. Dazed, he shook his head, though speedily brushing off my attack.

Finally having time to react, I thrust my sword towards him, feeling the tip connect with his doublet, but unfortunately there was still too much space between us to drive my sword into his chest.

Now we were both equally as exhausted, and the pace of the fight slackened. Hota had ignored his own plan and now fought with sheer anger, delivering only desperate and untimely blows. As he drove down his sword from above his head, I was able to dodge his frantic and untidy attack, leaving him to splinter the wooden fencing that surrounded the church.

I returned three pressing strikes, one to his head and the other two towards his torso. Hota now struggled to keep up with my surge and failed to counterattack. Retreating, he staggered with exhaustion to the oak tree, positioned centrally within the Square. Attempting to catch me off guard, he swiftly turned and clumsily lashed his sword out.

Equally dwindling, we sluggishly launched our blades, hoping to snatch victory, however neither one of us could gather enough momentum to deliver that crucial blow. Hota chopped down his sword, and aiming for my skull he roared, timing his assault with a burst of strength from a second wind. I barely managed to meet his assault, and our blades clashed together. The bones in my hand rattled from the force of the strike and caused me to lose my grip of the hilt of my sword.

As I leapt down to capture my weapon, Hota moved in and thrust the tip of his blade towards me, slicing into the flesh that covered my hip bone. My skin tore, triggering me to shriek. I desperately crawled on my hands and knees to regain my sword, but Hota was far too skilful not to take the advantage.

The sharpness of his cold steel pierced my calf and slid through my shin bone, and I screamed vociferously. Hota furthered his torment, lashing his boot into my ribcage and forcing me on to my back.

He panted heavily, glaring down at me. Chuckling, he placed the tip of his sword against my throat. "It saddens me to see an end to our feud, brother."

He pressed his blade against my throat, and I could feel my skin beginning to open, as he gently began guiding his sword. I raised my upper lip and sneered, masking my fear of death.

A voice called, demanding him to cease. Her smooth yet condescending tone was familiar. Hota rolled his eyes and growled, before kicking away my sword and angrily facing the person who had prevented him ending my life.

"He is worth nothing to us dead, brother. Your lust for revenge does not outweigh the chaos we can inflict with him at our mercy, especially now his whore claims my title."

Struggling to sit up, I winced at moving my wounded leg. Truda now stood next to Hota; she was dressed in thick animal furs and had decorated her face with black die. "Understand this, Jep. I am not sparing your life, just claiming it, in order to negotiate with your associates. My brother will still inflict death upon you, but only when I no longer need you."

"Brother?" I said.

"It seems my sister has got into the habit of saving your worthless life. It was she who advised me to reward you with forgiveness after you murdered our father, and then you betrayed us. I knew in my heart you could never be trusted," replied Hota.

Looking to the four Crooks who stood behind Hota and Truda, I remained sitting on the boggy ground and began to laugh hysterically.

"What amuses you?" asked Truda.

"I am just trying to work out which one of you is the bastard of your unhinged family. You have a following of sick degenerates. Bartering me will not change that, so I suggest you run me through."

Taking unkindly to my insult, Hota placed his boot onto the wound on my shin. Leaning down, he dug his heel into the gash, causing me to cry out.

"I do hope your manners and gratitude improve on the road," said Truda, haughtily.

A further Crook arrived, bringing a horse and wagon. I was roughly plucked from the ground and hurled into the back of the wooden cart. The Crooks heckled and tormented me, showing their delight in my capture. The wheels began to rattle, churning up mud from the boggy ground.

Tilting my head up, I looked back at the church doors, on which my mother's body so cruelly hung. Feeling the tears fill my blood shot eyes, I rested my head back down on to the hard wooden boards and stared up at the sky. Five crows swooped down working together, chasing away a lone buzzard, their quarrel above reminding me of the feuds that had existed in all parts of my life.

26

THE BUZZARD AND THE CROWS

Following the path south, Spike was now being ridden by one of the Crooks. Hota would often lean into the cart and eye me, spitefully. The uneven track made the journey uncomfortable, and with each bump, I murmured from the pain of the open wound on my shin. Blood now soaked my trouser leg, and it was only a matter of time before I could expect to bleed out.

Truda noticed the blood sodden cart and threw me a grubby cloth to wrap my leg in. My death on the road would be no use to any future trade or blackmail they had planned.

Setting up camp on the grass verge next to the path, the Crooks showed no concern for any outside intrusion. Filling themselves with mead, it wasn't long before their attention was drawn to me.

One of Hota's followers wrapped a rope around my neck, before dragging me head-first from the cart. The other four Crooks cheered, and even Hota and Truda were amused by the suffering and torment I was being forced to endure.

Sitting upright with my elbows dug into the dirt, I watched as one of the Crooks swaggered towards me. She hissed down at me; her narrow eyes decorated by paint. Spitting on me, she followed up by kicking me in my side, causing me to double over and clutch hold of my already damaged ribs. "That is for Dak, you pig turd."

The violence did not end there. The Crooks pounced on me like a pack of wolves, landing punches to my head and kicks to my torso. My eyes were now nearly swollen shut and my lips had ballooned. The final attack knocked my jawbone out of place and left me sprawled out, barely conscious, on my back.

"Enough, we need him alive," called Truda.

***

The jolting of the trundling cart caused me to groan and attempt to open my inflamed eyelids. The brightness of the daylight caused me to squint and blurred my vision. I noticed the buzzard hovering above, and I couldn't help but believe it was the same bird I had seen back in Somerby. The sight of its wings spread, soaring through the air, gave me hope and a sense of guardianship.

I could hear the flowing water of the great river breaking against the rocks. Cheering came from the front of our party, but however I adjusted my head to see what was causing the commotion, the front of the cart obstructed my view.

A loud thud came from the foot of the wagon, causing my body to jolt. Hota and another Crook had tossed the corpse of a regal guard by my feet.

"Feel free to share your bleats with this one," chuckled Hota.

The Crown's guardsman lay with open eyes staring blindly towards the sky. His throat had been slit and his claret tunic was drenched in his blood, his life taken easily without remorse. Unable to turn my sight away from the river's patrolman, I felt numb, sighing, before dropping my head back down, knowing that my outcome would not be too dissimilar.

Two further voices had joined us at the bridge. Truda applauded their efforts in securing the crossing into Thear's southern divide. "What rumours come from the city?"

"The Crown cares little for the north, we are free to roam," replied a voice of a stranger.

"I will not roam, I will rule. We continue with our plan, meeting at the southern shores. There we will be able to prepare and keep view of our enemies."

"What about the pig? They will be looking for him," said the newly arrived man.

"Like most that are forced to endure Jep's tiresome behaviour, I believe they will have grown weary of him by now," interrupted Hota.

Truda joined me in the wagon, shoving the guard's body aside. "Oh! I do hate the smell of the dead, they have a certain reek to them."

"Why not discard him in the river?" I mumbled.

"My brother wishes to tease you."

"His very existence achieves that."

"I have a much more imaginative way to unsettle you. You are the only person that will bait that pathetic wench into a reckless reaction. I remember the way in which she fluttered her eyes at you." Leaning her mouth closer to my ear, Truda whispered, "And then you will see her ploughed and hacked, and only then will my brother be allowed to avenge our father."

Ignoring her, I stared through the splintered wood of the cart, gazing across at the stone walls of the bridge, listening to the water as it splashed on the surface of the river. Truda stood angrily at her failure to get any reaction, gripping her hands on to the side of the wagon, "You picked the wrong side, Jep."

Hota called out, ordering that we were to come to a halt. Hearing the fluster in her brother's voice, Truda began to lean her head over the wall of the cart, to see what had caused the hold up on the bridge. I felt the cart dip, prompting me to look down at where Truda stood. She stared towards the far side of the crossing, the whites of her eyes bulging from what confronted her.

Her head jerked back, and she squeezed her grip tighter on to the sidewalls of the wagon. Inhaling, Truda wheezed, her breathing became raspy and disjointed. She peered down at me, giving me a look of dismay.

As I heard the squelch from the weapon being withdrawn from her back, Truda's body was pushed down on top of the dead regal guard. Blair stood at the end of the wagon with the hood of her robe covering her hair.

The blood from the sword's edge ran down its handle and dripped on to her knuckles. Blair watched on, revelling in Truda's suffocation, listening with satisfaction to her gargling as the Crook's lungs began filling with blood. Unable to hold herself back any longer, Blair leapt forward on top of Truda, plunging her sword into the Shadow Crook's chest.

Roaring with antagonism, Blair now thrust at Truda again and again frantically, disregarding the blood that was splashing on to her face. Seeing her avenge Fawkes' death with his own sword, it was clear Blair's innocence had disappeared. She was now a warrior and no longer a defiant servant girl.

Finally leaving Truda's mutilated corpse, Blair got back on her feet and noticed my disfigured face and bandaged leg.

Hearing the commotion and panic that came from the remaining Crooks, I asked Blair to help me up. Perching myself against the front plank of the wagon, my heart pounded at the image of what met us at the entrance of the bridge.

The Governor sat mounted and armed with a mace in his hand. Standing next to him was Chenchi, who grinned back at us, with his sword resting against his thigh.

Hota looked on with dread, emulating the same expression on the faces of his six followers. The Shadow Crooks demanded direction from their leader, who remained flabbergasted, knowing too well the abilities and threat from the men who stood before him, poised to attack.

Hota's attempts to steady his agitated horse triggered four of the Crooks to retreat from their floundering headman. Sprinting past the cart, Blair raced forward to intercept the fleeing Crooks.

"No, do not allow retribution to be your demise, just look where it has got me," I called.

Hota guided his horse a few paces behind the two lingering Crooks, struggling to settle his agitated animal. The Governor jumped down from his own steed, pulling loose his sword.

Now armed with a mace in one hand and his sword in the other, he strode forward, closing in on the Crooks. Chenchi attempted to join our senior, but he was ordered to hold back by the Governor.

Hota anxiously took a fleeting glimpse back at me, before scanning the bridge for a way to escape. I turned my attention to the other entrance of the bridge, to witness Detector Flint and Sword Lev blocking its path, intercepting and stabbing their swords down through the escaping Crooks.

Watching the Governor strut forward, I felt tense, frustrated by the fact I was unable to join the fight.

I looked back at Blair as she smiled, confident in our Governor's abilities and willingness to engage our enemy single handed. The two Crooks withdrew their weapons, one a short sword and the second, an axe. Charging forward, they attempted to rush and overpower the Governor.

The Governor eyed both the Crooks, showing no sign of unease at them racing towards him. Looping his mace skilfully in his hand, he tilted his chin down towards his chest and observed the impending attack with hooded eyes.

The first Crook swung his axe towards the Governor, who reacted calmly, stepping back and dodging the enemy's assault. Within close range, the Governor swung his mace upwards, guiding the weapon towards the Crook's head, slamming the steel spikes into his face. Releasing hold of his mace, he allowed the man to crash to the floor, with the weapon embedded in his jaw.

The Governor then tackled the second Crook, permitting his opponent's over-animated thrust of his sword. Side stepping and leaping behind the man, the Governor shoulder barged him in the back, causing the Crook to lose his balance and stumble, whilst trying to turn to face our adept leader. With two fast and precise blows, the Governor sliced his sword across the man's stomach, causing him to fold over, clutching at his wound. Delivering his second strike, the Governor ploughed his sword down between the shoulder blades of the hunched over Crook.

Withdrawing his weapon, he turned around, squinting at Hota. Plucking his mace from the chin of the dead Crook, the Governor proceeded to stalk towards Hota.

With his sword in hand, Hota heeled his horse's sides and rode furiously towards our leader. The Governor paused, showing his composure, observing Hota and his beast racing closer to him.

Undeterred, he launched his mace into the air, causing it to spin towards Hota, allowing the ball of spikes to penetrate the Shadow Crook's chest.

Knocked from his horse, winded and gasping for breath, Hota lay sprawled out on the ground, incapacitated and now finding himself at the mercy of his former senior.

Harshly pulling out the spikes from Hota's chest, our Governor glared down at him with menacing eyes. Grabbing the scruff of his doublet, he heaved Hota from off the ground, dragging him towards the edge of the bridge.

Hota squirmed before attempting to resist and break free from the Governor's hold. Hurling our adversary at the bridge wall, Hota's face bounced off the stone.

Bloodied and breathless, Hota was slumped against the wall. Dazed he looked up at his tormentor.

The Governor leaned his head close to the Crook and yelled in his face, "You spinelessly took the lives of honourable Swords. My Swords! For that I judge you and am here to deliver your punishment."

Kneeling before the fallen Crook, the Governor wrapped his arm around the back of Hota's head, pulling his face closely into his chest, before whispering in his ear.

Hota gulped and his eyes widened as the Governor gradually slid his blade into his abdomen before slowly dragging it upwards through his stomach. Retching, Hota coughed out blood from his mouth, and attempted to grab onto the Governor's arms, whilst gasping for air, finally breathing his last breath. Pulling back his sword, the Governor stared at Hota's corpse and sighed.

"You look terrible," called Flint, who now stood at the foot of the wagon, observing the state of me.

"He always looks like that," said Blair.

The Governor approached the front of the cart and observed my wounds. "We start together, and we finish together, that is the Blue Sword way."

Lev had wandered over to Hota's body and dragged the Crook's torso on to the wall. Lifting the legs, he began shoving the body over the edge of the bridge, to fall with a splash into the river, before smiling back at us. "The fish will be thankful for the gesture."

"Did you apprehend the others?" asked the Governor.

"We executed three of them, but one escaped. It seems Lev's aging bones have got the better of him," replied Flint.

Feeling my leg buckle, I stumbled, falling down. Blair insisted on getting me back to Stanford.

Setting off, I looked up at the clear blue sky, keen to see the buzzard that had previously hovered above. Yet it was nowhere to be seen; in its place was the rare sight of four crows circling above us.

Relieved and satisfied by Hota's downfall, I gazed up at the crows, and could not help but suspect I had misjudged the meaning of the buzzard that had followed us from Somerby. It was the crows that represented guardianship. The crows were my companions and saviours, and Hota was my buzzard.

My eyelids felt heavy, and the sky became blurry and hazed. The last thing I felt was the dampness and the cold from my blood-soaked trousers. Slowly everything went dark, and I was aware of nothing more.

27

BLUE SWORDS

Walking through the gates of Stanford over two winters ago, I had been nothing more than a peasant boy, my only offering being a foul stench. Luck had favoured me, combined with the ability to choose my words wisely. In a town divided by both kindness and cruelty, I had managed to uncover the right path, a path that had led me to the Blue Swords and an opportunity to work under Sword Fulten's guidance.

My time in Stanford had been short in comparison to most dependable residents, yet it had been fruitful. I do not deny that my actions may had been clumsy and at times imprudent. But my adulthood did not start out with me being a convenient heroic figure. Like most in our lands; I was to be taught to endure hardship and be made to appreciate the importance of growth.

Baroness Ivy was free from the wickedness imposed on her by Baron Asher. She was now in her rightful place as Baroness and ruler of Stanford. The people adored her and were sure to be elevated by her leadership, and I was the foolish poor boy, who fell for the temptations of forbidden love.

Knowing now that her duties outweighed her desire to love me, I could only pray that our love would rekindle in the afterlife.

***

Awakening from my dream of Lady Ivy, I was astonished to find the Baroness herself seated by my bed as she awaited my recovery. Her face brightened at seeing me rouse and she carefully leaned towards me, gently kissing my forehead.

With her fingers tenderly resting on top of my hand, she blinked away a tear from her eye. "You are the most stubborn, yet invincible man I know."

Grunting, I laughed quietly. "I should have continued as Carre's farm hand."

"Well, if you had, we would now be under the rule of heathens."

"We have lost so many to this fight," I mumbled, wincing as I strained to sit up.

"But their audacity has allowed us to live freely, and for that our fallen will never be forgotten, Jep."

Noticing the gold necklace that hung from her neck, I grinned. "Your appointment has been confirmed by the Crown?"

"I received word only a few days ago. In truth I have not offered a promising start, I have been distracted ensuring care is provided for a wounded Sword."

I lifted my hand, placing my palm gently against her cheek. "I will forever envision what our life together could have been, but I am able to comprehend that your people's need for you is greater than my own desire."

"May we revisit our love in another lifetime?" whispered Ivy, leaving us both teary eyed. "Will you stay? Help me build on all we have achieved?"

"I will always fight by your side when needed, my Lady, but for now, there is much I am to explore."

Our lips met and we kissed for what felt the final time. Watching the Baroness walk away from the guest chambers of the Grand Hall, I gulped away the lump in my throat.

***

Baroness Ivy had offered Emil a position within her household, but Emil had declined the offer after Abbot had taken up a temporary role as a labourer on Carre's farm. Both my sister and I had been welcomed at some point to Western farm with open arms. Dam relished having another strong-minded woman on the farm, ensuring that the stubborn men were kept in line.

Gibbon refused to leave my side; he followed me around like a faithful dog, ensuring that I was left to heal in peace. It was nice having my childhood friend close, but at times his overzealous waiting on me became a little stifling.

Baroness Ivy had ordered Seiloff to organise heightened patrols within the town, allowing my companions to concentrate on rebuilding the lock up. Flint had refused to return to the city with Chief Muir until the town had recovered from the Shadow Crook's invasion.

As the days passed, Baroness Ivy became more distant, and her visits decreased. Her new role kept her engaged and I understood that she wished to remain free from idle gossip and rumours.

Blair looked in on me from time to time, grumbling about her and Isa's new position, serving the Great Hall. She had pleaded with the Governor for a chance to try out for the up-and-coming Sword trials, however he had determined that she was still too immature in age and would be required to wait a further two winters before she was eligible to attend the trials.

Whether her tenacity allowed her to believe it or not, Blair was destined to become a Blue Sword. Lev had made a point of honouring our late companion's memory by continuing to mentor the girl until the day she was ready to wear our crest. With the pledge of the Stanford Swords behind her, Blair was certainly not going to let her femininity be a barrier and had been marked to be the first woman to serve. She would just need to wait and allow maturity to take its natural course.

***

As I limped towards the Market Square, our town was illuminated by the late spring sun. The people were energised and happiness enhanced the ambiance throughout the town. The Viking Invader Tavern once again bustled with life, and the repeated calls of traders could be heard bellowing from the Square.

Families rushed to get the best viewing points for the trials, with excitable children keen to witness the harmless combat. The day of the Blue Swords trials were upon us and I was enthused to see Rye put to the test.

My loyal friend Gibbon had also agreed to attend and with me acting as his sponsor, had been invited to try out in the hope of joining our crest.

The longstanding venue had been moved away from the Square. The arena had been precisely marked out at the bottom of the hill, by Western farm. Baroness Ivy had funded the event, promoting it as more of a celebration, rather than a formal assessment.

Lady Ivy was seated on a finely crafted wooden platform that had been built on the top of what was once named Baron's Hill. The pillars of wood supporting her cover had been engraved and carved with images of acorns and foliage.

The Baroness sat admiring the spirit of her people. She was dressed in a voluminous green gown with long sleeves and tightly fitted doublet underneath. Her feathered head scarf complemented the extravagant jewellery she displayed around her neck. Her angelic smile beamed, and she shone brightly watching over us.

The crowds had arrived in large numbers, all lapping up the early entertainment that was on offer from inside the arena. The locals laughed and jeered at two foolish jesters, balancing on stilts and attempting to chase each other on the grass. The humorous acts were dramatized by musical minstrels who played their instruments on the edge of the arena.

Pulling up the rope, I entered the arena and made my way towards the table positioned at the foot of the hill. Two navy blue flags, both embroidered with the *BS* emblem, identified the trial section.

Lev and Chenchi stood clapping and relishing in the less formal festivities. "You managed to hobble in," smiled Lev.

I looked behind him to see our Governor looking rather sour faced, seated at the table. "What troubles him?"

Chenchi tutted, "Don't mind him, he is bitter, and it seems, not an admirer of all the pleasures."

"Apparently it isn't representative of our traditions," shouted Lev, over the rowdiness of the crowd.

Flint was sitting next to the Governor, and on seeing me he raised his eyebrows, with an awkward expression on his face. The Governor leaned back in his chair, puffing.

I smiled at my senior, "Not a supporter of the celebrations, Sir?"

"Our trials have become a spectacle, a parade, it sickens me to see our traditions flaunted like a tacky play," he scoffed.

The Governor barked at Lev, ordering him to gather up the contenders. "Let's get this over and done with."

Lev strutted to the centre of the arena, wearing a navy-blue cloak that flowed stylishly down his back. Lev's appearance brought the music to an immediate halt, before he called out loudly for the arena to be cleared. "All those who are to be assessed, step forward and form an orderly line outside the tent."

The large number of men who emerged from out of the crowd, caused me to raise my eyebrows in surprise.

"I predicted as much," moaned the Governor. "They swing a sword in the face of a Crook and now they all think they're noble bloody knights."

At least sixty men had approached the open tent which sheltered the table and now formed a straggly line, all eager to gain the responsibility and virtuous title of a Blue Sword.

Lev stood before the men. "You are in for a treat today, gentlemen, acting as your assessor, we have Detector Flint. Our esteemed Detector has taken time away from pruning his hair and reading pointless parchments, all to help us identify the town's next cohort of Swords. When indicated, you will present yourself to both him and the Governor immediately. There will be no dawdling."

Examining the line of contenders, I noticed Rye stood three down from the front of the queuing men. He was jittery and unable to raise his gaze from the ground. Gibbon stood out the most, his thick set and enormous height overshadowing the rest of the challengers.

The biggest revelation was noticing Abbot poking his head out from behind Gibbon's back, also waiting to be considered.

"Abbot? I had no idea he was trying out," I said to Chenchi.

Chenchi folded his arms proudly. "Ah yes, I sponsored him, a man willing to take on your sister has more than earned the right to a seat at our table. Besides, look at him, small, with flame coloured hair? The man has been angry since birth, just what we need."

Standing a few paces away from the Governor's table, I watched the contenders moving away from their verbal assessments, some departing with pride filled faces, and others appearing downhearted and sullen by their rejection.

Rye stood before the table with his chest puffed out and his back straight. Unable to hear their exchange of words, I squinted, attempting to observe his facial expressions. Finally, the farmhand turned back, facing the arena. His demeanour gave little away, triggering me to cough in order to catch his attention. He beamed and bowed his head, indicating his success.

Lev strolled closer to me, tilting his head near my ear. "Pathetic, isn't it?"

"What is?" I asked, already knowing full well the grumbles he was about to relay.

"In my day, trials would be gruelling and last for days. Now it's a quick lick of the arse and any indication you can hold a baton without wetting yourself, and our crest is yours."

Chenchi brazenly called forward Gibbon. Both men had met before and developed a harmless rivalry after gambling on an arm-wrestle back in Somerby. Judging by the way in which they both arched their backs and glared at one another, their competitiveness had found its way to Stanford.

Gibbon had been talking at the table for some time now. Observing the perplexed expressions displayed on both the Governor and Flint's faces, I decided to step closer and eavesdrop.

"That's right, he is lucky he didn't have it hacked off," said Gibbon.

"I have heard enough," interrupted the Governor.

Flint raised his hand. "No, please do carry on."

"Well, it made him itch you see. The thing looked like it had been stung by bees. I did warn him, be mindful of those roaming girls. So, in the end I took Jep to see an old hag in the village, she had all sorts of concoctions, squared him right up, she did."

Laughing, Flint looked to the Governor. "Well if that isn't coming to one's aid, what is?"

The Governor shook his head impatiently. "I give up! Very well, attend before sundown for combat assessment."

Gibbon walked away appearing rather pleased with himself, winking merrily as he passed me by. I glared back at him for his temerity, knowing that Flint would never let me live this down.

At the end of the initial trials, Flint stood to stretch his legs, and catching sight of me he walked over. "I do worry for the future of our organisation; your man Rye was successful, as was the babbling oaf."

"What about Abbot?"

Flint patted my back, boldly. "Unfortunately, not, but I wouldn't fret, he has your sister to offer him comfort. This is all very diluted, a desperate way to seek new Swords. If you accept my offer, I will show you a far deeper side to the Blue Swords than you can ever imagine," he said.

"Thank you, I have made my decision."

"I leave at first light, with or without you," insisted Flint. "Oh, and I hope all is well down below," he whispered conspiratorially with a wink, gesturing towards my crotch.

I cursed Gibbon.

***

Rye had proven his worth and displayed promising abilities with a peace baton. His athletic physique meant he could dodge Chenchi's attack and react with adequate counters. Dam bellowed encouragement from the other side of the rope, motivating and spurring on the young farmhand.

The crowd roared with excitement on seeing him triumphantly avoid defeat at the hands of Chenchi. Rye had been successful, and with his proposal of appointment within the Swords, was now on the path to becoming a confirmed Blue Sword.

Gibbon marched towards Chenchi and the two gigantic men eyed one another. Chenchi threw Gibbon a peace baton, and my childhood friend scrunched his face, frowning and showing dissatisfaction with the wooden stick. "It is a mere child's toy."

"Well then, it shall not hurt when I spank you with it," threatened Chenchi.

Gibbon didn't hold back; he thundered towards Chenchi, attempting to deliver a decisive blow. Chenchi was far too dexterous to allow Gibbon's temper to disarm him that easily. Kicking Gibbon's legs away from his body to cause him to stumble, Chenchi side swiped his own baton into his opponent's chest.

Floored and winded, Gibbon managed to regain his composure and reached out, grabbing at Chenchi's ankles, pulling him off balance. The ground trembled as Chenchi's mass crashed down on to the grass, triggering a gasp from the excited audience.

Bear hugging each other, they rolled around in the mud, prompting laughter from the rest of us who watched. I looked over to the table, witnessing the Governor placing his forehead against the palm of his hand, mortified by the spectacle.

Eventually he stood furiously, knocking his chair backwards from the table. "Enough."

Chenchi continued, leaning over Gibbon and delivering punches to his head, forcing the Governor to call out for a second time.

Chenchi reluctantly stepped away and hovered over Gibbon. Extending his arm, he offered Gibbon a hand to his feet. "You can hold your own; and here was me thinking you were all wind and no puff."

Gibbon began brushing down his trousers. "You punch like I imagine you hump, with a lack of passion."

Chenchi turned to face the crowd. Raising his peace baton, he shouted vociferously to the local people, boasting his victory.

Gibbon sulked. However, he grew tired of hearing the chants generated by the gathering of people, all applauding Chenchi. Charging towards the showboating Blue Sword, Gibbon hooked his arms around Chenchi's waist, sending the men hurtling back down to the ground.

Chenchi wheezed, struggling to catch his breath, which allowed Gibbon to take advantage of the floored Sword and prise the baton from Chenchi's hand.

Now it was Gibbon's turn to brag of his conquest. The Governor marched towards Chenchi, demanding he got to his feet, before angrily yanking the baton out from Gibbon's grasp. "I sense you will be bothersome, yet as the rules stand, I am in no position to create a fuss.

Report to the guard barracks at dusk."

Gibbon cheered, encouraging a further reaction from the local people, who displayed their delight at his appointment. I approached Chenchi, who scornfully watched Gibbon playing to the audience. "I will insist on being his tutor. That way, I can walk him until the soles of his feet bleed."

"I am sure you will both learn to play nicely."

I congratulated Gibbon and he beamed back at me, thrilled at successfully being recruited into the Blue Swords. "These southern folks need us northern men to educate them."

"I have no doubt you will make a fine Sword."

With the trials completed and new recruits appointed to our crest, I felt satisfied and able to confirm my decision on where my future should lead me.

28

BAND OF BLUE

I joined the rest of my companions in the Dirty Duck tavern, and we enjoyed its humble surroundings. The crackling logs on the roaring fire were enough to offer a calm and comfortable setting.

Free from rowdy locals wanting to brawl, it was the perfect location for us Swords to enjoy our ale and not worry about outside meddling. Lev spent most of the evening propping himself against the serving table, enjoying a flirtatious conversation with the golden-haired serving girl.

Gibbon had sunk far too many ales, losing sense of Chenchi's zealous observations of him. Abbot brushed off his rejection admirably and allowed himself to enjoy the cosiness of my sister gazing at him, whilst seated on his lap. The sight was both humble and repulsive at the same time.

"What now for the two of you?" I asked.

Emil looked down at Abbot, fluttering her eyelids. "We shall farm, and live at peace."

"I will drink to that," Abbot said, guzzling the remaining ale in his cup.

"What of your fate, Jep?" asked Chenchi.

"I am to travel to Alma and take Flint up on his offer of a scholarship."

Gibbon quickly leapt up from his stool. "You're going to leave me here alone to indulge these placid southerners?"

"Sit down, you oaf," chuckled Chenchi. "Do not fear; you will be under my wing, and I have great plans for my new toy."

"Did I hear right? Jep is departing, abandoning us?" cried Lev, whilst returning to the table with more beakers of ale.

"Now the Baroness is done with him, he must seek a new venture," slurred Gibbon.

"That sounds about right, you conquer this town and move on to the next. Let us hope our gracious queen is able to resist your charm, we all know of your yearning for powerful women," smiled Lev.

Rye interrupted us and raised his beaker. "Jep has proven to us all that no matter if we were born in pig muck, we can still stand our ground against the world."

Lev playfully clipped the back of Rye's ear with his hand. "You speak gibberish, boy, it is me you have to convince of your worth, or I will have you returned to the pig muck."

Chenchi pushed back, causing the feet of his chair to grind across the floor. Standing, he tilted his cup towards me. "You are the most obstinate man I have ever needed to endure, yet I value you as a brother. My sword will always be yours, whenever you need to call on it. Go, and give those Swords a taste of country Blue."

His words prompted merriment from my companions, and they began pounding their beakers on to the table, causing a rowdiness within the Dirty Duck.

***

Leaving the tavern, I muttered in Abbot's ear, asking him to join me outside. Startled, he looked at my sister for reassurance.

Joining me on Main Street, he raised his open hands. "I know what you're about to say, Jep. You have my word, I will protect her with my life."

"Apart from the Swords, Emil is the only family I have left. She deserves happiness, and if you have the right intentions by her, you should see to it that you both become wed."

"Thank you Jep, it is all I have ever dreamt."

Stepping away, Abbot called out to me. "You know that will make us family?"

Turning around to face him, I smiled. "I have always seen you as a brother, Abbot."

***

Before entering the barracks, I peered up at the balcony to Baroness Ivy's chambers. I took a moment to ponder on our time together and reflect on the adventures we had shared. Lady Ivy's new appointment had not allowed me to deal with our circumstances any easier. In truth, I longed for her, and leaving was my own way to ease the pain in my heart.

I ran my fingers over the nicks and scars that now marred the skin on my face. Each one was a reminder of Stanford and what I had fought for. It was not the people I battled to protect, it was Lady Ivy and I knew that however far the distance I put between us, I would not stop loving the Baroness of Stanford.

The empty quarters gave me the chance to gather my belongings and prepare for the long journey south to the City. Whilst rolling my furs, I heard the door creak open. Looking up, I found the Governor now stood at the edge of the walkway. "So, the rumour is true, you have finally accepted Flint's offer to become a Detector."

"Sir, I was going to inform you of my intentions."

Waving his hand forward dismissively, the Governor walked towards me and perched himself on the foot of the adjacent bed. "You do not need to justify yourself to me, your decision is a wise one."

"I wanted to wait until after the trials before I left."

"I knew that was why Flint lingered around the town, he was waiting for you to accept his proposal. I have not always been very tolerant of you Jep, it is no lie that I have found you somewhat indignant and at times arrogant. But that said, I have always respected you. You fight like a cornered wolf and in your heart you care for those less fortunate than ourselves. You are a natural guardian of the people and for that you are most deserving of our crest."

Reaching out his hand, the Governor stood over me, grasping my shoulder. "There will always be a place for you here, boy, whether you wear a black or blue tunic. Fulten would be proud of what you have become."

Before exiting the barracks, the Governor called out to me for a final time. "Do not forget, I have need for a Sergeant, so don't stay away too long."

Once the Governor had left, I began mulling over his heartfelt words and was forced to clear the lump in my throat. He was a fierce leader, but one who I respected and would very much miss.

***

The dawn sun blistered through the splinter roof of the barracks. I crept out from my bed, passing Chenchi, who snored like he was taking his last breath. Wandering down to the river, I was keen to wash my face in the water.

Rustling came from the hedgerow behind me, followed by Blair's appearance.

Turning back to the river, I proceeded to wipe away the water from my face. "Do not tell me you're still sulking, girl?"

"Not sulking, just thinking, that is all."

Approaching her, I placed my hands on her shoulders. "Your only impediment is time; you are set to become the most formidable Blue Sword Thear has ever seen. Fawkes has passed on his legacy to you, and now Lev will guide your training until the time comes."

"You always promised to be my tutor."

Sighing, I glimpsed at the river's bank and then turned back to her, smiling. "You do not want me, I am the runt of the litter, whiny, troublesome and not to mention destitute."

"You do grumble a lot," laughed Blair.

"I swear you will alter the course of many lives in your time, you will stand and represent all those fearless warriors that have been overlooked by our prudish society."

"Like Sheron," Blair replied.

"Yes, like Sheron. Do not allow petulance to overshadow your true abilities, never stop fighting and always stand your ground, even when it is breaking you inside."

Blair stared up at me with a tear falling from her eye. "I don't want you to go."

Pulling her close, my heart began to pound as she sobbed into my chest, Blair had become like a little sister to me, and I had grown to love her dearly.

Stepping back, I eyed her. "Come now; wipe away those tears and show this town who you really are."

***

Once back in the courtyard, Blair returned to the Great Hall to notify her mother of my impending departure. Gibbon and Chenchi stood outside the barracks, awaiting my return. Lev proceeded across the courtyard, gently tugging Spike by his reins. "He is saddled and ready to be reunited with his friend. One last thing. A saying that us Blue Swords like to use, is the description 'shit lodestone'. My advice is stop being one when you get to Alma, you attract a lot of unwanted grief, Jep."

I patted my stallion's neck. Chenchi called to me. Holding out my arm, he unexpectedly pulled me close and embraced me. His bulging arms crumpled into my back, squeezing the air from my lungs. "Jep, we will always be the Band of Blue."

Flint appeared from the side path of the Grand Hall, cantering his horse towards us. "Enough of all these shameful sentiments. The next time you see Jep, he will be a Detector, primed and enhanced in black."

"You mean, he will fear the night skies, and only come out in daylight?" taunted Chenchi, receiving an approving nod from Lev.

Leaping up, I sat mounted on Spikes back. Smiling down at my companions, I bowed my head. Steering Spike to turn around in the direction of the gate, I noticed the Governor standing at the top of the stairs, leading to the entrance of the Great Hall.

Beside him stood Isa and Blair. Isa smiled, raising her hand, offering me a farewell. A shadow reflected from the stone wall above them, catching my eye. Baroness Ivy gazed down at me, with her hands resting over the balcony of her chambers.

I saw her take in a deep breath and for an instant we both paused, fixing our gaze on one another. The courtyard went silent, and from a distance we had our final stolen moment.

***

Flint remained silent, allowing me to soak in the memories that reflected back at me throughout the town. Seeing the Viking Invader Tavern, I thought of Jen, and the Square made me reminisce on the pork slabs that I had so often relished with Fulten.

Taking a final look over the town from the peak of the hill, I glanced between the ruins of the lock up and Western Farm. Exhaling, I took a few moments to recollect both the friends and foes that I had encountered during my time in Stanford.

"Come, let us find new adventure," called Flint.

***

Alma was situated on the southern coast of Thear, meaning we had several days of travelling ahead of us. Riding alongside Flint, he began cducating mc on thc city, and it wasn't long bcforc hc noticcd my vacant expression. "One thing you will learn as a Sword, is that people move on. It will do you well not to become too attached to your peers."

As we entered the meadow, Flint regained my attention. "The city is less forgiving. You will find even the gentler folk can direct hostility towards us Swords. After a reunion with the Chief, you will be enlisted into our scholarship and will undergo intensive educational training. Do not be fooled, becoming a Detector takes much more than waving a wooden baton in the air. I will show you a side of enforcement that you never knew existed."

"Even though I am apprehensive, I am eager to learn," I replied.

"You have the makings of a fine Detector, now let us go and ruffle some feathers."

This story continues in:

Book Three of The Crimes & Crests Saga
Blue Swords – The Detector

ACKNOWLEDGEMENTS

To all the people who have sent me messages of encouragement and kept me writing.

And to my team of friends, who have helped me shape this novel:

Kelli Sandells

Sue Mackenzie

Ian Halsey

JP

ABOUT THE AUTHOR

James Horton left his hometown in rural Lincolnshire to join the police service in London at the age of nineteen. Serving as a police officer in several units, James has had his eyes opened to the highs and lows that come with serving as a constable. Suffering a stroke at the age of twenty-seven, James turned to historic action novels to help settle his mind and aid his recovery. After his recovery, James decided to start writing his own novel, combining a career in the police and his passion of medieval stories.

Due to the overwhelming and incredible support received from his readers, James will be donating his profits from Book One and Book Two of the Blue Sword novels to the Stroke Association, UK.

Available worldwide online and from all good bookstores

Michael Terence Publishing

www.mtp.agency

www.facebook.com/mtp.agency

@mtp_agency

Printed in Great Britain
by Amazon

64733670R00166